# PAPPY
# MOSES'
# PEANUT
## PLANTATION

# MICHAEL EDWIN Q.

# PAPPY MOSES' PEANUT PLANTATION

*Pappy Moses' Peanut Plantation* by Michael Edwin Q.
Copyright © 2018 by Michael Edwin Q.
All Rights Reserved.
ISBN: 978-1-59755-482-4

Published by:     ADVANTAGE BOOKS™
                  Longwood, Florida, USA
                  www.advbookstore.com

Library of Congress Catalog Number: 2018908252
1.  Fiction:: African American - Woman
2.  Fiction: African American – Historical
3.  Social Science - Slavery


Edited by: Melissa Foster Follis
Cover Design: Alexander von Ness

First Printing: October 2018
18 19 20 21 22 23 24    10 9 8 7 6 5 4 3 2 1
Printed in the United States of America

# Chapter One

# That's the way God planned it

"The Lord knew what he was talking about when he said, 'It ain't right for a man to be alone! That's why he took one of Adam's ribs and made him a woman as a companion." Harriet Garrett slammed her teacup down, spilling its contents. "I'm not saying marriage is heaven on earth; it's hard work, just ask Mr. Garrett, but it's worth it." She took a deep breath and sat up in her chair. "I'm just sayin' it ain't natural for a young, good-looking plantation owner like you to surround himself with nothin' more than a few field hands and a bunch of darkies. A man needs a wife. That's the way God planned it."

Harriet Garrett picked up her teacup; her head bobbing up and down agreeing with herself. Charlotte Buchman and Abigail Cutter bobbed both their heads in harmony with Harriet. The Reverend Thaddeus Pleasant reached across the table, placing his hand in a fatherly fashion on Josh's hand.

"Listen to them, Josh. Listen as if listening to your own mother. For this is true motherly advice. In First Corinthians, Saint Paul said if you want to stay in the service of the Lord, and give your all, you are best to stay single. You are running a peanut plantation, my son. You need all the help you can get in a life partner."

Josh removed his hand from under Reverend Pleasant's. "If you recall, Saint Paul said that it was best to remain single and marry only if the burning passion is too much to bear. I handle my passions quite well, thank you."

Just then, a black woman, one of the kitchen help, entered the study. She placed a wicker basket covered with a towel down at the center of the table where they sat. It was clear she was no ordinary plantation slave. She walked tall and proud, her head held high, like African royalty. Her skin was a deep shade of brown without blemish. Her face was long and slender with high cheekbones, far apart eyes that glistened, and a perfectly shaped mouth that looked like two dark budding rosebuds. She wore a housedress of the highest quality, nothing a slaveowner would buy or allow a slave to wear. It was finer than any housedress the ladies seated at the table owned. The women eyed her up and down in silent jealousy. Her long willowy hands were well-kept. Unlike slave hands that appear gnarled and scarred from hard labor, her hands looked pampered. She reached across the table, pulling away the towel from off the wicker basket, revealing a dozen fresh baked biscuits.

"Hot biscuits?" she asked in regal tones. In just speaking those two words, it was obvious to all seated this was no ordinary, uneducated southern slave.

Charlotte Buchman rested her elbow on the table, holding her spectacles on her nose, eyeing this kitchen slave. "Pretty little thing, isn't she?" Charlotte commented, as one might admire a child. "It's almost a shame she's a darkie."

"It's what they call *Black Pretty*," Abigail Cutter announced to all. "I suppose you can find some beauty in all God's creations, if you look hard enough."

"Her name is Ellie. She runs the kitchen, in fact the entire house. I don't know what I'd do without her," Josh said this as he looked with sympathetic eyes at Ellie. For just a moment, the two shared a smile.

Entering the room, carrying a tray of soft butter, honey, and homemade jams, was a young slave girl, maybe eighteen or nineteen years old. She stood only an inch shorter than Ellie. It was clear they were relatives, having many body and facial likenesses.

"This is Ellie's daughter, Becky, short for Rebekah. She works here in the house, also," Josh said as the young woman placed down the tray.

"She has her mother's good looks," clucked Charlotte Buchman. "I don't think I've ever seen such a light-skinned darkie, in all my years. Do you know who the father is?"

"I couldn't say," Josh said, feeling all eyes on him.

Harriet Garrett leaned towards Charlotte Buchman, whispering loud enough for all to listen in. "Probably one of the foremen working here, I suspect." She looked across the table at Josh. "A foreman, I would guess to say. Some men have no control or scruples; you can't even leave them with barnyard animals."

The Reverend Pleasant dabbed the beads of sweat from his forehead and prayed a silent prayer the topic would turn.

Josh smiled nervously, clearing his throat. "That will be all, ladies. Thank you," Josh told the two slave women. He held up the teapot, swirling it to judge how much more tea it held. "Oh, and have Pappy bring us a fresh pot of tea, please."

Harriet Garrett snickered at Josh's attitude towards his slaves. "'Please?' 'Thank you?' 'Ladies'...? My, aren't we modern? Maybe we should have asked them to sit and have tea with us?"

"Perhaps Josh is just being tactful?" suggested Abigail Cutter.

"Then would you say Mr. Lincoln is just being tactful?" Charlotte Buchman blurted out. All the ladies laughed.

"Ladies, please!" Reverend Pleasant said, using his napkin to daub more sweat from his brow and upper lip, clearly embarrassed for himself and Josh.

A short, stout, old black man entered, carrying a fresh hot pot of tea on a tray. He wore a dark suit with tails. From ear to ear was just a semicircle of white, billowy hair around his balding head. His beard was white, cropped close to his face, more sparse whiskers than beard. His black face wrinkled from the years. There was sadness in his eyes. His hands were the hands of a slave, gnarled and scarred. He moved slowly, his old bones creaking like aged dry wood. He placed the teapot in the center of the table.

The ladies were still laughing; the sight of the old man only increased their laughter.

"Oh my, what do we have here?" Harriet Garrett said to the others, eyeing the old man from head to toe.

"It's the black Methuselah!" exclaimed Charlotte Buchman, stirring up more laughter.

"Ladies, please! You're embarrassing our host," insisted Reverend Pleasant.

When the laughter died down to muffled giggles, the introductions Josh made. "This is Pappy Moses; Pappy, as we like to call him; he's been here from the start. I inherited Pappy when I inherited the plantation. He's the father of Ellie, the slave you just met, and the grandfather of Becky."

"You mean to say this ugly old goat sired those two lovely creatures?" questioned Abigail Cutter, in disbelief.

Pappy calmly bowed slightly at the waist, smiling wide, showing his straight white grin to all. "All educated peoples know a man gets his looks from his father and a woman gets hers from her mother. Zipporah, that being my wife, may she rest in peace, was a beautiful woman. That's why my babies is beautiful." He looked directly into the eyes of Abigail Cutter. "You, my dear lady, must have been born in a barn because I is sure your momma walked on all fours."

"Well, I never!" Abigail Cutter shouted with her eyes wide and shooting fire.

"That doesn't surprise me at all," Pappy said through his smile.

Josh jumped from his seat, standing between Pappy and the table to protect the old man, in case someone threw something at him. "Pappy, that's no way to speak to our guests."

"I should say so," insisted Harriet Garrett. "What sort of man are you, Joshua Nunn? If one of our slaves spoke to one of our guests like that, my husband would whip his black skin right off his back!"

"Oh, I couldn't do that," Josh said. "Pappy's been like a father to me."

7

That statement did not sit well with his guests. The room got so quiet that you could hear a feather fall. Josh stuttered out what he thought would clear the air and change the mood.

"I mean, Pappy ain't nothing but a dumb old black man who ain't got a lick of sense left in his broken-down old body. Still, he's as faithful as an old hound dog. He's just old and don't know what he's saying. Don't the Bible say we need to treat our slaves with gentleness and simpletons with kindness? Pappy ain't nothing but a whole lot of both. He's been a slave all his life and a simpleton ever since he got old. Ain't that true, Reverend?" Josh looked to Reverend Pleasant for support.

"Yes, Josh, I believe you're right. I don't remember where the verses are, but I do remember the Bible saying something to that effect. Not in those exact words, mind you, but I do believe it does," Reverend Pleasant agreed.

Josh turned to Pappy, placed his hand on his shoulder, gently turning the old man toward the door. "That will be all, Pappy. Why don't you go to your room and have a lie down. I think you're having one of your spells, again."

The old man never stopped smiling. He shuffled forward and started to leave. Josh stood watching him, not returning to his seat till he felt safe that Pappy was far down the hall.

The mood changed; everyone went silent. A maternal feeling came over Harriet Garrett and it shown in her eyes. She spoke softly and gently to Josh. "Dear Josh, you're still a young man; you have so much left to learn. Do you know why you are the owner of the *Bush Plantation*?"

Josh shrugged his shoulders. "Because I inherited it?"

"You poor, sweet innocent boy, no, that's *how* you came to own this plantation. The reason you are the owner is because you are *white*! The reason they are slaves is because they are *black*! That's the way God planned it. They are like children needing guidance and a firm hand. No one benefits if you do not do your duty! It's in the Bible. Am I not right, Reverend Pleasant?"

The Reverend, clearly befuddled, squirmed in his chair. "Not in so many words, but I'd say it does imply that."

Josh looked at the Reverend as one looks at a traitor to the male cause in the war of the sexes. The old preacher knew better, but years of marriage had taken much of the wind out of his sails. He saw it as a battle already lost. Josh was a sinking ship; and like any self-respecting rat, Reverend Pleasant had jumped overboard.

Harriet Garrett continued. "I'll tell you what, my boy. I'll make you a proposition that will benefit us both. My husband, Tom, ran our plantation all his life with an iron fist. We've never lost a slave, and we get the most work out of them. Most of the plantation owners in Georgia look up to Tom. They all come to him for advice, and he's always willin' to give it, and it'd please him to help you anyway he can."

Josh looked confused. "I am always open to friendship, as well as advice offered by someone of experience. Tell me, what I could do for you?" he asked.

"You can teach Tom about raising peanuts. As you know, we've farmed nothing but cotton on the Garrett Plantation for three generations. Since this war with the Yankees..."

Abigail Cutter put in her two cents. "The war won't last long, now that Texas joined the Confederacy."

Harriet Garrett continued, ignoring the interruption. "As I was saying, this war with the Yankees has made it near impossible to import and export goods. It is best to grow local crops for local customers, at least until this blasted war is over. If you could give my Tom, in fact all our husbands, some peanut-farming pointers, we'd be most grateful."

"It's bound to be a short war with Texas in the fight," Abigail Cutter said, determined to put the same two cents in.

"Gee, ladies, I don't know what to say," Josh admitted humbly.

"Just say 'yes', my boy. We are in your hands."

"Since you put it that way, how can I not say yes? Of course, I will help you anyway I can."

"Bless you, my boy. I'll tell my Tom when I get home. He and the other plantation owners will contact you about when they will come to visit at your convenience, of course, sir." Harriet Garrett let out a long sigh of relief. "I'm so glad we settled that."

"We haven't settled what we originally came here to settle," insisted Reverend Pleasant.

"What's that?" asked Charlotte Buchman.

"Finding this young man a suitable mate!" demanded the Reverend.

Josh raised his palms in hopes of halting all at the table. "No, please, that's not necessary. I'm perfectly happy the way I am."

"Nonsense!" Abigail Cutter said. "You're too young to know what true happiness is."

"Besides, we have a plan," Charlotte Buchman said.

"A plan?" Josh questioned. He looked to Reverend Pleasant in one last attempt for support, "A plan?"

"They have a plan," the Reverend stated, as if it were inevitable.

"Each of us will select an eligible young woman and arrange for the two of you to meet under the best of circumstance, of course. Don't worry; we will use great discretion at every turn of these endeavors," Harriett Garrett announced.

"I still think we should consider the widow Desman. You won't have to teach her a thing. I mean, she's already broken in."

"He's not buying a horse, Abigail," Charlotte Buchman remarked.

"Don't I have a say in all this?" Josh complained. He looked once again to Reverend Pleasant for help.

"Don't look to me, my boy. My wife is behind them completely. Just be glad Mrs. Pleasant had the Ladies Quilt Circle today, or you would have had four ladies instead of three to contend with. You might as well learn it while you're still young. In the war between men and women, your only hope of survival is to surrender. Resistance is useless."

"Then it's settled. Each of us will communicate with you through the post. We will let you know whom we've selected and where and when you can meet them," Harriett Garrett said. She stood up, which seemingly signaled the others to stand. "Well, it's been a slice of heaven but we need to be off."

Taking the Reverend's advice, Josh caved into their demands. He walked them through the house. "I'll see you to your carriage."

Outside, in front of the Bush Mansion, Josh stood close by as they seated themselves in the two horse carriage. The driver, a small, young black man, gave each woman a helping hand up. Before getting in, Harriett Garrett turned to Josh. "My Tom will contact you about setting up a meeting."

"I will be waiting patiently," he said, kissing her hand and then helping her to her seat. He closed the door of the carriage as the driver got in place.

Harriett Garrett smiled at the other ladies. "Oh, this is going to be fun."

"Get on, now," hollered the driver as he slapped the reins down on the horse's backs. Josh watched as they rode out the front gate, waiting till he could no longer hear the sound of rolling wheels. He never truly appreciated how peaceful and quiet the plantation could be until that moment.

He felt exhausted. He felt like he'd just run a race. He slowly marched back into the house, back to the study and sat at the table, staring quietly at empty teacups and plates covered with biscuit crumbs. The rustle of petticoats broke the silence. He looked up to see Becky sit down across from him. She took one of the now cold biscuits; split it open and poured honey over it. A few drops of the sweetness dripped on her finger, she licked them off.

"Daddy?" Becky asked. "Do all white women get ugly when they grow old?"

Josh smiled, shaking his head. "No, my darling, not all do. My mother, your grandmother, was beautiful up till the day she died. You have her eyes, you know."

"Do I really?" Becky smiled at the thought and then at her father.

Ellie sat down next to Josh, placing her hand on his. "Are you all right, sweetheart?"

He sighed. "I feel like they bound me, tied me, and then hung me up to dry for a month in the chicken coop."

"They did sound like a nest of chickens," Becky laughed.

Pappy walked up slowly behind Josh and swatted him hard on the back of the head. Josh held his head in pain, looking shocked at the old man. "Pappy, what'd you do that for?"

"No reason at all! I guess I'm just havin' one of my spells." Pappy sat down and began to rant at Josh. "After all I ain't nothin' but a dumb ole black slave without a lick of sense, a simpleton! Don't you worry none, though; 'cos I is as faithful as an ole hound dog. Oh, oh, I feels one of my spells comin' on again." Pappy reached over and popped Josh hard on the top of his head.

Ellie jumped up, wrapped Josh's head in her arms to protect him, and kissed the top of his head. "Now, Pappy, you stop hitting my sweet husband like that. What else was he suppose to do?"

"That's right," Josh pleaded. "I didn't mean what I said, but I had to say what I said. We've got to keep up appearances."

Ellie came to her husband's defense. "You know Josh loves and respects you, Pappy. We've got to keep up appearances. He only said what he said for the good of the family."

"Appearances, my eye! He said what he said for the good of the family? I suppose he was just thinkin' 'bout the good of the family when he agreed to go courtin' all the single woman in the county."

"You didn't agree to that, did you, sweetheart?"

"Well…"

"Did you, sweetheart?"

"What was I suppose to say, that I'm already married? Then when they ask me who I'm married to, I can say you. They'd burn down the plantation and string us all up!"

"You're not going to go courting these women, are you, sweetheart?"

"Well…"

Becky looked up from her biscuit. "Daddy, if you and momma split up, do I get to live with her or do I have to move in with you and some white lady?"

"Nobody's splitting up, baby. Don't even think that," Josh said.

"I asked you a question, Josh," Ellie demanded. "You're not going to go courting these women, are you?"

"I've got to at least meet them, honey. We've got to keep up appearances."

"That's not the answer I expected to hear. Oh, oh, I think I feel one of my spells coming on."

She slapped the top of Josh's head, storming out the room. Josh jumped up and ran after her.

Pappy couldn't stop laughing. He cupped one hand next to his mouth and shouted, "What's ya fussin' for, Ellie? He's just thinkin' 'bout the good of the family!" Still laughing, he smiled at Becky. "Don't worry, pumpkin. You can always live with Pappy."

# Chapter Two

# The Family Meeting

Sunset! The colors of yellow, purple, orange, and rose erupted along the horizon and reflected in the clouds. To the east, darkness approached and stars began to take their places in the night sky. There was just enough light left in the world to walk about slowly. They left their homes, each carrying a chair. They entered the barn, lined up the chairs theater style. Kerosene lamps on all the posts lit up the barn. Everyone sat and waited. The plantation foremen were all young white men, students from The Southern Seminary out of Newberry, South Carolina. They'd offered their services as mock-foremen. After six months, they would leave and then be replaced by a new group from the seminary. They stood in the back near the barn door. They'd come to listen. This concerned them, too. Pappy entered the barn with his daughter, Ellie: his son-in-law, Josh: and his granddaughter, Becky. Becky took a place standing with the foremen. Pappy, Ellie, and Josh sat at a long table set at the back of the barn, in front of all.

"Good evening, everyone," Pappy said loud enough for all to hear.

"Good evening, Pappy," responded all, like they do when they reply to the preacher every Sunday at church.

"I call this family meeting to order," Pappy announced. He looked around till he saw the face he was looking for. "Ezra, come on up here and tell everyone how we stand this month."

A tall, somber-looking young man of twenty-five, Ezra was the plantation accountant and family scribe. Pappy selected him for the job not only for his mastery with numbers but for his eagerness to try harder than most, which Ezra prided himself in. After one year in the position, he stood with confidence as he spoke to the family with nary a hint of the stutter, which plagued him since he could talk.

Ezra stepped up to the table carrying a large, leather-bound ledger under his arm. He placed it on the table and opened it.

"I'm sorry to say profits are down. This war's making it harder to trade. The good news is we're still in the black, but profits are half of what they were this time last year."

"Cousin Ezra," Ellie asked, "how do we stand with lost family members?"

"That is the best news of all, Cousin Ellie," Ezra said, smiling at every face looking at him. "We now number thirty-seven family members with only eight more to go."

The barn filled with handclaps and cheers.

The barn door opened. Like a dark cloud raining on a parade, in walked Judd Taylor, a bounty hunter from out west. He'd switch from bounty hunting to tracking down runaway slaves or, as in this case, missing family members that were slaves. It was just as profitable, but a whole lot safer. He was good at what he did. He'd track down more than twenty family members, bought them, and brought them back to the Bush Plantation, reuniting them with the family. Pappy never trusted him as far as he could throw him. Still, he figured as long as there was money to be made, Judd would do as he was told and be loyal for the time being. Just one look at him, and you could tell he was a mean one and not on the up-and-up. He was middle-age; tall and slender, with long white hair on his head, short white whiskers on his face, and deep-cut lines in his face that made him look older than his years. He always wore black: black western boots: jacket and pants: shirt and ribbon tie: and a wide-brim, round-top, western hat that always shaded his eyes. Everyone watched in silence as he slithered up to the front table.

"Mr. Taylor," Pappy said. "They tell me ya have good news for us."

Judd Taylor stood before the small audience; his steel blue snake eyes became fine slits. He pushed away the flap of his jacket, exposing a gun and holster on his hip. He rested his hand on the hilt. "I've found Nathaniel Brown."

The crowd was silent for a moment; then someone hollered from the back. "Cousin Skeeter, you found Cousin Skeeter? Where'd you find him?"

"He's working on a plantation in Alabama."

Adeline Brown, an elderly, heavyset woman stood up, nervously wringing her apron with her hands. "Sir, you found my son, Nathaniel. How does he look?"

"He looked just fine. I'd say his master treats him well. There were no marks on his body that I could see."

"Mr. Taylor," Pappy interrupted. "Was his Massa not willin' to sell Nathaniel?"

"No, he was willin' to sell the slave."

"Then may I ask why you didn't buy him?"

"The slave's owner wanted one thousand dollars."

A voice shouted from the second row. "A thousand dollars! Heck, Cousin Skeeter don't weight no more than a hundred and twenty pounds. That's little more than eight dollars a pound. The boy just ain't worth it."

The entire group burst into laughter. It was either laugh or cry. They knew no matter what the price was, they had to pay it for one of their own.

Pappy again questioned Judd Taylor. "Mr. Taylor, it is true Nathaniel ain't nothing more than a skinny boy, but we do love him. Could ya tell us why his owner is asking so much?"

"As the owner explained, he didn't want to break up no family. Nor did he want to be saddled with a grieving wife and children. If you want Nathaniel, you got to take the lot of them; and the cost is one thousand dollars."

Adeline Brown jumped from her chair. "Sir, are you saying my boy is a married man and I'm a grandmother?"

"Two times over, they got two young boys. That's Nathaniel, his wife, and the two boys; that'll be one thousand dollars plus my usual twenty percent."

Pappy looked to Ezra. "Ezra, can we afford it?"

Ezra ran his finger across some of the lines in his journal. He shook his head. "It's gonna leave us with not much left, but I guess we can."

Pappy turned to Judd Taylor. "You'll have your money in the mornin'."

Judd bowed agreeing. "Then if you'll excuse me, I'm going back to the house to get some sleep. I'd like to leave at first light."

As he walked through the crowd toward the barn door, people nodded and spoke their appreciation. "Thank you, Mr. Taylor. God bless ya, Mr. Taylor." He ignored them all. When he'd closed the barn door behind him, everyone stood, taking up their chairs.

Pappy banged his hand on the table. "Hold on, hold on, everybody. The family meeting ain't over by a long shot. Josh here, he's got something important to say." Pappy nodded to Josh who stood up to address the family.

If anyone were to question the veracity or depth of Ellie's love for Josh, they need look no further than into her eyes when she looked at him. She was never more proud of him with his confidence and commanding personality than when he addressed the family at these meetings. Dressed in his jacket with tails, white lace shirt, riding britches, and boots, he truly looked the master of the plantation. His long, full, wavy black hair was combed back with his ear-length sideburns cut close and sharp. His eyes were gentle and childlike, his face strong and beautiful like an ancient Roman hero chiseled in marble by one of the old masters. His skin was as pure-white ivory as her skin was pure ebony. From the beginning, they knew their love would never be easy, only that it would be worth it.

Josh began to speak. "As you know, profits have been down because of this war. At some point, we need to discuss what other crops we need to plant and if we should also take on livestock to turn a larger profit. Still, we live under a blessing. Other plantations are not doing as well; many have put everything into cotton, and the cotton market is down. Some of our neighbors have asked me to teach them on growing peanuts. I've agreed to help.

"This brings up another serious problem we need to face. We will see more than the usual amount of strangers, nonfamily, on our property. It's been brought to my attention by my concerned neighbors, these other plantation owners, that I am too softhearted and kind with my slaves. In exchange for me teaching them peanut farming, they plan to teach me how to run a plantation with an iron fist and get more out of my slaves."

"You know what they can do with that iron fist," shouted a young man seated in the back. The entire crowd burst into laughter and cheers.

Pappy bounded on the table. "Stop it! We need to take this here seriously. The world is at our door, and we need to give them the appearance we is on the up and up. Please, continue, Josh."

Josh nodded to Pappy. "When these folks are here, I may have to speak harshly to some of you. I ask your forgiveness in advance, and I ask you to bite your tongues." Josh pointed to the seminarians standing in the back. "You foremen will have to do the same, maybe push a few of the men around in full view of the visitors. Does anyone else have any ideas?"

There was a long silence as everyone thought. Florence Monroe raised her hand.

"Yes, Flo, any ideas?" Josh asked, pointing her out.

She stood up. "Each of us – men, women, and children – should put one set of old, torn and dirty clothes aside. We'll wear these clothes whenever the visitors come."

"Great idea, Flo!" Josh complimented.

Florence continued, "Most important, ladies, never wash these clothes. We may not smell good, but I'm sure that's what these folks expect." Again, there was laughter, nervous laughter.

Clarence Brown stood up. "I been thinking. We still have the wood from when we knocked down the old smokehouse. It's old wood, dry and nasty looking, which is why we knocked down the old smokehouse in the first place. Now, I know we were going to use it to burn in the new smokehouse; why don't we nail the old pieces of wood on the front of our homes. It'll make them look run-down. We can still keep them looking nice on the inside; but the outsides would look like your typical slave shacks."

"Clarence, you're a genius!" Ellie remarked, to the handclaps of the others.

"Anyone else with any good ideas?" Josh asked.

Amos Monroe stood and walked to the front without a word. "This is what we need to show them," he announce to all. He unbuttoned his shirt, took it off, and turned to expose his back to everyone. Everyone grasped at the sight. There were deep black scares in his brown skin, scares left from the whip. "Twenty-four lashes for stealing a potato. Twenty-four lashes for trying not to starve to death."

The sight of it made Josh's voice quiver. "How many others have whip marks they'd be willin' to show?"

A dozen hands went up, mostly men but a few women, too.

"Fine, but those look like old wounds," Percy Brown shouted.

"That's easy to put right," Pappy said. "Daub them with some fresh chicken blood; they'll look like they just happened."

"Very well," Josh said in conclusion. "Tomorrow, Ezra will give Judd Taylor the money for Nathanial and his family. Pappy and he will see him off. Ladies, start putting some old clothes aside for your families. The men and I can begin putting up false facades on the homes with the wood from the old smokehouse. I'll let everyone know when the strangers are coming as soon as I find out."

All eyes fixed on Pappy. "Any other matters we needs to discuss?" Pappy said, waiting for a reply. There was none. He slapped the tabletop. "I call this family meeting over and done with."

The kerosene lamps they blew out. Everyone left the barn holding their chair. They moved slowly and carefully through the dark to their homes. It was time to put the youngsters to bed. There was a soft light in every window. The grown-ups would be up till late talking. There was much that needed discussing.

# Chapter Three

# You're a fine man, Joshua Nunn

The next day, all hands on the plantation got busy. The women selected old clothing, cutting slits in them, pounded them on rocks, and then dragged them in the dry brown dust. The children gathered buckets of dry, grimy, light-brown sand they found on the roadside a half mile north of the plantation. Then the women lay the clothing in an empty field, first a layer of clothing, then a layer of dusty sand, then another layer of clothing, and then another of sand. Layer on layer till the pile was waist high, and then they covered that with more sand. Old shoes they hit with rocks to make them look shabbier, the shoelaces they removed; they cut holes into the soles.

The men, including the seminarian foremen, lead by Josh, loaded the worse-for-wear, dried-out, brown wood from the torn-down old smokehouse onto carts. They hammered and nailed the wood pieces here and there on the slave's houses. They paid no mind to workmanship. It was all done haphazardly; if a piece of wood was too small or too big or perhaps didn't fit right, well then, all the better. They did some other makeovers. With a horse team and plow, they put furrows in the road running through the slave quarters. All flowers and bushes they dug up, planting them around the main house. Anything aesthetic they removed. By the end of the day, the slave's quarters looked as rundown, unpleasant, and uninviting as any other shantytown in the South. Nothing left to do except wait.

That evening after dinner, Pappy sat on the veranda of the main house, smoking his pipe. A two-horse carriage came trotting through the front gate and up to the main house. The driver was the same young fellow from the other day who drove the ladies and the Reverend. He sat up straight and proud, looking down on Pappy.

"Is your Massa at home?" the young man asked.

"What kind of way is that to talk to your elder?" Pappy said, blowing smoke into the air. "No excuse me, sir, or good evening. Not even howdy doo!"

The young man rolled his eyes in frustration. "Good evening, sir, is your Massa home?"

"That's better! Whatever it is, ya can tell me, and I'll tell him."

"Massa Garrett gave me a message to tell to your Massa. He didn't say to leave the message with some ole house monkey."

"A house monkey?" Pappy shouted, jumping from his chair to the side of the carriage. "You know what you is, you is a...a...a whippersnapper. You know what a whippersnapper is, boy?"

"Sounds like some kind of bird."

"It ain't no bird. Ya ain't just a whippersnapper, ya is a young ignorant whippersnapper!"

"Yeah, well at least I ain't no ole house monkey."

Just then, the front door opened; out stepped Josh. "What's all the hoopin' and a hollerin' about?"

Pappy shook his finger at the young man. "This young, sassy Philistine come here to get his mouth washed out with soap."

The young man rolled his eyes again and then fixed them on Josh. "Massa Garrett tell me to go ask Massa Nunn if it be all right for him to come and visit Massa Nunn in three days."

"Three days?" Josh repeated thoughtfully. "I guess that would be fine but I thought Tom Garrett wanted to come out with some other farmers."

"I hear Massa say he want to come out by he self and find out what kind of man be Massa Nunn, first."

"Fair enough, you tell Mr. Garrett I'll expect him at noon for lunch."

"Oh, Massa can't be here till two."

"Very well, you tell him I'll be waiting."

"Thank ya, sir." The young man nodded his head, gave a last cross-eyed look at Pappy and drove off.

"Where ya goin', boy? I was just fixin' to get the soap out to wash out your Philistine mouth!" Pappy shouted.

The young man hollered over his shoulder, "House Monkey!"

The three days of waiting for Tom Garrett's arrival were trying for all hands on the Bush Plantation. The decision was that everyone should wear only their shabby clothes during the entire three days. No one was to bathe and brush or wash their hair; men would not shave. It was a terrible time for all. Only the children were happy.

The morning of the day Tom Garrett was to arrive, Pappy and Josh gathered all hands in front of the barn. Pappy looked at them like a general inspecting his troops. He placed his hands on his hips, bent backwards, laughing at the sky as loud as Gabriel's trumpet.

"Ya sure is the filthiest bunch of folks I ever did see," Pappy said, still laughing. "And you smells as bad as ya look." Josh put his hand over his mouth, trying not to laugh; but he couldn't help it. Pappy's laugh died down to one of his wide smiles. "But ya is the most beautiful peoples I ever laid my eyes on. Ya pulled together like a true family that ya is, and I'm proud of each and every one of ya."

The entire family applauded and cheered.

"Now everyone get in your places and wipe them smiles off your faces. Ya is in misery, remember. I wants ya shufflin' your feets with your heads bowed low. Ya is slaves working day and night on the meanest plantation in the South, run by the ruthless Massa Joshua Nunn."

The family burst into laughter, the last laugh of the day. When the laughter died down, everyone lowered their head, getting into character. They moved slowly, with lowered heads, dragging their feet, as they each went to their assigned job.

Pappy placed his hand on Josh's shoulder. "I guess I best be goin' back to the house and make some lemonade and lay out the whiskey for our guest."

"Lemonade and whiskey? I don't get it, Pappy," Josh said.

"Simple, we don't know what sort of a man this Tom Garrett is. If he be anything like his wife, he be wantin' lemonade. But seein' how most often opposites attract – and she the kind of woman that can bring a man to woe – I'd say it be wise to bring down the whiskey, too."

Tom Garrett said he would visit at two. He was a man of his word. You could set your clock by old Tom Garrett. At two o'clock, he road through the front gate as fast as a banshee with the angel of death at his heels. Josh and one of the young boys greeted him in front of the main house. Garrett sat tall and straight in the saddle with an air of arrogance and pride. When he dismounted, he was still straight and tall. A man in his mid-sixties, years of hard labor left him still a powerful figure. His skin was tan and cracked from spending his days in the hot cotton fields, overseeing his plantation and slaves. He wore simple farmer's clothes, a long-sleeved shirt, black pants, and a wide-brim straw hat, typically worn by plantation owners when in the fields. There was a coiled bullwhip on his hip, attached to his belt. He walked to Josh; the two shook hands. Garrett's grip was excessively powerful, partly to size-up Josh and to some extent just to show-off and prove he was still able to put a much younger man on his guard.

"It's a pleasure to finely meet you, Mr. Nunn. I heard so much about you."

"As well, I you, sir," Josh replied. He looked to the young boy. "Peter, see to Mr. Garrett's horse."

"Hold on there, boy," Garrett said. He reached into his saddlebag, pulling out a book. Then he looked young Peter in the eye. "Walk him a bit before you tie him up and see that he gets some water."

"Yes, sir," Peter said, taking the horse's reins.

"Shall we sit for a moment?" Josh proposed, pointing to a table and chairs set out on the veranda.

Pappy watched from the window of the study, sizing up the man. "Better get the whiskey," he concluded to himself.

Once seated, Garrett began. "Mr. Nunn, I'll come straight to the point. I believe an alliance between you and I can be very beneficial to us both."

"How can I help, sir?" Josh asked.

"As you know, this war with the Yankees has put a damper on the cotton trade. Many of the cotton farmers in the area are considering growing other crops, at least until this thing blows over. I, myself, have already planted some root crops: potatoes, carrots, and yams. Besides cotton, nothing grows as well in this rich Georgia soil as peanuts. I never thought much for peanuts. I'd rather give them to the hogs than eat them myself, but these are desperate times. If you could see your way to educating us cotton farmers in the ways of peanut farming, we'd be in your debt. As I mentioned, we'd only raise peanuts until this cursed war is over. After that, you have my word as a gentleman that we will go back to farming cotton and the peanut market in these here parts will return to you, sir."

Just then, Pappy walked onto the veranda carrying a tray. On it were a book, two glasses, and a bottle of Kentucky bourbon.

"It's a mite early in the day, but I don't mind if I do." Garrett smiled as Pappy poured the whiskey.

"Here is the book you wanted from the library, sir" Pappy said, handing it to Josh.

"Thank you. That will be all, Pappy."

"Pappy!" Garrett exclaimed. "My wife told me about you. You're the insolent house darkie who insulted her and her friends!"

Pappy's face went solemn. He bowed his head in remorse. "Sir, forgive me and give my sincere apology to your misses. As Massa told the ladies, I ain't nothing but a foolish ole darkie with not a lick of sense in my being, and getting worse with every day. I has these spells, too. Sometimes I don't even know what I is sayin' or doin'. I begs your forgiveness."

Garrett didn't know what to say. As Pappy turned to reenter the house, Garrett noticed a slight smirk on the old man's face. "You see that, sir," he shouted, pointing at Pappy. "That man is playing you for a fool, sir, which brings me to my next point. I'm much older than you, Josh; I've had to deal with slaves all my life. I know what goes on in their heads. I know all their tricks, and I know how to handle them. I can help you get a better grip on things here at the Bush Plantation."

"I appreciate that, sir," Josh said. "Still, just because I'm soft-hearted with some deranged old house darkie I've know since I came to the Bush Plantation, does not mean I run my field hands in the same manner."

Garrett held up his hands, shaking his head. "Please, sir, don't take any of my words as an insult. I have the greatest respect for you. You're young and still wet behind the ears with so much still to learn. You've spent too much of your time alone on this here plantation. It's time you reached out to others, and they'll reach out to you. All the plantation owners in the county must work together during these troubled times. I offer you my years of experience freely and humbly."

"Then I accept them freely and humbly," Josh said.

Garrett took a long swallow of whiskey and then placed the book he held in front of Josh. "I found this book to be most helpful. I would feel honored if you took it in friendship."

Josh held it up. "*How to Get the Most from Your Slaves*...sounds most interesting." Josh took the book that Pappy had brought out and gave it to Garrett.

"*Peanuts for Profit*...now that's the ticket," Garrett laughed, the drinks were loosening him up.

"It's still early," Josh said. "Let's have a few more drinks, and then I'll give you a tour of the plantation.

"Sounds like a plan," Garrett said, holding out his glass.

Garrett drank three whiskeys to Josh's one. His speech began to slur, his footing sloppy, but his posture remained upright. Josh first took him to the fields.

"Read the book I gave you and let the others read it, too; then all of you can come out; and I'll teach you about peanut farming what books can't," Josh said, presenting the acres of plowed land with a wave of his arm.

Next, they toured the slave quarters. It surprised Garrett to see that the Bush Plantation's slave quarters looked far worse than his slave's quarters. All hands kept their heads down as they passed, even the children. Few spoke, but those that did carried fearful respect in their voices. "Afternoon Massa...Good day, Massa." Garrett looked impressed. All hands looked filthy, ragged and miserable.

"Good gracious, man; don't your people ever wash?" Garrett proclaimed as he caught the stench of folks who, unbeknown to him, had not washed for days in honor of his visit.

In front of the barn was a wooden wheelbarrow. A thin black man lay in it asleep. His long legs and arms hung over the sides. His head tilted back, he snored loudly, his mouth opened, and flies buzzed around his head. It was Amos Monroe. Josh marched up to the wheelbarrow with Garrett close behind. Josh kicked the side of the wheelbarrow; Amos went flying, falling to the ground at their feet.

"Wake up, you good-for-nothing; wake up!" Josh bellowed.

Amos woke; acting startled, he jumped to his feet. "Massa, I was just getting some hay from the barn."

"So you thought you'd just take an afternoon nap!" Josh shouted into Amos' face. As planned, two field hands were walking by. "You two!" Josh barked. "Take this man into the barn and hold him against one of the posts." He turned to Amos. "Two dozen lashes!" Amos went limp as the two men dragged him into the barn.

"May I borrow your bullwhip, sir?" Josh asked Garrett who immediately handed it over.

"Do you need any help, sir?" Garrett asked, still slurring his words.

"Thank you, but this is nothing new for me. I can handle it on my own. I won't be a minute. Please, wait here." Josh, bullwhip in hand, entered the barn. Garrett stood outside, swaying a bit, listening and waiting.

Inside the barn, Amos removed his shirt and hung it on a nail. They placed an old saddle over the wall of an outer stall.

"Hold him tightly!" Josh ordered, loud enough for Garrett to hear outside. He unraveled the bullwhip, made a firm grip on the hilt, tossed it back behind him, and then wheeled it forward. The sound of the bullwhip cracking against the leather of the old saddle was sharp and loud. It made Garrett squint his eyes and cringe.

"Oh! Massa, please, don't! Massa, please!" Amos hollered, as loud as he could.

"Hold your tongue! This is what happens to lazy good-for-nothings. Hold him tight, boys." Josh let the bullwhip fly again. The snap of the whip was like a gunshot.

"Ooooooh!" Amos howled like a wounded hound dog.

The sight of Amos with his head tilted back baying like a wild animal was too much for the other two men to bear. They began to laugh. In turn, Amos began laughing also. They each placed their hand over the other's mouth to muffle the laughter. This only created more laughter. Crack went the whip against the old saddle.

Amos pushed the hand from away from his mouth. "Ooooooh!" he wailed. They placed their hands over his mouth before he could start laughing again. Josh continued to whip the old saddle. The sight of the three covering one another's mouths got to Josh. The laughter was contagious. To stop his own laughter, he placed his handkerchief in his mouth. He bit down hard, continuing to lash out at the saddle.

Seeing Josh with the handkerchief dangling from his mouth was comical torture for the other three. Still holding each other's mouth, they fell to their knees. Every now and then, they'd take their hands off of Amos' mouth longer enough for him to let out a bloodcurdling howl.

Finally, as Josh came to the last few lashes, he took the handkerchief from his mouth. "Twenty-two, twenty-three, twenty-four, that's it; let him go," Josh announced. The three men stood up, trying to compose themselves. One of the men, biting his lip and tongue, opened a jar containing fresh chicken blood. He dipped the end of the bullwhip into the fluid. Then he poured the rest onto Amos' back; the liquid dripped down onto his pants, but some of it remained in the scars and crevices in Amos' back.

"Are you ready?" Josh whispered. They nodded. Each man took Amos from under his arm. Amos went limp, as if dead. They left the barn. When Garrett saw Amos' blood-soaked back, his eyes went wide. The men carried Amos' slacked body to the slaves quarters, feet digging furrows in the dirt.

Josh called out to them. "You tell him if I don't see him working in the fields tomorrow, he'll get another twenty-four." Josh handed the bullwhip back to Garrett. There was blood dripping from the tip. "Oh, I'm sorry. Allow me," Josh said as he used his handkerchief to clean off the leather, staining the white material a bright red. He smiled at Garrett. "Shall we head back to the house for another drink?"

With a tear forming in the corner of his eye, a drunken Garrett looked sternly into Josh's face. "I've under estimated you, sir. Forgive me. You're a fine man, Joshua Nunn."

# Chapter Four

# How to Get the Most from Your Slaves

The evening after Tom Garrett's afternoon visit to the Bush Plantation, tortuous screams echoed throughout the slave's quarters. Every child who had not washed in the past three days was placed into a tub of hot soapy water and scrubbed raw. Women washed and combed their hair. Men shaved away their three-day stubble. Everyone put on fresh clean clothing.

At the main house after dinner, Pappy stood in the hallway spying on Ellie and Josh who were in the library. They were skimming through the book Tom Garrett gave to Josh.

"Do you believe this drivel?" Ellie said, turning the pages randomly. "It would be funny if it wasn't that so many people take this so seriously."

"I really should read it from cover to cover," Josh said. "If I'm to deal with these men, I need to know what makes them tick."

Ellie closed the book. "Some other night, I can't take much more of this. Let's go upstairs, I'm tired."

"A bit early to go to sleep, isn't it, dear?" Josh asked.

"I said I'm tired, not sleepy."

"Oh!" Josh said, smiling knowingly.

Pappy smiled to himself, his old mind remembering about such things. He hid behind the grandfather clock as they left the library and walked up the stairs. Alone, he entered the library. He took the book from off the table and fanned through the pages. He seemed disappointed to find there were no illustrations, only words.

"What are you doing, Pappy?" He spun around; Becky stood in the doorway.

He held the book up. "Could ya read this to me?"

"Oh, is that the book Tom Garrett gave Daddy? Momma was telling me about it. She got my interest; I'd like to read it, myself," she said, entering and taking the book from her grandfather. "Sit down, Pappy. I'll read it; I mean, we'll read it together."

They sat at the table facing each other. Pappy sat up straight, his hands folded carefully in his lap.

"Pappy," Becky asked, "how is it you never learned to read?"

"When I was young, I was a slave on a cotton plantation. We never had no need or time to learn how to read and write. Besides, it was against the law to teach a slave such things, as I believe it still is. I made sure your mother learned to read and write, and ya do it even better than her, and your children will have it even better. This I swear to ya, Rebekah." He stopped talking for a moment, staring out the window into the darkness as if looking into the distant future. Then something brought him back and he pointed, tapped his finger down hard on the book that Becky held. "Go on, pumpkin, read for your grandpa."

"It's late, and it's a long book, Pappy; but I can at least read the introduction."

### HOW TO GET THE MOST FROM YOUR SLAVES
*By Ichabod Norton*

"There's a side note," Becky said. "It says here that Ichabod Norton is a professor at Criterion University. He teaches a course in Human Behavior, and is an authority on Civil Law. He holds a Doctor's Degree in Theology from Boswell Christian Seminary."

"Human Behavior, Civil Law, Theology…what that mean?" Pappy asked.

"It means he's studied and teaches the laws of man and heaven," Becky replied.

"Really?" Pappy said. "Read on, I gots to hear this."

Becky continued reading.

*Introduction*

*You pass by a farm and see a farmer beating his horse with a rod. You ask him why he's beating the horse, and he tells you he is trying to teach the horse who is in charge. You would think the farmer a fool. You come on a man and his child. The child is insolent and disobedient, but the father spares the rod and lets the child go unpunished to do what he pleases. You would call that man a fool.*

*I bring up these two scenarios to make a point. Owning a Negro slave is in some ways similar to each, and the answer to how to handle your slaves is somewhere between both stories.*

*Owning a Negro slave is similar to owning a horse. You've made an investment that needs to work for you. Unnecessary cruelty will not get you the most out of your investment. The* horse you beat to show who holds the upper hand will turn on you. It will find ways to hide from you and not give you a good day's work; and when you're not looking, it will bite you as soon as look at you. Still, the horse that does not pull his weight, that's coddled and given sugar and apples, is no more motivated to work than the horse that's whipped for no reason.

There are similarities between a Negro slave and a child. Both should not be left to their own devices. Both are filled with vinegar, mischief, and poor judgment. Always guidance is needed or they will run amok and become disobedient slackers. When this happens, punishment is sadly the only solution.

So, where does that leave us? When should we punish? When should we reward? How great is the punishment, and how great the reward? What can be done with a runaway? All these will be addressed in the next few chapters. First, we need to understand where and at what level the Negro slave stands in God's creation and plan. We need to look at this logically, with good business sense, as well as Biblically.

First, the Negro's black skin is not the mark of Cain as so many, even some preachers, claim. If that were true, that would make the Negro our distant cousin, distant but still part of the same family. They are not part of the human race, distant or otherwise.

Don't be swayed by obvious similarities such as arms, legs, fingers, and toes. Remember monkeys have all of these and are still part of the animal kingdom. As well, don't be fooled by smiles, laughter, tears, the ability to solve small problems, even a caring manner. These only place the Negro at the top of the animal kingdom, making them perfect for their lot in life — subservient to mankind.

In the next few chapters we will cover such topics as punishment and reward. How do you select a slave? How much should I pay? What should I expect from my investment? Is it ethical to break up a Negro family? Can I get better specimens through forced breeding? When should I sell a slave, and when should I just cut my losses and remove the useless? All this and more we will cover. When we finish, you will be a slaveowner who is wiser, I hope wealthier, and closer to God.

Beaky closed the book and laid it on her lap. She wore a solemn worried face as she looked up at her grandfather. "Why, Pappy, you're crying!"

# Chapter Five

# Good news, Bad News

It was just a few minutes after high noon when nine-year-old Minnie Brown came running up to the main house followed by a group of other children from the plantation. Pappy stepped out on the veranda to greet her. He was laughing.

"Hold on there, child. Where's the fire?"

"They're coming!" Minnie said, out of breath from running, the other children standing behind her.

"Who's comin'?"

"We were playing on the road and..."

"Hold on there," Pappy said, the smile left his face. "Ya were playing off the property? Ya know you're not supposed to leave the plantation."

Minnie and the others turned to stone. They knew he'd them caught in the wrong.

"Never mind, child," Pappy said. "Tell me what ya was saying."

"It's the white man in black."

"You mean Mr. Taylor."

"Yes, Mr. Taylor. He's riding this way on a horse. There's a black family with him in a wagon. They're coming this way."

"Good work, children," Pappy said. He went to the dinner bell that hung at the end of the veranda, which they used as an alarm. He rang it loud and long.

The field hands stopped what they were doing, the women left their chores; everyone ran to the main house. Judd Taylor rode through the front gate followed by an open wagon. The children ran alongside the wagon. The small caravan stopped in front of the main house. Everyone remained silent. Then Adeline Brown pushed her way through the crowd, rushing to the wagon with tears in her eyes and her arms spread wide.

"Nathanial! You've come home!"

"Momma!" cried Nathanial as he jumped from the wagon into his mother's arms.

The others then gathered around to welcome him. The women hugged and kissed him; the men patted him on the back "What happened, Cousin Skeeter? You used to be as thin as a rail."

"Blame it on my wife's cooking," he said helping his wife down from the wagon. "Momma, this is my wife, Alice." Adeline wrapped her arms around the woman and kissed her cheek. "These here, Momma, are your two grandsons, Harry and Henry." The two boys dove off the wagon to their grandmother.

"I wish I had more arms," Adeline cried, to everyone's laughter.

As the celebration continued, Pappy and Josh took Judd off to the side to speak with him.

"We thank you again, Mr. Taylor," Pappy said.

"I'm just doing what ya paid me for." Judd said this in a way that suggested he had no heart for what he was doing. "We need to talk later. I have some information I'm sure you want to hear."

"Later, after dinner," Josh said.

"Have someone take care of my horse. I suppose I'm stayin' in my usual room?" When neither of them answered, he took it as a yes and entered the house.

Once the festivities ended, Josh invited Nathanial and his family into the library of the main house.

"You folks must be hungry," Josh said. He turned to Ellie. "Sweetheart, could you please stir up some food for our new family members?"

Ellie left, taking Becky with her. Nathanial and his family looked confused. Just the sound of a white man calling a black woman *Sweetheart* sent them into terror.

"Allow me to explain," Josh said. "As you can imagine, this is not your normal Southern Plantation. Everything you see is a sham. My name is Josh Nunn. I may give the impression I run and own this plantation, but I don't. I'd like to introduce you to the real owner of the Bush Plantation, Moses Brown." He pointed to Pappy who stepped forward.

Pappy explained, "I started this plantation with my partner who was a white man. When he died, he left everything to me. Legally, I ain't allowed to be the owner, so everything is in my son-in-law's name, Joshua Nunn. Yeah, he married my daughter. A white man and a black woman married; don't look so banjo-eyed. As ya see, the workers here are all family. Each, like yourselves, we bought with money made from the plantation. The white foremen are from a seminary school in South Carolina who gives their time. They's here for show only and ain't nothing to be feared. You's be given a home, small but clean, and jobs to do. Our goal here is to buy every known living family member in the south."

"Then what, Uncle Moses?" Nathanial asked.

"Then we skedaddle. We heads on out of here."

"Where to, Uncle Moses?"

"North, as far north as Canada if we has to, someplace where we ain't slaves anymore. Someplace where we can live free. Now, get yourselves into the kitchen and eats up. When ya is done, we'll show ya your new home."

"Thank ya, Uncle Moses. Thank ya, Cousin Josh."

As Nathanial and his family left in search of the kitchen, Judd Taylor was coming down the stairs. He entered the library.

"If you two gentlemen are free, I see no reason we should wait until after dinner to have our meeting."

"One moment, sir," Josh said, closing the library door for privacy. The three sat at the table near the window. Josh took up a box, opened it, offering it to Judd. "Cigar?"

"Don't mind if I do." Judd took one, rolling it between his fingers next to his ear. "Fresh!" Then he ran the length of his under his nose. "Nice!" He lit a match with one hand; he bit the end off and spit it to the floor. With a few puffs the area was under a cloud of cigar smoke. He fanned the match cold and tossed it to the floor. "I've got good news and bad news. Which would ya have first?"

"Give us the bad news first," Pappy said with a sigh.

"I've track down three of your relatives on your missing family members list. They're all dead. There was John and Arthur Monroe and Celeste Brown."

All three men remained quiet for a long time. Finally, Pappy broke the silence. "Celeste Brown, she was my sister's youngest. How did they die?"

"Does it make any difference?" said Judd. He was right. Knowing how they died would do nothing but add to the sorrow. Still, his unwillingness to tell them made it clear their deaths had not been natural.

"I hate to bring this part up; but ya do know that dead or alive, I still get my finder's fee," Judd said, still sending up cigar smoke.

"We understand. You'll get your money," Josh said, sounding put off by the man.

"Ya says there be good news," Pappy remarked. "Tell us the good news."

"I've tracked down Aaron and Miriam."

"Ya found my brother and sister!" Pappy cried. "Where have they been? Why didn't ya buy them?"

"I got wind of them when I was on my way to fetch Nathaniel and his family, so I had one of my men check it out. It seems they were both working on the same plantation. I'd planned to visit this plantation, but I was too late. Its owner's been in financial straits for sometime. He was forced to sell most of his property, including his slaves. He sold them to a slave trader who plans to sell them at auction next month in Coopersville."

"Coopersville, why that's less than a day's ride from here," Josh said.

Judd continued. "Now, I'm sure ya want to go to the auction to bid on them. Just keep in mind, if ya buy them or no, I still get my finder's fee."

"Don't worry," Josh said. "You'll get your money."

# Chapter Six

# The Legend of Bernie Bush

That evening after dinner, Pappy sat alone on the veranda watching the sunset like he did almost every night. Becky brought him out a tall glass of buttermilk, his favorite.

"Why that's might kindly of ya, pumpkin. I was just thinkin' about ya, child. Sit down, sit down and spend some time with Pappy."

"You were thinking about me, Grandpa? What were you thinking?" Becky said, sitting down.

"How pleased I is. How fine ya be growin' up."

The smile left Becky's face. "Pappy, when I read that book to you, you cried, why?"

"Ya know, pumpkin, tears ain't nothing but salty water, and ya can't tell the difference 'tween tears of joy and tears of sorrow. I was cryin' tears of sorrow for the way the world is and the things I seen, and I was cryin' tears of joy because ya ain't never seen that part of the world, and I hopes ya never does."

"Pappy, what was it like being a slave?"

"It's like livin' against nature, a life of contradiction. Ya is alive, but ya ain't got a life. You is a man, but they calls ya boy. They tells ya to pray to God, but ya must worship the Massa. Thee Lord say ya ain't supposed to put no one afore him, but the Massa say he come first. I don't understand. There be a Massa who thinks 'cos they feeds ya, clothes ya, and don't beat ya, they is good men. I say if ya try to own something that belongs to Thee Lord, ya ain't so good as ya thinks."

"Are you angry, Pappy?"

"Not no more. I was when I was young, though. I was a big ball of anger and hate. No, not no more, now that we gots hope."

"Pappy, do you really think someday we can get the family together and go north?"

"Of course we will, child. I promised Bernie Bush on his deathbed that I would."

"Bernie Bush! Bush...you mean like in the Bush Plantation? You never did tell me the story of you and Bernie Bush and how you wound up the owner of this plantation."

"I did, too. I told ya when ya be eight years ole. I guess it's time to tell ya again, now that ya is grown. First, take a sip of this here buttermilk. It's too big for ole Pappy; I needs your help. If I drinks it all, I'll be up all night with the vapors." Becky took a few sips. "That's good. Now wipe your lip." He handed her his handkerchief. "All right, the story of me and Bernie Bush goes like this.

"Like I said, when I was young, I was filled with anger and hate. I worked and lived with my family on a cotton plantation in Mississippi. I was the youngest. There was my father and mother, Amram and Jochebed, your great grandparents. With us were my older brother and sister, Aaron and Miriam. I was a sassy boy, always ready to fight at the drop of a hat. The owner of the plantation was named Ferric Khane. Now, Massa Khane was pure evil. His plantation ran on sweat and blood, our sweat and our blood. I seen him whip slaves to death just for fun. I hated Massa Khane; I would have killed him with my bare hands if not for my parents. I knew if I acted up or ran away, he'd take it out on my folks. So I obeyed, bit my tongue, and bided my time. When I was twenty-one, my father died, his heart gave out in the middle of bailin' cotton. A year later, momma died; sometimes I think just to be with papa. Not less than six months later, Massa Khane sold my sister and brother. I was alone in the world, and I felt I had nothing to lose. So one hot day out in the field, when Massa Khane started whippin' me for not workin' fast enough, I picked up a stone and smashed his head like a hen's egg."

"You killed a man?" a wide-eyed Becky asked.

"Lord forgive me; I did. I was a young fool. All the other field hands saw it. Thankfully, none of the foremen were close by. The other hands just stood there with their mouths open, not sayin' a word. There was nothin' left for me to do but run; and man, did I run. I ran out of Mississippi, through parts of Tennessee and Arkansas, clear into the Missouri. It took me a long time. I kept off the roads, livin' on roots, berries, frogs, and toads."

"You ate frogs and toads, Pappy?"

"Sure did. Raw ones, too, 'cos I was afraid of lightin' a fire that maybe somebody might see. It wasn't till I was in the forests of Missouri did I stop my runnin' and started livin' like a caveman. I ate fish from the streams, made traps for squirrel and rabbit. I was becomin' a real mountain man. I smelled like a cow blossom, my hair was out to here, and my beard was down to there.

"One night at the foot of a mountain, I decided to get some sleep. I rested my head against the trunk of a tree and covered myself with dry leaves to keep warm. I was just about to fall asleep when I think I see a flicker of light some one third up the side of the mountain. I sit up and look hard. Sure nuff, there was a glowing light on the side of the mountain. I get up and goes to find out what it be. When I get to where the light is, I see an ole white man diggin' a hole in the ground to the light of a kerosene lamp. When I says he was ole, he looked as ole as that mountain. His hair and beard was whiter than his skin, which was wrinkled as the leaves at his feets. He was short and thin. He was smokin' a pipe, and the smoke went clear up to the sky.

"Then I see what he diggin' a hole for. The body of an ole black man was lying at his feets. He was diggin' a grave. Now, I thought I was bein' real quiet like, but the ole man speaks out, 'I knows you out there. I'm too ole to play hide-n-seek, so ya best come out.' I don't know why I did, but I came out of hidin'. 'Ya kill him?' I asks, pointin' to the dead man. He say, 'No, he got hit in the head with a rock when the cave done caved in on him. He was my partner. We've been workin' that gold mine together for nearly a year. Rocks gave way and killed him.' The ole man reached down and took something out of the dead man's pocket and handed it to me. 'Here, ya might as well have this'. I says, 'I can't read, sir. What do it say?' He say, 'It says his name is Jethro Kenite; and he's a freeman, black; but he ain't no slave. Ya might as well keep it. Ain't gonna do him no good, no more'.

"Once we finished putting Jethro in the ground, the ole man fell to his knees and prayed to heaven. 'Dear Lord, this here's Jethro Kenite, a good man and a true believer. He's was my partner. He's as dumb as the dirt that surrounds him, now. He's a good honest man, a hard worker, and a good friend. He was always the best of company, which I will surely miss; and I'm sure you're learning to appreciate. He is a blessing to know, I guarantee. We thank you for the loan; and we give him back to you, no questions asked. Amen'. The ole man used the shovel to work back up onto his feets. We went back to his campsite that was in front of their gold mine. We feasted on hardtack, beans, and black coffee. Afterwards, sitting by the campfire, we got to know each other.

"His name was Bernie Bush. From back east, as he put it. It was hard to tell how ole he really was; he just looked real ole. He done everything and seen everything across this great continent, from the Atlantic to the Pacific, from Canada down to Mexico. He'd been a cook in a lumber camp in Hudson Bay, worked on a shrimp boat out of New Orleans, hunted gators in Florida, wrangled cattle in Texas, and about another dozen other odd jobs. Finally, one day he got tired of working for other folk. He took to minin' abandon gold and silver mines that no body owned any longer. He'd partnered up with Jethro Kenite, a free black man, when they were both worked the shipyards in Boston. The abandon mines didn't have enough in them to support a full diggin' crew, but it was enough for two miners to live off of. After years of minin' together, they never hit it big. Right there and then, Bernie Bush asked me to be his new partner. He figured a young buck like me would be a help in his ole age. He told me he'd teach me how to mine and he promised even if we never got rich, we'd make a good livin'. Before goin' to sleep that night, he handed me a pair of scissors and a straightedge razor. He say, 'There's a creek down yonder. Tomorrow, you clean up, cut your hair, and shave. If you're gonna use ole Jethro's name, you need to do right by it; and if you're goin' to be my partner, ya need to show a little self-respect. This ain't no place for a boy; this calls for a man; and that's what ya gonna be startin' tomorrow mornin'.

"Bernie was true to his word. We mined together years, never gettin' rich, but livin' high on the hog. We even had a little nest-egg put away for a rainy day, and built ourselves a cabin. Bernie and I became the best of friends but it was more than that. He became the father, brother, and family I'd lost so long ago.

"One night, Bernie sat smokin'; and he say, 'Ya know, Moses, neither one of us ain't getting any younger. We need to find us a little place, a farm maybe, and just live off the fat of the land'. I thought he was jus' talkin' till he shows me a deed for some property in Georgia. 'I'm takin' my share of the money', he says, 'and I'm leavin' for Georgia. If ya don't want to come with me, I understand. Still, I sure would be pleased if ya did. Do I still have a partner?' He held out his hand; we shook on it; and the next day, we left for Georgia.

"Now, this whole plantation didn't look like it does now, when we got here. There was just an ole one-room shack, a chicken coop that couldn't hold water, and a barn that we were afraid to walk inside because it looked like it would fall any minute. We got some livestock and planted a vegetable garden. That sayin' about livin' off of the fat of the land, well I don't know what land they is talkin' bout; but this ain't it. We worked twice as hard as when we was minin'. What with milkin' cows, feedin' chickens, haulin' hay, mendin' fences, and all there is to runnin' a farm, we did never get no sleep. It was twice as hard for me 'cos I was the younger and the stronger; and whenever a stranger came around – which was seldom, thank goodness – I had to go into my slave act. 'Yes, Massa Bernie; no, Massa Bernie' it was degradin' to my young man's pride.

"One day, Bernie comes back from town; he walks into the shack holdin' a small shrub. I say, 'What ya got there, Bernie?' He say, 'It's our new crop that's goin' make us rich; it's peanuts'. I say, 'Bernie, ya crazy'. I guess he wasn't so crazy because we started growin' and sellin'; and we couldn't do it fast enough. The demand got so great, within a few years this whole area was nothin' but peanuts as far as the eye could see. Got so we couldn't run the place ourselves, so we came up with a plan. We'd buy slaves..."

"Pappy, you bought slaves?" Becky sounded displeased.

"Now, let me finish, pumpkin. The plan was that we buy slaves and pay them just like they do with white farmhands. We'd give them a home, food, and a paycheck. Now, at anytime, they could buy their freedom papers for the cost they were bought for. Some took us up on it; others just stayed on, worked, raised families, and had a good ole life. Only they had to act like slaves whenever a stranger come by, which they gladly did.

"The years went by, and we did better than well. Bernie had this monstrosity of a house built. He wanted to name it the Bush and Brown Plantation; but that was crazy, so we just named it the Bush Plantation.

"I remember it like it was yesterday. Bernie and I were at a slave auction to get some new workers. That's when I saw her, Zipporah, your grandmother. I whispered to Bernie that I didn't care what it cost, but we needed to buy that slave no matter what. He say, 'What for? She's a cook and we do all our own cooking'. I say, 'That there is the woman I am gonna marry'. I knew it the moment I set eyes on her. Bernie say, 'Ya crazy'. We bought her for two hundred dollars, best money I ever spent. Now, just because ya buys a woman, don't mean she gonna love ya. That woman was contrary from the day one. I had to court and woo that woman for two years; but eventually she said yes and we got married."

"Did you love her, Pappy?" Becky asked.

"Love her, ya bet I did. We was so happy, I wanted to change the name of the plantation to Paradise Plantation, but Bernie say, 'Ya crazy'.

"In our second year of marriage, it happened. Bernie and I took Zipporah with us to the slave market. Her eyes bugged out, she points to some skinny black slave on the auction block and whispers to Bernie and me, 'That be my brother, Shamus,' so we bought your Uncle Shamus for two hundred and ten dollars. That's how it all started. We started trackin' down family members from mine and your grand momma's side of the family and buyin' them from all parts of the south. One day we'll all be together, and we can skedaddle." Pappy went silent with a dreamy look in his eyes.

"Don't stop now, Pappy. What about my momma?" Becky asked, bringing her grandfather back to the moment.

"Well, not that we weren't tryin'; but it took nearly five years to get that woman in the family way. I was so happy. Yet, like Job, everything turned around in one day. Zipporah died givin' birth to Ellie, your momma. I wanted to die; and if I didn't have a newborn child that needed me, I would have laid down and just let it happen. Ellie became my whole life, and now that I got ya, pumpkin, my life is even better." Pappy reached over and brushed Becky's cheek. "Ya is as beautiful as your grandma."

"Then what happened, Pappy?"

"Early on, we knew no one would believe only one ole white man was in charge of all these here slaves. So, Bernie made arrangements with a South Carolina seminary that we knew were sympathizers to send some of their students to pose as foremen. We offered to pay them for their services, but they refused money 'cos they believed in what we was doin'. Every year, the seminarians would leave and a new batch would come to take their place. One year, when your momma just turned eighteen, your father came with the new group of seminarians."

"Daddy was going to a seminary?" Becky said, sounding surprised.

"Sure nuff. Ya didn't know that? He was plannin' to be a preacher, but only one look at your momma and that thought left his mind in a hurry. The minute they saw each other, they went moon-eyed. They says they in love. One day, your momma and daddy comes to me; and he say, 'Mr. Brown, I'm askin' ya for your daughter's hand in matrimony'. I says, 'Ya crazy'. Your momma always knew how to get me to do and say anything she wanted, so I says 'Yes'. We had Pastor Jeffrey, the black preacher from the next county come and do the weddin'. I always worried if we'd done the right thing. Yet, when I looks at you, pumpkin, I'm glad they did what's they did."

Becky smiled shyly.

"Life is funny. It don't always do what ya wants it to do. The only thing ya can expect from life is that it will do what ya least expect it to do. If things is bad; and ya thinks things couldn't get worse, they will. If things is going good; and ya thinks nothing can go wrong, then they will. First, Bernie began to slow down, then he sat all day on the veranda hollerin' orders at everybody; then he watched from his upstairs window; and finally he was confined to bed. On his deathbed, he called me the son he never had; and I called him the father I never knew; we cried our eyes out. Though in between the tears, we had a lawyer come; and Bernie signed everything over to your father. We had to do something. He couldn't leave it to me, so we took a chance. I have to admit we made the right one. Plenty men would see all the power and money and either have me sold or killed. Your father's always been honest and true to his word. He only acts like the owner in front of strangers, otherwise he respects me and allows me to run my place like I likes. I'm mighty proud of him; but don't ya tell him I said that!"

"Oh, I won't, Pappy."

"So, besides your birth, pumpkin, ain't nothing changed much since. We drudge on like Noah slowly building his ark. Only Thee Lord sent Noah the animals two by two, and we got to buy our family members one at a time. When we done, we gonna skedaddle to freedom and not look back."

# Chapter Seven

# Somewhere between
# Angels and Animals

Josh's first thought was to hide the letter from his family, especially from Ellie; but his conscience got the best of him. It would be childish, not a way for a grown man to act. Still, he thought of ways to present it to her that would keep a lid on her hot temper. Perhaps, if he made light of it, treat it like a joke, or mention it in passing like some folks speak about the weather? His instinct for self-preservation was running high. Becky with her young mind would have a million questions. Pappy was sure to say something to make it worse. It was not going to be easy, especially with Ellie. Sweet dear Ellie, the love of his life, she deserved more, it's true. What was he to do? During dinner, he unfolded the letter, placing it on the table, pointed at it and puffed out a chuckle like someone who'd heard a bad joke but wanted to remain polite.

"Do you believe that Charlotte Buchman? She's determined to match me up," Josh said, shaking his head.

Ellie took up the letter and read it out loud.

*My dear Mr. Nunn,*

*As keeping with our last conversation, I will be the first to introduce you to what I consider a first-rate candidate for a wife, my cousin Fiona Bredworthy who will be visiting me for the next two weeks. If not for her spiritual calling that being working with her brother, the Reverend Bredworthy in mission work, someone would have snatched her up years ago. Now, the poor dear has been left lonely in the world, like yourself, looking for a proper mate.*

*She is a cultured, well-groomed, Christian woman. As for her outward appearance, which I know is just as important as the inner to a man, have no fear. I can say with confidence, few women can hold a candle to her, very much like me when I was her age.*

*Please, allow me to be so bold as to invite Fiona and myself for tea next Wednesday. If this is not acceptable, please let me know. Otherwise, you can expect us at two.*

*I feel certain you and she will hit it off.*

*Your friend, confidante and Cupid,*
*Charlotte Buchman*


Becky placed her corncob on her plate and looked blankly at her father. "Daddy, if you marry this woman, do I have to call her momma? I'd feel funny doing that. Can't I just call her Auntie Fiona?"

Josh shot a stern look across the table, shaking his finger at his daughter as he spoke. "I know you're trying to be funny, Becky; but this is no time for jokes." He took the letter from Ellie. "Do you believe the nerve of that woman? I'll just write her first thing in the morning, telling her no way."

He was just about to rip the letter up when Ellie took it back. "Oh no, you don't. Those women are going to keep pushing women at you till we do something to stop it."

"Like what?" Josh asked.

"We're smart people; we'll think of something. We've got to nip this thing in the bud."

Josh felt a surge of relief. He never could figure woman, least of all Ellie. To hear her talk like that was a weight off his mind. All this time, Pappy continued eating, giving little or no attention to the matter.

"Well, Pappy, I'm surprised you've got nothing to say about the matter," Josh said.

Pappy looked up from his plate. "Me?" he asked, pointing innocently to himself and then sucking on his teeth to get a corn kernel out from between them. "Me? I'm just plum amazed."

"Amazed at what?" Josh asked.

"Ya is the first man I ever known who asked his wife if he could go courtin' another woman, and lived to talk about it, and even get her permission to go do it! Of course, she be wantin' to go with ya when you do; but hey, ya can't expects everything."

"I know what I'll do. I'll just call her stepmother. I mean, after all, that is what she is," Becky said, trying to hold a straight face.

Josh jumped from his chair and rushed towards his daughter. "I know what you need, young lady…a good down-home tickle. He pushed his fingers into her sides; the girl curled up in her chair.

"No, Daddy, don't! You know I'm ticklish!" she shouted as she laughed and wiggled.

"Josh, stop it! You're gonna make her throw up!" Ellie said, between her giggling.

Pappy just shook his head in disbelief, grabbing another chicken wing. "This family, sometimes I wonder." He looked up to heaven. "Zipporah, look what ya and I started."

\*\*\*

39

Pappy greeted the carriage when it arrived. He stepped from the veranda, held out his hand to help Charlotte Buchman down. She quickly pulled her hand from him.

"Oh no, not you, get away from me, don't you touch me!" Charlotte Buchman shouted.

Josh rushed to the carriage, offering his hand.

"Keep that horrible man away from me," she continued. "I don't even want to see him."

"I think it would be best if you go help in the kitchen, Pappy," Josh said as he helped Fiona Bredworthy down from the carriage.

Charlotte Buchman made the introductions. "Mr. Nunn, allow me to introduce my cousin, Fiona Bredworthy. Fiona, this is Joshua Nunn." He bowed at the waist and she gave a slight curtsy. She offered her hand, wearing a black crocheted glove that exposed her fingers. Josh took her hand. It felt like a cold dead fish caught in a net. He decided kissing her hand was too forward, and instead gave it a gentle shake.

The two ladies dressed in true southern belle attire with parasols, bonnets, and overly wide hoopskirts. In the dining room, sitting with hoopskirts was difficult and awkward. They tried not to look uncomfortable, but it was obvious. Ellie and Becky quietly served tea and biscuits. Though she knew it didn't really matter, Ellie felt relived to see Fiona Bredworthy's physical shortcomings.

There was no easy, quick or flattering way to describe Fiona Bredworthy. It was difficult to estimate her true age. She began acquiring an elderly look and demeanor at age twelve. She was a hatchet-faced woman with a long, sharp nose and an Adam's apple worthy of any man. She was beyond slender and best described as boney. Her dark black hair she parted in the middle with each side plastered flat to her head. Her eyes were as pale as her skin and she wore a constant expression on her face that made it impossible to tell what she was thinking or what did, or did not, impress her.

"It's so good of you to have us for tea," Charlotte Buchman announced, as if it were all a big surprise and not well-planned.

"It's a honor to have you ladies here today," Josh replied. He turned to Fiona Bredworthy. "So, Miss Bredworthy, what brings you to Georgia?"

Charlotte Buchman corrected Josh, "Oh, Mr. Nunn, please call her 'Fiona'." He thought this strange, but ignored it.

"You must call me 'Josh'," he said, not sure who to direct the statement to. "So, Fiona, what brings you to Georgia?"

She intertwined her fingers as if about to pray and rested them on the table. "It's been years since I've visited dear Charlotte. I thought it about time. Besides, my brother is on sabbatical."

"Fiona does missionary work with her brother," Charlotte Buchman added.

"Yes, my brother is the Reverend Thomas Bredworthy. Have you heard of him?"

"I'm afraid not," Josh said.

"For years now I have been his right hand. Thomas' mission is very unique."

"Oh, and how's that?"

"We travel spreading the word of the Lord to the black slaves of the South."

Josh smiled with a look that showed he was impressed. Listening in from the hall, Ellie tilted her head to Becky. She too wore a look of being impressed.

"That's very commendable," Josh said. "After all, they are God's children, too."

"I wouldn't go so far as to say that," Fiona Bredworthy said. The smile and agreeable look left Josh's face. "We just believe the black slave has a soul, but not on the level of a white. We teach them the word of God so they may enter heaven. After all, who else will do the work they were born to do? Certainly not the angels; man is just a little below the angels. If we had to do menial tasks in heaven, then it wouldn't be heaven then, would it? The black slave should feel privileged to serve whites in heaven, as they should here on earth."

"Let me get this straight," Josh said. "You preach to black slaves so they can go to serve the white man in heaven. You say they have souls, just not souls at the level of their masters. If so, you must believe that animals, who also serve man, have souls, and black slaves are no better than animals."

"Not at all," Fiona Bredworthy replied. "The soul of the animal is even lower than the slave's. True, animals serve man, but they serve the slaves, too. Also, they can be food for the slave as well as the master. So obviously, animals are lower than both master and slave."

"Interesting," Josh said, sounding put off. "If the black slave's status is somewhere between whites and the animal kingdom, would you say he is more man than animal or more animal than man?"

"All this serious theology is bad for the digestion," Charlotte Buchman said. "This is a visit with good purpose. Let's keep it light, children."

Ellie rolled her eyes at Becky and then pointed to the kitchen. They disappeared into the kitchen and then came out, Becky holding a food tray and Ellie with a ceramic pitcher. Becky placed a bowl and a spoon in front of all at the table.

"Fresh cut peaches, how wonderful," Charlotte Buchman exclaimed.

Ellie held out the pitcher. "Would you like some fresh sweet cream, ma'am?"

"I'd like some, girl," Fiona Bredworthy said, holding out her bowl. Ellie carefully poured a stream of white cream over the peaches in her bowl.

"I'll have some, too, girl," Charlotte Buchman said.

Ellie smiled direct into her face and poured. Only the stream of cream never made it into the bowl, but cascaded into Charlotte Buchman's lap. The woman jumped to her feet.

"Watch what you're doing, you fool. Look what you've done." She looked at Josh. "If you ask me, she did this on purpose!"

Josh rose from his seat. "Mrs. Buchman, I'm very sorry."

"I'm so sorry, ma'am," Ellie cried, placing down the pitcher. "Follow me out to the kitchen; I'll have you cleaned up in no time."

Charlotte Buchman followed Ellie out of the room. Josh sat with Fiona Bredworthy in an uncomfortable silence. Becky appeared in the doorway. She curtsied and spoke in her best plantation slave manner.

"Massa Josh, Miss Ellie say come quick. She can't get the water pump to work."

Josh wiped his hands and lips with a napkin, rose and bowed. "If you would please excuse me, Miss Bredworthy. I'll be right back." He followed Becky to the kitchen.

Alone, Fiona Bredworthy lifted her teacup high enough to look at the inscription on the bottom to see who made it.

"Can I pour you more tea, Missy?" Pappy asked, slowly walking to the table.

"Oh, gosh and golly, you nearly scared me half to death, creeping around like that. Yes, I'd like some more tea, please."

She held out her cup; Pappy poured her more tea.

"We is so glad ya come here today, Missy. Massa Josh needs to meet a good Christian woman like you. He need to find a good wife to get him to give up his evil ways." Pappy placed the teapot down and started for the door.

Fiona Bredworthy's interest became aroused. "Old man, tell me what do you mean by *evil way?*"

Pappy worked back to the table. "Well, all in all, Massa Josh is a good man. It's just this livin' alone makes it hard for a man not to go astray. I'm sure a good Christian woman could get him back on track and give up his evil ways."

"Again, I ask you, *what* evil ways?"

"Well, Massa Josh likes to gamble: cards, horse racin', cockfights, and dogfights…it don't matter. Every month he lose more money than he take in. That sorrow makes poor

Massa Josh drink: wine, whiskey, brandies…it don't matter. He gets himself good and drunk; and when he's good and drunk, he likes to go down to the slave quarters."

"The slave quarter…you don't mean…?"

"Yes I do, Missy. He got him some lady friends down in the slave quarters. Normally, Massa Josh ain't like that, but whiskey can make a man colorblind."

"I see," Fiona Bredworthy said. "Thank you for the warning. What is your name, boy?"

"Pappy, Missy."

"Well, Pappy, I'd appreciate it if you keep this under your hat."

"Mums the word, Missy, mums the word."

Just then, Charlotte Buchman entered, followed by Josh.

"There's that terrible man, again. Keep him away from me, keep him away!"

"Pappy, go back into the kitchen, please," Josh asked.

"Fiona, can you see a stain on this dress? Be honest."

"There's still a wet spot; but I'm sure once it dries, you won't be able to see it. Your dress is white, as was the cream."

"That's true. I didn't think of that."

"I'd feel better if you allow me to reimburse you for the dress," said Josh.

"Nonsense, my boy, it wasn't your fault. If you went around paying for every mistake some darkie made, you'd go broke."

Becky was in the hallway holding her mother back from rushing in and pouring the remaining cream over Charlotte Buchman's head. There was a long moment of silence before Josh spoke up.

"So, Miss Bredworthy, I mean, Fiona, tell me more about your mission work."

She closed her eyes, placing her hand on her forehead. "Cousin Charlotte, may we leave? I feel one of my headaches coming on. Please, forgive me, Mr. Nunn."

"Of course, I'll see you to your carriage," Josh said.

"Oh, you poor dear," Charlotte Buchman said. She turned to Josh. "This is all too regrettable. Perhaps, we can come back another day."

"I don't think that will be possible, Cousin Charlotte. I forgot to tell you I received a letter from Thomas yesterday. He's been called to do some preaching in Mississippi, and he asked me to join him. I'll be leaving in the morning. It was a pleasure to meet you, Mr. Nunn."

"The pleasure was all mine."

Out in the hall, Ellie whispered to Becky, "That's one down and two more to go." They quickly tiptoed back to the kitchen.

# Chapter Eight

# The Trip to Coopersville

Ellie, Josh, and Pappy discussed long and hard if they should allow Becky to go with her father and grandfather to Coopersville for the slave auctions.

"We've worked so hard to protect her from the evils of the world," Ellie argued.

"All the more reason she should go," Josh replied. "We can't hide her away from the world forever."

"She's a smart girl. We've taught her well. She understands these things. There's no need for her to confront these things face-to-face," Ellie said sorrowfully.

Pappy reached out, taking Ellie's hand. "Ellie, ya can talk till you turn blue tellin' someone about what an apple tastes like. Ya might get close but it ain't the same as sinkin' your teeth into one. One bite and ya knows what he is talkin' about."

"She's not a baby anymore," Josh said.

"She'll always be my baby," Ellie said, biting her lip to hold back the tears.

"Ellie, sweetheart, you've got to let her grow up."

"I want to go, Momma. Please, let me go." They turned to see Becky standing in the doorway. "Please, Momma."

Ellie took a long time to answer. "You promise to stay close to your father and grandfather, and do everything they tell you?"

"I promise, Momma."

"Very well, then you can go."

Becky ran to her mother, throwing her arms around her. "Oh, thank you, Momma, thank you."

Holding her daughter, Ellie looked to Josh and Pappy. "If anything happens to this child, don't come home."

********

In the morning, they started off for Coopersville. Josh at the reins of the two horse buckboard wagon, Pappy sitting at his side, and Becky in the back with her arms around a lunch basket.

"Are we there yet?" Becky asked after an hour traveling. There was a giggle in her voice.

"That's not funny, Becky," her father said, trying to hold a straight face.

Another hour later, Becky started rummaging through the basket. "Can we stop, Daddy? I sure am hungry."

"I don't know," Josh said.

"Why not?" Pappy said. "We've made good time. We is almost there. I know ya is hungry 'cos I sure am."

Josh stopped the wagon; they sat on a large rock by the side of the road, eating their lunch. Josh stopped and sat up and listened.

"Do you hear that?"

"Hear what, Daddy?"

"I got ole ears; I don't hear nothin'," Pappy said.

"Shush, just listen."

They stopped eating and listened. The sound of horse hooves became louder as they slowly came closer. The sound of squeaky wagon wheels echoed all around, and then the distinct sound of chains rattling.

Coming down the road was a slow-moving caravan. In front was a lone horseman. A three-day growth on his beard, his clothes wrinkled and soiled, and a flat-brimmed black hat shading his dark, deep-set eyes. A double-barrel shotgun rested on the horn of his saddle. Behind him was an open wagon with two men on the buckboard holding rifles. Attached to the back of the wagon was a long line of fifteen black slaves, chained one behind the other. Bringing up the rear was a young boy of maybe twelve with a swagger of confidence and a look of distain found only in older men. He, too, had a double-barrel shotgun.

The leader held up his hand as a silent command. The convoy stopped. He looked down, speaking only to Josh.

"Good day, sir," the man spoke in a gravely voice.

"Good day," Josh replied.

"Are ye headin' on yonder to Coopersville for the big slave auction?"

"Yes, we are."

"Will ye be sellin' or buyin'?"

"I'll be buying."

"That be a shame, sir. The older man there ain't worth a plug nickel, but I'd pay handsomely for the girl."

"She's not for sale," he said calmly. Becky's whole body stiffened.

"That be a shame," the man repeated. "Since ye be buyin', I'll give ye first pick at me merchandise before we get into Coopersville, and ye have to pay the commission."

The chances of any of his slaves being Uncle Aaron and Aunt Miriam were slim to none, but it was worth a look. Josh stood and started down the line with Pappy at his side.

"Does the old darkie do thy thinkin' for thee?" asked the man.

"Some men have a green thumb for farming; others know good horseflesh when they see it. This old man knows a good slave when he sees him."

"Does he, now?"

There were very few old folks in the line. When they came to the end, Josh looked at Pappy. The old man shook his head. They walked back up to their own wagon.

"Sorry, sir, there isn't a single one I'm interested in."

"Truly, ye say? I call them fine specimens. I'd be lettin' ye take any of them off me hands for a lowly price."

"Not today, sir." Feeling uneasy, Josh walked to their wagon and slowly took up a rifle he kept under the buckboard.

"Ye sure ye wouldn't want to give up on the girl?" He smiled. Every other tooth in his mouth was missing. He slipped his finger onto the trigger of his shotgun.

"I told you, she's not for sale." Josh raised his rifle, pointing it at the man.

"Ha, ha, she not be worth it." He said, easing his finger from the trigger. "We be seein' ye in Coopersville. Ye have a good day, sir." He motioned his hand forward and the column started to move again. They passed slowly like a funeral procession. One look at the slaves spoke volumes about human misery and suffering. They looked unwashed, overworked, and underfeed, with no hope in sight, life with no hope. They dragged their feet, the chains clanging. They looked down as they passed, ashamed to look into a human face. Pappy looked down, not wanting to bring shame on them. Becky watched with wide eyes, her heart breaking. Josh looked at Becky, wishing he could protect her forever from the world, all the while knowing the folly of such longing.

"There was something familiar about that man," said Josh to Pappy. "I can't put my finger on it."

"Strange, I felt that, too," Pappy said.

********

On any ordinary day, blustering and hectic would not describe Coopersville; but this was no ordinary day. With a slave auction in town, the atmosphere was carnival. Tables from the town's shops lined the streets, restaurants, and bars, put out to peddle their goods. Everything from hand-painted music boxes, homemade rock candy, farm needs, kitchen needs, lace by the yard, cooked potatoes with all the fixings, to hardboiled chicken eggs, pickles, boiled peanuts, and shots of whiskey by the glass. The crowds walked the streets, elbow to elbow. They'd erected a large wooden stage in front of an old barn where they kept the slaves.

A small man wearing an undersized Bowler hat, his large belly trying to pop off the one button of his brown suit, stood center stage, ringing a handbell.

"Come one, come all, selling a slave, selling a slave, top quality. Come one, come all."

The crowed flocked to the stage. The small man stopped ringing the bell.

"The auction will start in one half-hour. Meanwhile, the merchandise will be put on display for your close inspection." A group of armed guards brought the slaves out from the barn and lined them up in front of the stage. There were men, women, children, couples, elderly, and full families. The salesmen made the slaves jump in place to show how spry they were. People prodded them, felt their muscles, looked in their mouths for coated tongues and counted their teeth.

Josh, Pappy, and Becky walked down the line of human commodities. Pappy tapped Josh's arm and pointed. Near the center of the line was an elderly couple. The gray haired old man was tall and held the shrinking old woman in his arms close to his breast. Pappy walked up to them and looked her in the eye. At first she looked right through him, and then her eyes caught sight of his. So many years since they were young, so many years since they last saw one another. The body may change but the eyes stay the same for life; the eyes never lie and show the true self.

"Moses?" she whispered. She looked up at the man holding her. "Aaron, it's Moses, it's our brother, Moses." A look of amazement washed over Aaron's face; Miriam began to cry.

Pappy put his finger to his lips, "Shush, everything gonna be all right."

Meanwhile, at the end of the line, Becky stood before a young slave. He wore more and heavier chains than the others. His teeth grinned hard in his mouth. People were afraid to approach him. His face filled with hatred and it was in his eyes. He growled and spat at everyone like a wild animal. Becky stood before him. When their eyes met, all anger left him. Her heart went out to him, she nearly cried. He calmly looked at her. She smiled and he smiled back.

Josh took hold of Becky's arm pulling her away, then he grabbed Pappy's prying him from his siblings, and the three found a place in front of the stage. The auction was about to begin.

"How much do you think Uncle Aaron and Aunt Miriam will cost?" Becky whispered to her father.

"It better not be more than 750 because that's all we've got," he whispered back.

The small man returned to the stage, ringing his handbell. "Come one, come all, selling a slave, selling a slave, top quality, low prices. Come one, come all. Our first offering is a family. The parents are still young and no strangers to hard work. True, the youngin' are small, but so is their price. Think of it as an investment. They won't stay small forever. Now, we do like to keep couples, families, and relatives together. Still, if only one or two catches your fancy, don't hesitate to bid on just the slave or slaves you want. The customer is always right."

The auction moved quickly for the next hour. Finally, they placed Aaron and Miriam on the stage.

"Next we have a brother and sister. Now, I know they're old, but you'll never find a harder working, more reliable, more obedient pair in the lot. They'd be good in the kitchen, food service, anywhere in the house, and they're good with children. What are my first bids?"

The crowd remained silent for a few seconds, and then someone hollered, "Two hundred!"

"Two hundred?" the small man questioned. "That's only one hundred apiece. I can get more for children. Folks, these are slaves with talents and abilities that took years to instill. Do I hear four hundred?"

Josh took the lead, "I bid two twenty-five."

"I've got two hundred and twenty-five. Will someone make it three hundred?"

The person who bid two hundred raised the bid. "Two hundred and fifty."

"Two fifty? Playin' it safe, aye?" the small man said. "Well, I understand. Do I hear three hundred?"

In hopes of eliminating the other bidder, Josh shouted out, "Three hundred!"

It worked! The other bidder shook his head and walked away. For a full minute there was silence, not another bid.

The small man raised his hand, ready to point at Josh. "Three hundred goin' once, Three hundred goin' twice..."

"Four hundred!" a bid came from the back. The crowd turned to see who it was. In the back, stood a handsome, well-dressed, gentleman. His dark mustache was long and well trimmed. He wore a bunch of lace at his throat. His suit, tails, and top hat were robin blue. His collar and headband were dark blue satin.

The small man was in a hurry to close the deal. "Four hundred once, twice. . ."

"Five hundred," Josh shouted.

"Five fifty," the gentleman replied.

This went on for five minutes. The bid increased in increments of fifty with first Josh ahead, then the gentleman, and then Josh, back and forth till the bid stood at seven hundred and seventy-five, with the gentleman in the lead.

"Would you care to bid eight hundred, sir?" the small man addressed Josh. Josh shrugged his shoulders in hopelessness, bowed his head and shook it.

"Very well, seven hundred and seventy-five goin' once. . ."

"Wait!" the gentleman shouted. "This gentleman seems to have his heart set on these two old darkies. I am not an ogre, sir. Perhaps we can come to some gentlemen's agreement? If the auctioneer will grant us two minutes alone, I'm sure the sale can be finalized."

"You have my permission, sir," the small man said.

"Meet me behind the large tree over yonder, sir," the gentleman spoke to Josh.

Behind the tree the gentleman took off his hat; his entire demeanor changed. "I will come to the point, sir. I will be honest and straight as an arrow. I am not wealthy. I work for this auction company. My job is to bid and urge customers to bid higher. In your case, sir, I have made a miscalculation and have bid myself out of job." He reached into his inside pocket and took out a roll of money. "Here is two hundred. Bid eight hundred and they will actually only cost you six hundred. I suppose it worth two hundred to save my job." Josh looked at the money, but did not touch it. The gentleman counted out another hundred. "Very well, here's three hundred, but that's all I can afford." Josh took it. "Then we have a deal, sir?"

"We have a deal," Josh said. The two men shook hands and returned to their places.

"I trust you two have come to an arrangement?" the small man said. "Do I have a bid of eight hundred?" he asked Josh.

"Yes, sir, you do," Josh replied. "I bid eight hundred."

"I have eight hundred once, eight hundred twice, eight hundred three times, sold to the gentleman with the patience of a saint. You can pay for and claim your goods at the side of the stage."

Josh was taking his wallet out of his jacket when they ushered onto the stage the wild young man in double chains, who Becky shared a moment with.

"Next we have an exceptional specimen. Ladies and gentlemen, just look at those arms and legs. He could carry twice his weight in cotton."

"Why the chains?" someone hollered from the crowd.

"I'm not going to lie," the small man proclaimed. "He's young, sassy, and does not have his head on straight quite yet. Though the right owner, with a strong hand, could shape him up in no time and get more than his money's worth. Now, what's my opening bid?"

There was silence throughout the crowd. The young slave held up his muscle-bound arms, the chains dangling; he growled from the stage. "Who'll bid a thousand, two thousand; I'm worth twice as much as all of you. You see these chains? You better keep me chained, because I swear I'll kill you while you sleep. You won't get a night's sleep, wondering when I might strangle you with my bare hands!"

The small man hammered the handbell into the face of the young man. He fell to his knees, his lip bleeding. There were no bids, not a sound.

Becky moved in close to her father, whispering very low and soft so only he and Pappy could hear her. "Buy him, Daddy. Please, buy him!"

The three gathered in a small circle. Pappy spoke first. "Child, ya don't know what you're askin'."

"Yes I do, Pappy. That's the man I'm going to marry."

"Pumpkin, ya talkin' crazy."

"Why? Isn't that what happened with you and grandma?"

"It's not the same, child."

"Why, because I'm a girl? If it was true for you, it can be true for me." She looked at Josh with that look that melts the hearts of all fathers. "Please, Daddy, please buy him."

"I will, but under one condition," Josh said. "That no one is to tell him about the situation at the plantation. We will only when I believe him worthy of the knowledge. Until that time, he will believe he is a slave like so many other slaves on a plantation no different from any other in the south. Do you promise not to tell him?"

Becky nodded. Josh broke away from them and waved to the small man on the stage. "I bid fifty."

"Please, sir, let's be serious."

"I am serious! I bid fifty."

The small man waited. There were no counterbids. "Fifty once, twice, and three times, sold to the luckiest man of the day."

Later, Pappy pulled his brother and sister to the side. "I have so much to tell ya both, but it will have to wait. Trust me. I'll tell ya everything when we get home. Just remain silent during the trip."

The ride back was a quiet one. Josh and Pappy sat at the front of the wagon. Becky, Aaron, Miriam sat in the back. Also in the back, the young man lay on his back and remained chained. Josh stuffed a rag in his mouth because he wouldn't stop cursing his new master. Now and then, Becky wiped the sweat from his brow, which kept him calm. No one spoke a word all the way home.

Not knowing the time of their arrival, there was no one to welcome them when they returned to the Bush Plantation. Josh stopped the wagon between the barn and the main house. He took the chained young man to the barn as the others entered the main house. In the barn, Josh chained the young man to one of the posts in a way in which he could stand, sit, or lie down in the hay. He removed the gag from the young man's mouth.

"You have anything to say?" Josh asked.

The young man just stood tall, shooting a defiant look at Josh, one filled with anger and hatred. Josh knew there were no words that could cross that bridge at that time, so he remained silent and left the barn.

Walking back to the house, he met Becky coming to the barn, carrying a food tray.

"I imagine he's hungry," she said. "I also need to clean his wound."

"Becky, I can appreciate what you're doing, but I want to remind you what you promised. You must never tell this boy the truth about our family. All our lives are in your hands."

"I promise, Daddy."

"That's another thing. Don't call me Daddy in front of him."

"Yes, Massa," she said in a giggle, walking toward the barn.

She found the young man inside, sitting on the ground, his back against the post. He tried to ignore her as she placed the tray at his feet. She dipped a clean towel in a bowl of water.

"First, we need to clean that cut lip."

"What for, why do you care?" he said in a low voice, still not looking at her.

"Because infection is going to set in; and yes, I do care. Now, hold still." She dabbed the blood from his mouth with the towel.

"Ouch, that hurts," he said, recoiling from her touch.

"Big, tough man, what's your name?"

"What's it matter? We're just slaves, no better than a chicken or a horse."

"Well, I have to know what to call you. My name is Becky."

He sighed long and hard. "My name's Caleb, Caleb Jehu."

"I need to go back to the house, Caleb. I'll be back later for the tray."

"How can you be like that?" he asked. "How can you smile and be so happy? You're a slave!"

"It's not so bad. This is the best plantation in the South, and the Master is a good man."

"A good man doesn't own another man! If I ever get these chains off, I'll kill him with my bare hands! Oh, why am I wasting my breath on you? You're just like all the rest, just another ignorant picaninny!"

"You're a mean, filthy boy; next time, you can get your own food!" she said, bursting into tears as she stormed out the barn.

Meanwhile, Pappy and his siblings spoke not a word till they were standing alone in the library. With tears in his eyes, Pappy held out his arms to them. "Aaron, Miriam, thank the Lord!" They rushed into his arms; and the three cried, unable to speak. Finally, Aaron backed off, looking at Pappy.

"Moses, my brother, how old you look!"

"Ya ain't no spring chicken either." Pappy looked at his sister. "Miriam, you still look beautiful."

"That's because you're looking through ole eyes full of love. Remember, I'm the oldest of us three. It hasn't been that long since I've looked in a mirror. I know what I look like."

"Pappy?" said a shy voice at the doorway. They all turned to look.

"Aaron, Miriam, this is your niece, my daughter, Ellie."

"Uncle Aaron, Aunt Miriam!" cried Ellie. She ran into their arms; the tears began to flow again.

"My, my, she is a beauty. Your wife must be lovely, Moses."

"She was."

"Was?" Aaron asked.

"She died many years ago. Come, sit, we have so much to catch up on, and have I got a story to tell ya."

Just then, Josh entered the library. Pappy placed his hand on Josh's shoulder. "Aaron, Miriam, I'd like ya to meet Ellie's husband, my son-n-law, Joshua Nunn."

They stood speechless; staring in awe till Miriam spoke up. "Brother Moses, that story you want to tell us, something tells me it has more twists and turns than any other I've ever heard."

"We sure live in amazing times," added Aaron. "These are amazing times, indeed."

********

Later, Becky returned to the barn to fetch the food tray. She kept her head down, not wanting to make eye contact with Caleb.

"Becky," he said softly. "I'm sorry for the way I spoke to you earlier. Forgive me. It's not like me to be that way. In my defense, it's not everyday I get sold at auction."

"For fifty dollars, what a bargain," Becky added.

"Yeah, some bargain," he said with a hint of laughter.

"So, you can smile," Becky said.

The smile left his face as he looked solemnly into her eyes. "It's been a long time since anyone's been kind to me, especially like you've been, Becky. I think you're the sweetest, most beautiful person I've ever known."

Becky carried the tray to the barn door, turned and smiled. "Sleep well, Caleb. I'll come by in the morning with your breakfast."

# Chapter Nine

# Another Man's Poison

This time Josh waited until after supper. He read Abigail Cutter's letter out loud in a manner similar to a government official announcing a declaration of war.

*My dear Mr. Nunn,*

*When last we met, the other ladies expressed their concern that the Widow Desman would not be a suitable candidate as a wife for you. She was my first choice; and after giving it much thought, I disagree with my friends all the more. The Widow Desman possesses all the qualities to be a perfect wife; and being a widow, she's already broken in. She is a treasure, and her children are two lovely cherubs from heaven.*

*As I'm sure you know, next Sunday is the church barbecue. There are few picnic tables on the church grounds. My husband, Gregory, made arrangements with Reverend Pleasant to secure a table. It would be our pleasure to have you sit with us. I've asked the Widow Desman to be our guest as well. This way you two can have a leisurely afternoon getting to know each other. Please, say you will join us. Your life may be forever changed.*

*Sincerely,*

*Abigail Cutter*

Ellie smiled at Josh. "You're on your own with this one, my love," she said. "As a mixed couple, there are many things we cannot do together. Yet the one that hurts me the most is not to be able to go to the same church. In my heart, your God is my God."

"I've never thought of God as bein' black or white," Pappy added.

"Sometimes I even think of Him as a Her," Becky spouted out.

Everyone seated around the table stared at her, speechless.

"I mean, it could happen," Becky said defensively.

Miriam reached across the table, placing her hand on Becky's. "Child, starting tonight and every night from here on, you and your auntie are gonna hold a Bible study."

********

The Crusaders of the New Zion Church, led by Reverend Pleasant, sat on twenty acres of flat grassland. It was a white wooden structure on a beam platform, with windows on all sides and a tall spire with a bell that folks heard for miles. It was large enough to seat the one-hundred-person congregation, though full capacity they achieved only on Christmas and Easter.

Josh and the Widow Desman sat in the front pew with, thankfully, Abigail and Gregory Cutter sitting between them. Reverend Pleasant spoke for an hour and a half on the Beatitudes applied to everyday life. After that point, he began losing folk's attention. The sweet aroma of slow-cooked beef filled the church. The smoke circled, snaking from pew to pew, tweaking every nose. All eyes were on the windows, and all minds remained focused on the activities outside. Reverend Pleasant was no fool. He knew a hungry stomach will always win over a hungry soul. So he cut the sermon short. They stood, ending with a chorus of Rock of Ages, and then rushed to the nearby picnic grounds.

A team of men oversaw the cooking. They kept the fire hot, but the flames down. The side of beef was on a spit that the small boys took turns spinning. Now and then, one of the men dunked a mop with a cut-down handle into a bucket of sauce and slobbered large strokes of the nectar along the side of the meat. Droplets of beef fat and sauce fell onto the hot coals, hissing and sending up a scent that had everyone salivating.

The women of the church hurried about covering one table with bowls of salads and vegetables, another with breads and deserts.

Before food service, everyone stopped and bowed their heads as Reverend Pleasant said grace. Seated with Abigail and Gregory Cutter were the Jeffersons, Liam and Prudence, two old friends of the Cutters. Seated on one side of the picnic table were the Widow Desman and Josh.

"You must call me 'Evelyn'," she said, smiling at Josh.

"You must call me 'Josh'."

An assessment of the Widow Desman would depend on whose eyes you were looking through. Women often described her as pretty in the face, a compliment that ignored her other physical aspects, which most women tend to ignore anyway. Men fell into two camps of thought. There were those who professed being attracted to a woman with some meat on her bones. "Give me a big gal every time," was how they phrased it. The other group of men, not attracted to large women, called her *Buffalo Gal*, though never to her face. They also made crude and rude remarks in private, comparing her to common, large farm animals.

Her two young boys, Richard and Robert, nine and ten respectively, were rotund whirlwinds, running in circles, constantly shrieking in high-pitched voices.

"Richard, Robert! Richard, Robert!" The Widow Desman called them many times before they stopped and listened. "I don't want either of you boys going near the dessert table till you've been through the food line, filled your plates, and finished every bite." They nodded and ran off.

"Shall we?" Josh asked, pointing to the line forming at the food tables.

"My pleasure," Evelyn responded with a smile.

Standing in line, they made small talk.

"It's so nice of Mr. and Mrs. Cutter to invite us to sit with them," Evelyn said. "Do you realize we are probably the only two landowners in the county who are single? It's good that we get to know each other."

Josh nodded.

She continued. "After all, you never can tell what might happen. Who knows, the love of your life may live right down the road from you."

"Who knows?" Josh agreed, fighting the urge to make a run for it.

They each took a plate and started to make selections at the first table. Evelyn piled on salads, vegetables, and a mound of potatoes.

"Do you mind?" she asked, getting Josh to hold her full plate as she took another. At the next table, she formed a mountain of sliced beef covered with grilled onions and savory sauce. In gentlemanly fashion, Josh took her second full plate to free her hands. She took another plate and loaded it with slices of home baked breads and a slab of fresh churned butter.

Josh relieved her of this plate and placed all the plates on the reserved picnic table. He sat down. Evelyn returned with still another plate, this one covered with cakes and pies. The two of them sat alone. Clearly, the Cutters and the Jeffersons were allowing them time so they could become more acquainted. Evelyn arranged the four plates in front of her, liberally salting and peppering everything except the deserts.

"I normally don't eat this much," she said, "but it is a special occasion, and with all the effort everyone put in, I'd feel guilty if I didn't try everything." She looked across the table at Josh's plate. There was one ear of corn on it. "Aren't you hungry?" she asked, using her knife and fork to position her food for the attack.

"I'm starving; but I'm a vegetarian."

"A vegetarian, what's that?" she asked, cutting her meat.

"I don't eat meat or by-products from animals or anything thing that comes in contact with meat."

"You eat just vegetables?" she asked with her mouth full.

"Some vegetables, but not ones that destroy the plant when you harvest them, like potatoes, carrots, yams, and such. Also, no butter, cheese, or honey."

"Then, what do you eat?" she asked in mid-chew.

"Corn," he said, holding up the cob.

"Is this some kind of religious thing with you?"

"Somewhat, but it is cost-efficient and very healthy."

Her next question formed in her mind, but she felt uncomfortable asking it. As if he could read her mind, Josh answered it.

"I've eaten like this all my life. I'll never change. If I ever marry, it would have to be to a woman who feels the same."

"Getting acquainted, are we?" Abigail Cutter proclaimed as she and her husband sat down with their plates of food. The Jeffersons joined them.

Both Evelyn and Josh were oblivious to the conversation at the table. Josh just smiled and nodded, Evelyn kept her head down and her mouth full. Finally, when all her plates were clear, she placed her utensils down.

"It'll take a few minutes to round up the boys. I need to head on home before dark."

"Josh can take you home," Abigail Cutter suggested.

"I'd be pleased to," Josh added.

"No, that won't be necessary. Besides, I've got my buggy here." She stood up. "Well, thanks for having me and the boys. It's been fun." She looked at Josh. "It's been nice spending time with you, Josh. I'll be seeing you in church."

With that she rushed off, grabbed her two boys, jumped in her buggy and galloped off leaving a dust cloud behind.

"That's strange," Abigail Cutter said. "Joshua Nunn, what did you say to that sweet, beautiful woman to scare her off like that?"

"I didn't say anything," Josh confessed. "All we did was swop some recipes."

Josh got up, took an empty plate, and piled on potatoes, pea salad, and a fist-sized slice of beef covered with onions and sauce.

# Chapter Ten

# Good with Words

It was late. The barn was dark save for a low burning lantern far from Caleb's reach. He sat on the ground on the soft hay, chained to one of the posts. The barn door opened slowly, in walked Josh.

"I think it's time we talked," Josh said, firm but kindly. Caleb stared at the ground, ignoring him. "I gather you don't like the way your life is going." Caleb's head went up; he shot a look at Josh, expressing pure hatred. Josh continued, "What if I told you that it doesn't have to be this way? What if I told you that you don't have to be a slave anymore, you can be free?"

Caleb's eyes squinted. "I'd say you're a liar, the devil, or both."

Josh shook his head, sighing. "I don't blame you for feeling the way you do. I suppose I'd feel just the same if I went through what you've gone through."

"What do you know of what I've been through?" Caleb hissed through clenched teeth.

"You're right, I don't know," Josh said, "but I do know what's right and what's wrong, and I know slavery is wrong."

"Then why do you own slaves?"

"I don't really. I only do on paper. What if I told you every slave on this plantation is working their way to freedom, and I'm helping them everyway I can?"

Caleb stood up, looking Josh squarely in the eye. "Do you dangle a carrot in front of all your animals to get more work out of them?" Caleb spit in Josh's face.

Josh took out a handkerchief from his jacket pocket and wiped his face. "So, that's the way it's going to be. You won't even listen to me."

Caleb's eyes burned like hot red coals. "You think you've got them all fooled. Especially that sweet innocent kid, Becky; she thinks you really care. Not me, I see right through you. One day I'll kill you with my own hands; I swear I'll kill you."

Again, Josh shook his head. He turned and left the barn.

********

"Why did you buy this young man?" Miriam asked.

"It's because I never learned to say no to my daughter," Josh replied.

Everyone seated at the dinner table looked at Becky as Miriam questioned her. "Becky, sweetheart, I know you have a good heart; but why did you feel a need to save this particular young man?"

Becky looked to her grandfather. "Pappy understands why I did."

All eyes looked to Pappy. "I told the child a story about love at first sight, and she believed me."

"Was the story true or not?" Becky asked.

Pappy remained silent.

"Was it?" Becky insisted, almost in tears.

Pappy bowed his head and shook it. "Yes, it was all true."

"Pappy, what's this all about?" Ellie asked.

"I told your daughter how your mother and me met. I told her it was love at first sight and how I knew she was the woman I was gonna marry."

"So, you think this boy is your soul mate, just by looking at him," Ellie scolded Becky. "If you think you're going to marry this boy..."

"Hold on," Josh said. "Nobody's going to marry anybody. I've tried to talk with Caleb; it's like talking to a wall. He's just one big bundle of anger and hate."

"Maybe I should talk to him?" Becky asked.

"You'll do no such thing. We can't take the chance. There're too many lives involved. Promise me you won't say anything about our plans," Josh insisted.

"I promise," Becky said reluctantly.

Josh placed his hand on Becky's. "I know it's hard, but it's the only way. Tell me, what food have you been bringing out to barn?"

"Anything we have left over from what we eat."

"That won't do anymore," Josh said. "From now on, you make him something nutritious but more in line with what he'd get at any other plantation. If he thinks he's a slave, then we need to treat him like one."

"What are we going to do with this young man?" Aaron asked. "We can't just keep him chained up in the barn, day and night."

Just then, someone tapped on the wood frame of the dining room doorway; they all turned to see who it was. A tall, slender, young, white man stood smiling and holding his hat in his hand. He was blonde with fair skin. His eyes were dull baby blue; his Adam's apple prodded from his slender throat nearly as far as his chin. He wore a clean farmhand outfit, but nearly an inch of dry mud clung to his boots.

"You wanted to see me, Mr. Nunn?" the young man said.

"Lester, come in. Everyone, this is Lester Burton. Lester is one of the seminarians from South Carolina here to help us out as a foreman. Lester, I don't think you've meet my aunt and uncle, Miriam and Aaron."

"Sir, ma'am, pleased to meet you."

"Would you like something to eat?" Ellie asked.

"No, ma'am, we just ate, and I had plenty."

"Ya better eat whenever it's offered, son," Pappy said, smiling. "A fellow like ya needs to put on some weight. You're so skinny, I bet when it rains you got to run around in a circle just to get wet." They all laughed.

"Lester," Josh said. "We've got a young black man chained up in the barn. He's been a slave all his life; I think he's had a hard time of it. I don't think he's ready to accept or understand what we're trying to do here at the Bush Plantation. So, we're going to keep him in the dark. Still, we can't leave him chained in the barn all day. Last year, we started clearing the back forty. We felled all the trees, but most of the stumps are still there. If we can get those stumps up, we'd have more land for farming. The young man in the barn's name is Caleb. Tomorrow, I want you to take the buckboard, put all the tools you think you'll need, and get him to clear that land. I don't care how long it takes. You own a shotgun, Lester?"

"I got me a double-barrel, why?"

"I want you to stand over him with that shotgun. Let's help him believe what he's determined to believe."

********

The hot sun moved slowly across the sky. Lester sat on the edge of the wagon, his wide brim straw hat shaded his face; his shotgun hung in the crook of his arm. Caleb used a shovel to dig around the tree stumps. When there was enough root exposure, he used a long crowbar to pry the stumps up. This went on for days with both men saying nary a word between them.

"Why don't you take your shirt off?" Lester suggested. Caleb ignored him. "Would you like some water?"

"Why you so concerned about my well-being?" Caleb asked. "Is it compassion or are you feeling guilty."

"Guilty about what?"

"About owning slaves."

"Why would I feel guilty about that, I don't own no slaves."

"Then why you tryin' to be so nice?"

"I'm just trying to be Christian," Lester said.

"A Christian don't stand over a man, pointing a gun at him all day," Caleb declared.

Lester placed the gun on the buckboard next to him.

"I'll have that water now," Caleb said.

Lester reached for the bucket, placing it on the edge of the wagon. Caleb put down the crowbar and walked over. He reached out for the ladle hanging from the side of the bucket. Instead, in the blink of an eye, he grabbed Lester's gun.

"Get down from there," Caleb demanded, pointing the gun at Lester's chest. Lester couldn't move save for raising his hands high. "I said, get down!" Caleb shouted as he swung the butt of the gun around, catching Lester square on the jaw. Lester flew off the wagon and flat down on the ground. Caleb pointed the double barrels an inch from Lester's face. "Since you're a man of God, how about you meet Him right now?" Lester closed his eyes real tight. Caleb pulled the trigger. Click! The gun was empty. Lester swung his leg out, causing Caleb to back into the wagon. Lester jumped up. With his left hand he took hold of the gun; with his right he punched Caleb on the jaw, hard. Caleb fell to the ground.

"You tried to kill me!" Lester shouted.

"I couldn't! You didn't have any shells in it! What kind of man goes around with a gun and no shells?"

Being a seminarian, the missionary came out in Lester. "*Thou shall not kill* says the Bible, not to mention all that blaspheming you were doing. Didn't you ever read the Bible?"

"No, I never did!" Caleb growled as he rose to his feet, brushing himself off.

"Why not?" Lester barked.

"Because I can't read, you stupid hillbilly!"

A calm look washed over Lester's face. "You can't? Heck, I can teach you how to read." Lester walked to the front of the wagon, grabbed the lunch basket and his Bible. "Sit here. I guess it's always best to start at the front and work back, cover to cover. *In the beginning...*"

********

Becky thought she was hiding her true feelings from her family. Being older and wiser, they'd all lived through what she was experiencing, so they recognized it for what it was. Becky was smitten with Caleb. She stayed true to her promise not to say a word about the family to Caleb. Yet, when it came to bringing simple food out to Caleb in the barn every night, she crossed her fingers behind her back, and each night brought him a tray of leftovers from the family's supper. Each morning, she'd pack the lunch basket with as much goodies as she could lay her hands on, much to the delight of Lester as well.

Every night when she brought the food out to Caleb, she'd sit with him and talk. As time went on, these talks became longer and longer, till it was bedtime when she got back to the house. Josh and Ellie wanted so badly to say something to their little girl. That was the problem. Becky was no longer a little girl. She was a young woman who had to live her own life as she saw fit. So, Josh and Ellie kept hush; and with enough warnings, Pappy learned to bite his tongue.

Becky and Caleb talked about everything under the sun. Till one night, it all changed. It became personal.

"I don't like the way he looks at you," Caleb said.

"The way who looks at me?" Becky asked.

"Your master, he has a certain way of looking at you. I don't know what it is. I can't put my finger on it, but I don't like it."

"You're just imagining things." Becky tried not to laugh. She knew what that look was. It was the look of a loving father for his daughter.

Caleb placed his hand on Becky's. They'd never touched before. It startled her, but it felt good.

"One day, I'm going to run off to freedom, and I'm going to take you with me," he said.

"What makes you think I'd go? Besides, I don't go running off with any man, just because he asks me."

"I won't be just any man; I'd be your husband."

"You mean that you'd marry me?"

"Of course, I would. I'm a good Christian man, you know? At least I will be as soon as Lester gets me through this here book, and I get baptized." He placed his hand on the Bible at his side, the one Lester gave him. There was a pencil and paper. He picked up a folded piece of paper and handed it to her.

"Lester's been teaching me to read and write. I ain't much good at it yet, but I'd like you to be the first person I write a letter to."

Becky took the slip of paper and held it to her heart. "I'd be privileged." She hung her head, shyly. "Caleb, tell me why?"

"Why what?"

"Why do you want to marry me?"

"Because…"

"Because why?"

"Gee, Becky, I ain't no good at words, so I put it all there in the letter."

"Becky! It's time to for bed. Get yourself in the house," they heard Becky's mother call from the back porch.

"Coming," she hollered back. A moment of awkward silence lingered. Still shyly looking down, she spoke. "Caleb, since we're engaged, don't you think we should seal it with a kiss?"

"I suspect so."

They slowly leaned forward towards each other till their lips met. They kissed. It was worthy of a first kiss…soft, sweet, and memorable. Becky jumped up and rushed for the barn door. "I'll see you at breakfast," she said over her shoulder, afraid to look back and break the spell.

Later, alone in her room, she opened the note and read it. The handwriting was clumsy; the words were few and simple.

> *My name is Caleb.*
> *What is you name?*
> *I love you.*

She read it again and again through tearful eyes. She folded it and placed it under her pillow so she'd dream of him all night. Caleb was wrong. At least for Becky, he was good with words.

# Chapter Eleven

# Down to the Last Brown

The family meeting, usually scheduled at night, they held in the daytime. Only then was the barn empty while Lester and Caleb worked the back forty. Pappy pounded on the table for order.

"Cousin Ezra, would you please make your report?"

Ezra brought his leather-bought ledger, placed it on the table, and opened it.

"Money-wise, we's holdin' our own. I do pray we don't have no emergencies, cause if we don't, we be just fine." He turned a few pages to the back of the book. "As for the amount of family members still not bought..."

Pappy interrupted, "Cousin Ezra, sorry to break in on you like this. Before you go any further, Brother Aaron has something to say about this. Aaron?"

Aaron stood up in the middle of the crowd, his hands folded before him. He hung his head as if in shame. "My brother has shown me the list of family members. I'm so sorry to tell you this. I know for a fact that only one person on that list is still alive. The others are dead."

The family went silent, holding their breath.

"I know for certain as of three months ago that Jasper Brown, Millie Brown's boy, is still alive; and I know where he is."

Jasper's immediate family let out a sigh of relief and cries of praise and thanks to learn he was still alive. Those closest to whose names Aaron didn't call let out moans of despair and loss. Pappy waited for the moment to pass.

"We need to get in touch with Judd Taylor." Pappy was looking at Josh as he spoke. "Tell him we want to buy Jasper. Tell him we want Jasper first; but I want you to include the names of the other family members on the list."

"I don't understand," Josh said. "If they're dead, why keep them on the list?"

"Because, Judd Taylor may be good at what he does, but he's not an honest man. He's gone along with us so far because there was money to be made. When he learns there are no more family members for him to find, he'll know there's no more money to be made. He's probably figured we intend to skedaddle up north once the family is a whole. There are plenty of people who'd pay good money for that information. If folks got wind of what we were up to, the property would be lost; and everybody here would be sold into slavery, except you Josh. You'd go to prison. We need to keep him thinking there's more money to be made. By the time he figures it out, we'll be long gone."

********

The next day Josh rode into town and stopped at the Telegraph Office to get a message to Judd Taylor. Early on, they worked out a code so no one would be the wiser. The word *Client* was code for *Slave*, the word *Contact* was code for *Buy*. Josh telegraphed Judd the list of *Clients*, with orders that Jasper Brown, a resident at the Sherwood Plantation in Alabama, was to be his first *Contact*.

Just over a week later, Josh received a message from Judd Taylor. *Have found client, have not made contact. Will let you know amount needed.* Three days later, Josh received another wire from Judd, *Have made offer to owner of eight hundred, more than worth of merchandise. He declined. Need to know budget.*

This called for an emergency family meeting in the barn. Cousin Ezra, standing before the family, holding his ledger, did not have good news.

"We don't even have enough to cover Judd Taylor's first bid of eight hundred for Jasper, never mind trying to up the ante."

"Maybe we could sell something," Ellie said.

"What could we sell?" Josh replied. "We don't own anything of value except our crop, and that won't be in till next season."

"Yes we do," said a small voice from the back of the crowd. Everyone moved aside to give young Hattie Brown room to speak. She was a teenage girl, as thin as a beanpole, and shy and skittish as a squirrel. Everyone had to be quiet to hear her soft voice. "We do have something of value. We have the plantation."

"Are you saying we take a mortgage out on the plantation," Josh said. "The plantation's our whole life, it's all we have."

"The girl's right," Pappy said, standing up. "Jasper is the last relative we need to buy; and then it don't matter anymore. After that, we all gonna skedaddle up North and never come back again. If a promissory note from a bank will help get us all to the Promised Land, then so be it. The Bush Plantation was given to me, it belongs to me, and I say borrow on it and let them take it in foreclosure when we fail on the loan or sell it straight out. Either way, it's my decision, and I say do what needs to be done."

********

The Southern Farmer and Cattleman's Bank was an old establishment, in an old building, in an old part of town, run by an even older man, Bank President Cornelius Blackwell. The war put a damper on everyone's life, but not Cornelius'. The bank prospered. What with folks selling land at a third the price just to make ends meet, folks failing on loans, foreclosures on property, Cornelius and the bank were having a wingding of a time. They would keep this uphill climb just as long as the confederate dollar held its value.

No one knew how old Cornelius truly was. Some said he was a pallbearer at Methuselah's funeral. He married into money...not once, but twice. He'd outlived and buried both wives, the last one more than twenty years ago. He was a boney creature. His stringy hair was a mixture of shades of gray and white, as was his skin, his manner of dress was similar to the villains in the works of Mr. Charles Dickens. He stood, smiling as Josh entered his office.

"Mr. Nunn, what a surprise. Have a seat. Would you like a drink or perhaps a cigar?"

"No thanks," Josh said.

"Well then, I hope you don't mind if I do." Cornelius took his time to light a cigar and pour himself a brandy. He'd learned that making a client wait made them nervous, putting them off guard. Having the upper hand is like making the first move in chess. If you don't make any mistakes, do all the right moves, the game is yours from the beginning.

"So, Mr. Nunn, for what do I owe the pleasure?"

"Well, sir, recently I cleared forty acres at the back of my property. I'd like to start farming it, but that will take some doing. I'll need more equipment: perhaps a new barn, more workers, and of course someplace to house them."

"That's quite an undertaking, young man," said the banker, drawing on his cigar. "So I presume you're here to see about a loan?"

"Yes I am, sir."

"I suppose you'd like to put your plantation up as collateral? How much will you need?"

"I was thinking ten thousand; the land alone is worth that."

The banker put his drink and cigar down as he shook his head. "Mr. Nunn, you do know there's a war on, don't you? I agree your property is worth far more than ten thousand, and I'd gladly give you that amount if these were different times."

"Well then, how much can you give me?"

Cornelius took up a paper and pencil. He stared silently for a moment at the slip of paper, as if adding numbers in his head. He was doing no such thing. He knew the amount he'd offer the second Josh entered the office. He wrote a number down on the paper and slid it across the desk to Josh.

"Four thousand, I'm talking about all my acreage, the equipment, the house, and the barn!"

"I understood that to be the case. I wish it could be more, but you must remember that there is a..."

"A war going on, yes I know. What if I throw in all the slaves, too? That's thirty healthy men and women who are good workers, and that's not counting children."

Cornelius put on his thinking face again. "I could give you an additional two thousand."

"Didn't you hear me? I said thirty slaves!"

"Mr. Nunn, nowadays slaves are two for a dollar. The south is overrun with them. Remember, they have to be housed, clothed, and feed for a long time before I could sell them and make a profit. I'll tell you what I'll do; I'll up it another thousand. That's seven thousand; my best offer, take it or leave it."

Now it was time for Josh to put on his worried face. Seven thousand was far more than Josh thought the bank would offer.

"Well, Mr. Blackwell, you've got me over a barrel. I guess I'll take it."

"Wise choice, young man, wise choice, I'll have the contract drawn up immediately."

********

Sitting on the veranda of the main house, Josh read Judd Taylor's wire to Pappy. It was short and to the point. *They have declined new offer. What now?*

"How much did you allow Judd to offer for Jasper?" Pappy asked.

"I told him two thousand."

"Two thousand, and they still won't sell." Pappy shook his head in worry. "Wire Judd and tell him to get started looking for the others on the list. That will keep him busy and out of our hair."

"What are we going to do, Pappy?"

"There's only one thing we can do. If they won't sell Jasper to us, we'll just have to go get him."

# Chapter Twelve

# Thunder Down Under

The third and final letter came on a Friday night. The family was glad it would be the last time the local ladies of the county would impose on Josh, but the uncertainty of its content worried them. As they sat on the veranda of the main house after dinner, watching the sunset, Josh read it aloud, slow and clear.

*My dear Mr. Nunn,*

*I'm sorry I did not get with you sooner. I apologize for the discomfort and hardship you must have endured at the hands of my lady friends, Charlotte Buchman and Abigail Cutter. I met Charlotte Buchman's cousin, a nice girl, but clearly not your type. As for Abigail Cutter's choice of a mate for you, the Widow Desman, good taste and Christian charity forbid me to say what we both know of the woman. If only I had been the first to present my choice, all this could have been avoided. That was not possible. My choice being my niece, Charity Hope Mercy Goodman (I know it's a mouthful, but have no fear, everyone calls her Peaches) has only recently come to visit us from Dexter County. I've spoken to her about you, and I'm sure I've fired her interest. I've made her promise to visit you at your plantation. Being a shy child, I've promised not to accompany her. I realize this is highly unorthodox, but I do trust you, and I won't tell anyone if you don't. She will come alone this coming Thursday at noon. I feel positive you two will hit it off. I'm sure you are a perfect match for each other. I know you are a gentleman; but tread lightly, for she is a gentle flower.*

*With best regards,*
*Harriet Garrett*

"Does this mean I've got to change my name to Goodman?" Becky asked in jest.

"Don't be silly, child," Aunt Miriam kidded. "It's the wife who always takes the husband's name."

"Now stop that!" Josh shouted. "Nobody's gonna marry anybody! I'm already married, and happily, too!"

"Well, that's good to hear," Ellie said.

Josh looked at Pappy. "I suppose you've got some sly remark. Well, go ahead, have at it."

"What?" Pappy said, as innocent looking as can be. "I ain't gonna say nothin'…Mr. Goodman, sir."

********

For the next few days, no one in the main house spoke of anything other than the approaching visit of Harriet Garret's niece, *Peaches*. They decided to use the same strategy they used with Charlotte Buchman's cousin, Fiona Bredworthy. They'd portray Josh as a heavy drinker, gambler, and philanderer, clearly poor husband material.

The day of Peaches' visit, Josh sat on the veranda, waiting, mentally preparing himself. Pappy came out to join him. He carried a tray. On it were an uncorked bottle of bourbon and two glasses. He placed it on the table next to Josh, sat down and poured, filling both glasses to the brim.

"What's that for, courage?" Josh asked.

"Partly," Pappy smiled, holding up one glass handing the other to Josh. "Mostly, it's for looks. If you're supposed to be a drunk, it best be ya smells like one."

"I can do that by just swirling a mouthful and then spitting it out," Josh replied.

"True, but a glassy-eyed look wouldn't hurt matters. Down the hatch."

Josh took two sips and placed the glass down. "My, but that's nasty."

"I never been here nor there when it comes to drinkin'. I can take it or leave it. I do know one thing, though. The more you drink the better it tastes. Hold your nose and try to get some more down."

Josh held his nose and finished half. He held his breath and finished the rest. His eyes began to tear. Pappy refilled both their glasses. This time Josh downed half his glass without holding his nose.

"You're right. Once you get started, it don't taste so bad. It kind of grows on you." Pappy went to top off Josh's glass. Josh covered his hand over the rim of his glass. "No, I better not drink anymore. I've got to be sober enough to meet what's her name…Honeydew, Persimmon, whatever."

"You mean Peaches," Pappy said.

"Yeah, whatever, I knew it was some kind of vegetable."

"We need to make a toast," Pappy said, raising his glass. "Here's to Ellie, a good woman, daughter, and wife."

"To Ellie!" Josh countered, taking a drink.

"And here's to Becky, a great daughter and granddaughter."

"To Becky!" Josh shouted, taking another sip. He smiled at Pappy. "You know, you're not such a bad old geezer. A bit cantankerous at times, but I love you. You know I love you?"

"I love ya, too. Say, why don't we drink to that? Here's to love!" Pappy toasted. Josh downed his drink, placed his glass on the table and smiled at Pappy. "Son," Pappy said, "I believe ya is inebriated."

"Inebriated?"

"Intoxicated..."

"Intoxicated?"

"Ya is drunk, boy. Ain't a woman in her right mind that would have ya, now. Peaches is gonna take one look at ya and turn around and run to her auntie."

"Who's Peaches?" Josh asked.

Just then, they heard the sound of a galloping horse coming through the main gate. They looked up to see a large cowhand riding hellfire to the front of the house. He wore a large Texas-style cowboy hat, plaid shirt, blue jeans, and spurs on knee-high boots.

"Who could that be?" Josh slurred the question.

"Probably Peaches' boyfriend come to punch you in the nose," Pappy laughed.

The horseman stopped abruptly in front of them. Josh and Pappy waved the dust from the air.

"How can we help you, partner?" Josh asked. He'd used the word "partner" only because it seemed appropriate. The horseman dismounted.

"I'm looking for Joshua Nunn."

"What would you want of him?" Josh asked nervously.

"Just a word or two with him."

"Who might you be?"

The horseman took off his hat and hair fell down to his shoulders "The name's Peaches."

Josh and Pappy's jaws dropped. With closer inspection, though not so obvious, they realized that what they thought was a *he* was actually a *she*.

"So, you're Peaches. I'm Josh Nunn. It's a pleasure to meet you." The two shook hands.

"Would ya have a drink with us?" Pappy asked.

"Don't mind if I do. I'm a bit parched from all that ridin'."

"I'll just go get ya a glass."

"No need. I'll just take a few swigs straight from the bottle, if ya gents don't mind."

"Oh, we don't mind."

Peaches put the bottle to her lips, tilled back her head, and downed a quarter of the bottle. She was a remarkable looking woman. She stood no less that four inches taller than Josh, and must have had at least ten pounds on him. Her arms were thick, pressing against the material of her shirt. Close up, her feminine features, though few, were obvious. With her hair tucked under her hat, she could pass for a cowhand who just shaved real close.

"So, what is it you want to talk about?" Josh asked, sitting down, offering Peaches the chair next to him. He did his best to sit up straight and not slur his words. It was obvious he was drunk; and it was clear Peaches couldn't care less.

"Mr. Nunn, let me come right to the point."

"Call me 'Josh'."

"Josh, let me come right to the point. I'm sure you're a fine man; and someday you'll make some woman a fine husband. I tell ya, that woman just ain't me. I'm here only because of my Aunt Harriet. She means well, but she can be…"

"Pushy?" Josh added.

"I was going to say assertive, but I guess 'pushy' says it better. I'm just not in the market for a man. I've got plans of my own."

"Have another?" Pappy asked, handing the bottle once more to Peaches. She downed what was left, to the amazement of both men.

"What plans are you talking about?" Josh asked.

Her face lit up with a smile from ear to ear. "Ranchin', that's the life for me."

"What kind of ranchin'?" Pappy asked.

"Cattle and horses, but not just any cattle or horses: longhorns and quarter horses. That's what I want," she said with pride.

"Where you gonna do this ranchin'?"

"Australia!"

"Australia?"

"Yup, Australia. They got plenty of territory out there where a person can live the way they want, be they a man or a woman. So, ya see, Josh, there can never be anything between us. I hope you're not too disappointed?"

"Let's just say this wasn't what I expected, but I'll get over it," Josh said, offering his hand. "We can still be friends, can't we?"

She took his hand, smiling, pumped it like she was working a water pump. "I would consider it a honor and a privilege to call ya friend." She got up and walked to her horse.

"I'd appreciated it if ya made up something good to tell my Aunt Harriet, and please don't tell her about Australia."

Josh put his finger to his lips. "Mum's the word."

"Nice to make your acquaintance, Josh, and ya, too, feller." She tucked her hair under her hat and mounted her horse.

"Nice to meet you, too, Peaches."

With a jab of her spurs, her horse took off like lighting. They watched her ride off in a cloud of dust. Pappy placed his hand on Josh's shoulder.

"All I can say is, 'Heaven help Australia'."

# Chapter Thirteen

# Welcome to the Family

Becky gathered some hay into a pile and sat down on it. She enjoyed watching Caleb eat. He stopped in midbite.

"Why you looking at me like that?"

"I don't know. I like looking at you." She smiled. "So, Caleb, what did you do today?"

"What I do everyday, I pull tree stumps up in the back forty. What kind of question is that anyway?"

"I just think a wife should take an interest in her husband's work. After all, someday we'll be married. You did promise to marry me."

He put the drumstick down. "I did, didn't I?" He sat up straight. "Darn, if I didn't! I meant it to! In fact, let's get married soon, this week!"

The smile left her face. "Caleb, I didn't mean this week, just someday."

"Why not this week? We can run away together and get married."

"You mean elope?"

"No, I mean runaway. We are slaves, you know?"

"People just don't do that. I mean, I'd have to ask my…" she stopped short of what her mind wanted to say.

"Go ahead, say it. You'd have to ask your master. I don't believe you, sometimes. What does that man have on you? I don't understand."

"I can't explain it. He's been so good to me. I've known him all my life."

"He's own you all your life, you mean. That's it! Tomorrow we run off together. I want you to pack your things tonight and be ready to runoff when you bring me my dinner tomorrow night."

"Caleb, can't we just wait, be engaged for a year or so?"

"No! It's tomorrow night or never!" He reached over, took her in his arms, and kissed her long and hard. She melted in his arms. "Tomorrow night?" he asked softly.

She swooned, "Tomorrow night."

\*\*\*\*\*\*\*\*

In the early morning, Becky found her father alone in the library drinking coffee. He sat at his desk, his head low as he studied books on farming and peanut growing. He looked up to see his daughter. He smiled.

"Sweetheart, what is it?"

"Daddy, can we talk?"

"Oh, course, princess."

"I've been thinking."

"About what?"

She hesitated. "Daddy, how did you know you loved Momma?"

"I just knew."

"Yeah, but, when did you know? What first attracted you to her?"

"It wasn't what first attracted me to your mother that made me know I loved her. I was attracted to her the second I laid eyes on her. That got us talking; but it was the talking that made me fall in love. I got to see how beautiful she was inside, as well as out."

"Like what?"

"She's tender and understanding, she has a good heart. She's loving and easy to love."

"You think I'm like her?"

"In some ways, but you're your own person. Becky, does this have anything to do with Caleb?"

"Is it that obvious?"

"He seems like a nice boy, a little bit confused; but that's understandable. Listen, Becky, I'm your father, and I want to see you happy and I don't want to see you hurt. Talk to your mother; she'll know what to do."

********

Ellie, Aunt Miriam, and Becky spent the afternoon in the kitchen making bread. Once the loaves were in the oven, they sat on the back porch waiting.

"Momma," said Becky, playing with the edge of the tablecloth. "How old were you when you married Daddy?"

"I just turned twenty. Why?"

"I don't know. I was just wondering. I'm nineteen and a half."

"Why, you thinking of getting married?" Aunt Miriam asked.

"What girl doesn't?" said Becky, finally looking up.

"Well, I was older than you when I married," Ellie said.

"Only by six months."

"That's not what I mean. I was older in many ways then you are now. You're still a child."

"I am not a child! I don't feel like a child. I'm a woman just like you!" Becky protested.

"Listen, when I was your age, I had my father to look after; and I ran this house and still do. You've never had any responsibilities. I'm afraid that's mine and your father's fault, but it's true."

"I'll just be an old maid, I guess," Becky pouted. "Aunt Miriam, why didn't you marry?"

"I should take offense," Aunt Miriam laughed. "You putting marriage and old maid in the same breath and then looking to me."

"I didn't mean…"

"It's all right, child; I understand. Slavery…slavery is the reason I never married. The plantation I lived on didn't allow slaves to marry. Some of the larger, stronger girls were allowed to have children; multiply the master's wealth, so to speak. That would have been nice, to become a mother of a brood. I guess I was too small and ugly to let that happen." The sadness in her voice silenced them for a moment.

"Say, what's this all about? You're not falling for that nappy-haired Caleb, are you?"

"What if I am?"

"He maybe nappy, but he sure is handsome," Aunt Miriam added.

"Aunt Miriam, don't encourage her. And you, young lady, maybe you should stop taking Caleb his dinner?"

"You smell that?" Becky shouted.

"I don't care if you think it stinks or not," her mother scolded.

"That's not what I mean, mother. I think the bread is burning!"

********

Becky found Pappy and Uncle Aaron on the veranda, watching the sunset. There was a half empty bottle of bourbon on the table between them. They sipped at their glasses in silence. Pappy turned to see her and smiled.

"Pumpkin, you come to see your old grandpa?"

"I need some advice, Pappy."

"You want me to leave?" Uncle Aaron asked.

"No, Uncle Aaron, please stay. I need all the help I can get."

Aaron looked at his brother, "This sounds serious."

Pappy looked to Becky. "What's bother you, Pumpkin. Ask me anything."

"I want to know about love."

"Well, you came to the right place because I'm an expert in love. You know why?" She shook her head. "Because I been in love. Just like a swimmer gets to be an expert swimmer, by being in the water, I got to be an expert in love by being in love."

"It all depends on what kind of love you're talking about," Aaron added. "Some people love cornbread, some folk love corn liquor. Me, I once loved a horse named Bluebell."

Pappy slapped his brother's arm. "She's talking about the love between a man and a woman, and you know it. Quit trying to confuse the girl. Now, Pumpkin, who you in love with?"

"Caleb."

"You mean that boy we bought for fifty dollars and keep locked up in the barn?"

"That's him."

"Well, I don't know, Pumpkin, he don't seem too bright."

"No, Grandpa, he's very smart and he's very sweet."

"Sweet ya say?"

"He wants to marry me."

Pappy took a long drink of bourbon; he thought long and hard before he spoke. "As your grandpa, my first thought is to talk ya out of it. Speaking from the heart, person to person, I'd say love is the most important thing in the world and ya should take it wherever ya find it, even if it cost ya the world." He turned to his brother. "Ya got anything to add to that, Aaron."

Aaron finished his drink in one hard swallow. He stared at the ground as he spoke. "As a man who's never been allowed to love, I'd give my right arm to have someone."

There seemed nothing left to say. Becky went up to her room to pack.

********

After a long hard day, Lester returned Caleb to the barn.

"Do I have to wear shackles on my feet? It's so uncomfortable," Caleb pleaded. "My hand is chained to the post. I'm not going to go anywhere. Come on, Lester; show a little Christian Kindness."

Lester liked Caleb; he felt sympathy for him. He hated not having permission to let him in on the true nature and mission of the plantation. To treat him like a slave where slavery found no acceptance or tolerance weighted heavy on him. When Caleb begged for "Christian Kindness", his heart melted. He chained Caleb's right arm to metal ring set deep into a wood post.

"Wrap those chains around your ankles. If Master Nunn comes in, act like your feet are shackled. If he finds out, he'll have my hide."

"I appreciate this, Lester. You're a true brother in the faith."

"I just wish I had more faith in my brother. Promise me you won't do anything stupid."

Caleb did have a plan, but he didn't consider it stupid. Still, just to be on the safe side; he crossed his fingers behind his back. "Lester, I'm chained to a post, where do you think I can go?"

Lester sighed, walking out of the barn. "I'll see you in the morning," he called over his shoulder.

"I'll see you in my dreams," Caleb said under his breath.

There was a tool locker on the other side of the barn, but it was too far and the chain was too short. Caleb quickly sat down when he heard someone at the barn door. It was Becky with his supper.

"What are you doing here," he scolded. "I told you to not come tonight. I told you to be ready to run away with me."

"I just figured you were hungry. Besides, how are you going to get loose from those chains?"

He stood up, stepping out from the chains around his ankles.

"How did you do that?" she exclaimed.

"I have my ways. I'll get out of this thing, too." He shook the chain from his wrist to the post. "I won't need any help from you." He thought about asking her to fetch a tool from the locker, but his pride got the best of him. He'd free himself, sneak up to her room and off they'd go. "Now, get back in the house and wait for me to come get you."

She wasn't so much offended as surprised at his bossiness. "Yes, Master." She turned to leave. "I'll be back for the tray in the morning."

"By morning, we'll be miles away," he said with such confidence she couldn't help but believe him.

"I'll be in my room. Wait till everyone's asleep."

********

The next few hours, Caleb tugged at the chain. He heard the soft sound of creaking wood as the bolt that held the chain to the post slowly started to come out. He began pulling the chain from side to side to loosen it. Finally, it gave way; and he flew across the barn, landing on his back inches from the tool locker. In it, he found everything he needed.

He hacked and sawed till he freed himself of the shackles. He took the crowbar – in case he needed a weapon.

The night was dark; a light shown from a second-story bedroom. He thought of calling up to Becky but was afraid of waking the others. He walked around the house and barn – looking for a ladder but found none. There was only one thing to do…enter.

He moved slowly down the dark hallway to the foot of the staircase. He spread his legs, stepping on the outer part of each step so they wouldn't creak under his weight. He gripped the railing with one hand, holding the crowbar in the other. A thin light flared from under the bedroom door. He knocked gently.

"It is I, My Love. I've come to take you away."

"You're late," a voice said from within. The door opened. Aunt Miriam stood in her nightgown, holding a lantern. "About forty years too late, I'd say."

"What the…?" he said in surprise.

A strong hand grabbed his shoulder and spun him around. It was Josh. Caleb pulled back with the crowbar; but before he could swing it, Josh pushed him. Caleb tumbled down the stairs, falling flat on his face at the bottom of the stairs. Josh ran down the staircase, but in the darkness he stumbled, falling over Caleb. The two men jumped to their feet. Josh ran into the dining room followed by Caleb swinging his crowbar. Josh tossed dining room chairs in front of Caleb to try to trip him. Josh found himself trapped in a corner. Caleb swung the crowbar, Josh dodged to the right; Caleb tore a hole in the wall. Josh darted to the left; Caleb missed (another hole in the wall). He had Josh cornered. He was about to bring the crowbar crashing down on Josh's head when Becky grabbed hold of his arm.

"Caleb, don't! Don't hurt him! He's not my master, he's my father!"

Caleb turned to look at her. "Say what?"

Josh's fist caught Caleb square on the jaw. The force was so hard that Caleb rolled over the dinner table and onto the floor (unconscious). Becky fell to her knees, taking Caleb's head in her arms.

"Daddy, how could you do such a thing?"

"How could I…he was going to hit me with a crowbar!"

"I think you killed him!"

Pappy bent low to get a good look. "No, he ain't dead. He won't be able to talk proper for a couple of days; the side of his face is gonna swell up like a pineapple."

*********

When Caleb woke, he was lying on a divan. He felt something cool on the side of his face; it was a wet cloth. Sitting up, it fell to the floor. A wave of pain shot through his face and it began to throb. When his eyesight cleared, a very stern looking Josh seated in a chair a few feet away confronted him.

"Go ahead, son. I want to hear it. I want to hear an explanation," Josh said.

"An explanation….?" Caleb stopped midsentence. It hurt to speak. He began again, slowly. "An explanation…? I'm the one who needs an explanation! What kind of plantation are you running here, anyway?"

Josh's features softened and he sighed. "I suppose you're right. This is going to take some time, so sit back and put that wet towel back on your face and relax."

Josh told Caleb everything, from the story of Pappy and Bernie Bush, his marriage to Ellie to the birth of Becky, and finally the gathering of the family to the plantation and their plans. When he finished, Caleb stared in disbelief.

"So, what do you think?" Josh asked.

"What do I think?" Caleb replied, snickering. "I believe every word of it. It has to be true. No one could ever make up something so…so…made-up-sounding."

Just then, Becky entered with a fresh wet towel for Caleb. She sat next to him, dabbing the swollen side of his face.

"You poor baby, what did that mean old man do to you?"

"Be serious, Becky," Caleb said. "Why didn't you tell me he was your father?"

"Because I warned her not to," Josh interrupted.

"Now I know the true story," Caleb replied.

"So, now that you do, are you in with us or not?" Josh asked.

"I'm in deeper than you might imagine," Caleb said, looking at Becky. "Sir, I want to marry your daughter."

A rustling sound came from the doorway. Josh turned to see Ellie. After years of marriage, he could read his wife's thoughts just by looking into her eyes. She was unsure of her only child marrying. She held mix feelings. The mother in her wanted to say "No". The woman in her wanted to cry "Yes". Undecided, she'd leave it to her husband.

Josh turned to Caleb. "First you try to kill me, and then you want to marry my daughter."

"I didn't know, sir. I'm sorry. It does tell you one thing, though."

"What's that?"

"I'm willing to kill or die to be with her."

Josh tried to not look impressed with Caleb's answer, though he was. He turned to his daughter. "Becky, what have you to say?"

She never took her eyes off Caleb. "I love him, Daddy. I never knew I could find such joy being with and doing for someone else."

Josh thought long and hard before speaking, and then he smiled. "Well, it would seem there's gonna be a wedding."

"Ye-haw!" Pappy shouted from the hallway. "It took ya long enough!"

********

It was a beautiful day for a wedding. The sun was shining, the sky was clear, deep blue, and it wasn't too hot. Everyone at the plantation, dressed in their Sunday best, gathered in the clearing alongside of the main house. Folks put out their tables and covered them with food for the wedding feast. Flowers surrounded the area where the young couple would stand. Reverend Ellwood T. Gummer, the black pastor from Madison County came to do the honors.

Up in Becky's room, the ladies were putting on the last touches – weaving small flowers into Becky's hair.

"Sometime, today!" Josh shouted up the stairs.

Aunt Miranda's head popped over the banister. "Hush up; this is Becky's day, not yours. Now get yourself back in the kitchen and wait for your daughter."

Outside, Reverend Gummer took his place. Standing at his side were the groom and his best man, Caleb and Lester.

Lester whispered from the side of his mouth. "Relax, it's just a weddin' not a hangin'."

"I know," Caleb said. "A hangin' is easier."

In the kitchen, the ladies handed the bride to her father and went outside to take their places.

"You know, if it doesn't work out with Caleb, you can always come home," said Josh to Becky.

"That wouldn't be hard, seeing how Caleb and I are going to be living in the main house with you and Momma."

"I know," Josh said, laughing, "but it sounded like the thing to say."

"Daddy, there's no need to worry. Caleb and I are going to be just fine. He's a good man. You may not believe this, but he's a lot like you."

"Like me?"

"More than you'd ever want to admit."

Outside, the three-piece orchestra – a guitar, banjo, and fiddle – broke into the wedding march. Becky slipped her arm through her father's.

"Thanks for being such a good daddy, Daddy."

They slowly walked through the crowd to the front.

"Who gives this woman to this man?" Reverend Gummer asked.

"I do," Josh said as he placed Becky's hand into Caleb's. He smiled at Caleb. "Looks like that swelling went down real good." Caleb wasn't sure if Josh was making a joke or a threat. He was too nervous to answer. Josh took his place next to Ellie who slipped her arm into Josh's and the other into the crooked arm of Pappy.

"Our baby's growing up," Ellie said as she began to cry.

"She looks just like your momma the day we got married," Pappy whispered, holding back the tears.

Reverend Gummer was a good preacher. His wedding ceremonies were heartfelt and warm. He always gave the wedding couple good advice. Yet a nervous young couple can't hear over their own heartbeats. Good advice doesn't make any sense till the day it's needed. Reverend Gummer gave it anyway. He knew it would echo back at the right time. He was a wise old man.

"Now, by the power invested in me by the Great God Almighty Himself, I now pronounce you man and wife."

The crowd cheered; the three piece orchestra began to play. There was dancing, feasting, and laughter. Ellie, Josh, Uncle Aaron, Aunt Miriam, and Pappy circled the newlyweds.

"You do the honors, Pappy; you're the head of this household," Josh said to Pappy.

"First, we'd like to welcome ya to the family, Caleb. We've gotten ya both a wedding gift. When you go upstairs to Becky's room, you'll find a king-size bed, our gift to ya."

"Oh, Grandpa," cried Becky, wrapping her arms around the old man.

Josh motioned for Caleb to step to the side, so he could have a word with him.

"Yes, Dad," Caleb said.

Josh let out a long sigh. "First, don't call me 'Dad'. It makes me feel old. Second, whenever you walk out of your bedroom, please don't smile. As her father, I don't want to live with the images in my mind as to what put that smile on your face." Josh smiled, to make it friendly. Caleb smiled back.

"Whatever you say...Josh."

"Caleb, now that you're a part of this family, we've got to find you something better to do then haulin' up stump in the back forty," Josh said. "Have your honeymoon, but next week I'm putting you to work."

"Doin' what, Josh?"

"You and I are going to take a little trip together. We're going to get us a new slave for the plantation: a family member named Jasper."

The party went on well into the night. When it got dark, when no one was looking, Becky and Caleb snuck off upstairs to see their new king-size bed.

********

Hidden in the forest just off the Bush property, a pair of eyes watched the festivities: a group of evil men with evil intent.

"It's just as ye said, Brother Judd, there's something not right with this here plantation and these here folk."

"It's like I told ya, Brother Tobias," Judd said. "I've been buying slaves for Josh Nunn for a long time, and I think the buyin' is about to stop."

"I remember those folk," said Tobias. "I met 'em on the road to Coopersville, during the slave auction. They acted mighty suspicious."

"They're up to no good, I tell ya," Judd said.

The gold tooth in Tobias' mouth glimmered when he smiled. "I tell ye, it be worse than that, Brother Judd. This here be the work of the devil, I tell ye."

# Chapter Fourteen

# One Cotton Pickin' Minute

They headed west from the Bush Plantation with three horses, Josh riding one, Caleb on another, the third weighed down with provisions. When they found and freed Cousin Jasper, it would be his mount, for surely a fast horse would be the key to a successful getaway.

Becky and Ellie stood on the veranda waving goodbye to their husbands. They did not stop and go into the house until Josh and Caleb were well out of sight.

"If only I were twenty years younger; I would have gone with `em," Pappy said when he met them in the hall.

"I'm so worried," Becky said.

"Don't worry," Ellie said. "Caleb will be just fine."

"Oh, I'm not worried about Caleb. It's Daddy I'm worried about. I told Caleb before he left to watch over Daddy."

Ellie laughed. "I told your father to watch over Caleb."

Pappy shook his head. "If I were twenty years younger; I could have watched over both of them."

*********

As they rode in silence, Josh kept thinking he needed to say something to Caleb; and Caleb thought the same. After two hours, neither one spoke.

"This is ridiculous," Josh finally said. "We've got a two-day ride ahead of us. We need to talk!"

"I agree," Caleb said. "I want to talk. Do you want to talk?"

"Sure, I want to talk."

"Good; then you go first."

Josh thought for a moment. "I can't' think of anything right now. I mean, I want to talk. I just can't think of anything. You better go first."

"You want me to talk to you about me and Becky?"

Josh didn't have to think long about that one. "No, I don't think you should. I don't think I want to know. I mean, maybe someday, just not today."

Caleb looked frustrated. "You want to talk about you and Ellie?"

"No, I don't think I want to get into that right now."

"What about me and Becky having kids. You want to talk about being a grandpa and having grandkids?"

"Why, is Becky expecting?"

"No...not that I know of."

"What do you mean by 'Not that you know of'?"

"What do you think it means? It means I don't know!"

"If you don't know, why did you bring it up?"

"I don't know. I was just trying to think of something to talk about. You want to talk about grandkids or not?"

"No, not particularly; I don't know. What do you want to talk about?"

"I don't know. What do you want to talk about?" There was a long pause. "What about Pappy?" Caleb laughed. "He sure is a funny old goat."

"Yeah, you're right," Josh laughed. "He sure is a funny old goat."

They fell back into silence for the rest of the day.

********

Edom County was cotton country. Josh and Caleb passed plantation after plantation.

"What exactly are we looking for?" Caleb asked.

"The Sihon Plantation, its owner is a fellow named Eli Sihon. He's second generation cotton farmer, richer than Solomon, as shrewd as they come, and a hard man to do business with. I suspect he refused to sell Jasper just to be spiteful. He's got a mean streak, and he likes to have the upper hand."

"I don't know how we're going to find it. There's nothing but cotton in all directions as far as the eye can see," Caleb replied.

Just then they came on an old black man walking along the side of the road in the opposite direction. He walked slowly. He was thin and boney; his hair and whiskers were white. He hunched over badly, and he dressed all in black.

"Say, old-timer, can you help us? We're looking for the Sihon Plantation," Josh said.

The old man stopped and looked up at them. His face was stern.

"Ya might as well ask me how a man can get to Hell. I'd say read the Bible and jus' do everythin' contrary and you'll get there."

"There's got to be a clearer explanation on how do get there?" Josh said.

"There is," the old man said. "All ya have to do is use your senses. Do ya know what blood smells like? It smells like a slaughterhouse: hot, red, and foul. Jus' follow the stench of blood. Listen with your ears, and you'll hear the high-pitched howling of suffering. Hear the screams of mistreated slaves. He, who has a nose, let him smell; and he who has ears, let him hear. If ya can do all this, ya'll find yourself either at the opening to the Sihon Plantation or the gates of Hades."

"I take it you don't approve of Eli Sihon," Josh said. "Can't you just bypass your convictions for a moment and give us more direct directions?"

The old man sighed as if he'd failed. "Five miles ahead, on ya right, a brown wooden fence."

"Thank you," Josh said.

"Say, old-timer," Caleb asked. "Are you some kind of preacher or something?"

"No, I'm just what every man should be, a man of faith."

"What do folks call you?" Caleb asked.

"Enoch. Before my mother died giving me birth, they gave me the name 'Enoch'."

"Well, I'll tell you, Enoch..." Josh said, turning in his saddle to face the old men; but he was gone. As far as they could see, in both directions the side of the road was barren.

"Where'd he go?" Josh asked.

"I don't like this," Caleb said.

"Where'd he say the Sihon Plantation was?" Josh asked.

"Just five mile up the road, on our right; it's got a brown wooden fence." Caleb shook his head. "No, sir, I don't like this."

********

Caleb read the sign, "*Sihon Plantation*."

"You can read?" Josh asked.

"Why, does that surprise you? I ain't stupid."

"I didn't say you were. I just know that some people consider it a hanging offense to teach a black man how to read."

"Then they need to hang Lester because he's the one who taught me."

"Lester...really? That Lester's a good man." Josh rose in his saddle to see farther. "Well, I don't think it a smart move to ride through the front gate. We best go around to the back of the property."

"I hope you got a plan," Caleb said.

"Oh, I got a Jim-dandy of a plan."

"Really? Like what?"

"I'll tell you when the time comes. Don't worry. It's a good plan, it's bound to work; and I guarantee you're just going to hate it."

"Hate it? Why?"

"You'll see."

********

A waist high log fence bordered the back end of the Sihon Plantation. Josh and Caleb dismounted and stood looking over the fence. There were acres of cotton ready for picking. They could see off in the distance a group of slaves busy picking cotton. Two overseers sat on horseback, watching their every move, guarding them with shotguns.

"So what's this Jim-dandy plan of yours?" Caleb asked.

Josh went to the supply horse, reached under the saddle, and came up with a white sack (the kind used for cotton picking). He tossed it to Caleb who caught it.

"Oh no," Caleb said. "I ain't gonna go out there."

"Well, I certainly can't," Josh said. "All you have to do is cotton pick your way to the others and ask who Jasper is, and then the two of you can sneak back here. We jump on our horses and skedaddle."

"Hold on one cotton-pickin' minute, and forgive the pun. What makes you think it's that easy? If it was, why don't others just walk off?"

"Because they don't have horses, and they won't get far. They know it and the overseers know it. That's why they won't be paying much attention."

Caleb let out a long sigh and slung the sack over his shoulder. "Well, you're right about one thing."

"What's that?"

"Your plan, I hate it."

********

Caleb hunkered down low as he moved through the cotton to the group of workers. There were maybe thirty of them; old and young; men, women, and children. When he was close enough, he stood up and began picking cotton.

One of the men looked up at him wide-eyed. "Who are ya?"

"I'm looking for Jasper Brown. You know him?"

"Why? What ya want with him?"

"I'm his kin. I come to get him out of here."

"You crazy," one of the women said. "No one gets out of here, ever. Not even when ya die. They bury ya here in the field. They say it's good for the cotton."

*87*

Another man stepped forward. "Jasper ain't here; he's in the oven."

"The oven?" Caleb asked.

"It's a small, tall shack with just enough room for a man to stand up in. It ain't got no windows. They put Jasper in it yesterday for sassin' back. A man can cook to death in the oven. I ain't ever seen anyone last more than three days."

"Where is this…oven?" Caleb asked.

Just then the butt of a shotgun hit Caleb in the back of the head. He looked up from the ground, half dazed, at an overseer standing over him, pointing a shotgun in his face.

"I hear lots of talkin' but I don't see no cotton gettin' picked." The overseer reached down, picked up Caleb's sack, and looked inside.

The other overseer on horseback was behind him. "What's goin' on, Frank?"

"Seems this here boy don't want to work. He just wants to flap his gums."

"Throw him in the oven," the other said.

"We already got one in the oven."

"Good, then they'll both have company."

********

When they opened the door to the oven, Jasper covered his eyes from the sharp blinding light. He stood there leaning against the back wall, drenched in sweat. They tossed Caleb in and slammed the door shut. The two men were in complete darkness, standing chest to chest.

"Sorry about this," Caleb said.

"No need to apologize to me," Jasper replied. "Say, who are ya? I don't recognize your voice."

"I'm not from here, Jasper. My named is Caleb."

"How do ya know my name?"

"It's a long story, Jasper."

"Well, we got nothin' but time."

Caleb continued to tell Jasper the full story. From the legend of Bernie Bush and Pappy Moses Brown, all the way to the family's plan to head north to freedom and everything in between.

As the sun began to set, the heat in the oven started to subside. By late in the evening, it was tolerable. Around midnight, someone opened the oven door. It was Josh.

"I waited till I was sure everyone was asleep," Josh said.

Caleb held onto Jasper, helping him out of the oven.

"We need to hurry," Josh said. "The horses are waiting at the fence."

They turned to walk away. When they did, a large group of people confronted them. It was all the slaves of the plantation. The oldest man in the group stepped forward.

"Do not be afraid. We means you no harm."

"What do you want?" Josh asked.

The old man looked at Caleb. "This afternoon, when ya were explaining everything to Jasper, my grandson sat behind the oven, listening. We know everything." He turned to Josh. "We ask ya, no, we beg ya to take us with ya. It is easy to runaway; but if ya have nowhere to go, ya will be caught. Ya have such a place. Please, take us with ya."

"I don't see how we can do that," Josh said. "We wouldn't get far before they came after us."

"We've tied the overseers up in the barn. It will be hours before they can break themselves loose." He moved aside, someone shoved forward a scrawny, old white man. He was tied and wore a gag. "This here is Eli Sihon, our Massa. We've gone passed the point of no return. Once the overseers get loose and free him, they will hunt us down and kill us."

"I say we kill them first!" a woman from the back of the crowd shouted.

"No!" the old man shouted back. "That would bring us down to his level, and we are better than that!" He pushed his Master into the oven, slammed the door, and turned the latch. "That'll hold him long enough for us to get to where we needs to go."

Caleb looked at Josh. "We can't leave them here. It would be a death sentence. We have to take them."

"How?" Josh asked. "Someone's bound to notice such a large group."

"Just tell them you're a slave trader, and you're taking us to market," the old man said.

Josh sighed, shaking his head. "I don't know, one white man over thirty black slaves."

"One white man over thirty-four to be exact, thirty-five if you count your young friend here."

"What's your name?" Josh asked.

"My name is Levi."

"Well, Levi, tell your people to gather only their clothes for the journey and as much food as you can lay your hands on. Do you have any wagons?"

"Enough for the women and children; the men can walk."

"If you have any chains, I want you to chain as many folks as possible to make it look genuine."

"We have plenty of chains, thanks to Massa Sihon," Levi said. He looked hopefully at Josh. "Does this mean we're going?"

Josh looked at Caleb, then at Jasper, and then to Levi. "We leave at first light."

A cheer rose from the crowd.

********

Early the next morning as gold and rose colors appeared in the eastern horizon, and the west was still black with stars, they lined up *Wagon train style*. Everyone sat in one of the four wagons, chained to one another. Some of the men stood alongside the wagons, their ankles chained. Caleb and three of the other men drove the wagons. Josh was upfront, on horseback.

"Here goes nothing," Josh said as he signaled them forward.

They met few folks on the road. Surprisingly, no one gave them more than a momentary glance. A caravan of slaves on their way to auction was a common sight. The fact only one white man was in charge of so many didn't shock anyone. As Levi said, "It is easy to runaway; but if you have nowhere to go, you will be caught."

Later in the day, Josh rode alongside one of the wagons where Jasper sat in the back holding a small young girl in his arms.

"You feel any better?" Josh asked.

"I've had something to eat and drink, and I've rest some. I feel much better. Thank ya."

"I guess Caleb told you the whole story?"

"Yes, it's a miracle." Jasper smiled. "It's like a dream come true, only better. The dreams of slaves never come true. For the first time in my life, in all our lives, there's hope."

"Your Master, this Eli Sihon, tell me about him. What's he like?"

"He'd shame the devil. He's pure evil, and he enjoys it. That makes it worse."

"What do you think he'll do once he gets loose?"

"His pride has been hurt. He'll stop at nothing to find us. When he does, he'll kill us all. He doesn't care how much money he'd loose. No whippings and sending us back to work. He'll kill us all, even the children." Jasper hesitated a moment, "but I wouldn't worry about that."

Josh looked at him, confused. "You wouldn't? Why's that?"

"Because Eli Sihon is no more. Before we left, I killed him."

"Jasper, why would you do such a thing?"

Jasper lifted the young girl in his arms; he took her face in his hand and aimed her angelic eyes at Josh. "This is why!"

Josh made no argument. He rode back to the front of the caravan.

********

Tired and hungry, the line of four wagons slowly passed through the front gate of the Bush Plantation. It didn't take long for folks to take notice of the raggedy troop. When they got to the front of the main house, all the family had gathered. Pappy and the others stood on the veranda. They stopped; Josh sat up in the saddle and spoke out loud for all to hear.

"This here is Cousin Jasper..." Josh pointed to Jasper who stood up in the wagon. "Now, I know Caleb and I were supposed to just get Jasper back here with his family; but things don't always go as planned. It just got out of hand. These folks are from the same plantation as Jasper. I didn't have the heart to leave them. I'm sorry if I let you down but I ask you to search your hearts and welcome these folks."

Pappy stepped forward. "May we never turn away the hurting and the hopeless." He turned to the others. "See that these folks are fed and given a place to sleep." He looked at Josh. "Somehow we'll make this happen." Then he shouted as loud as his old lungs would let him. "The family is now altogether. Prepare! We march north to freedom!" The family cheered and welcomed the strangers. Jasper's mother held her son, and in tears she praised and gave thanks for Josh and Caleb.

When the crowd scattered, Pappy placed his hand on Josh's shoulder. "It was smart of ya to chain everyone up and make it look like a slave caravan."

"It was their idea," Josh said. "With their four wagons and our two, all we need to do is buy another three wagons; and then we can do the same. We can travel north disguised as slave traders moving slaves to auction. Of course, we'll need to buy us some more chain."

"My boy," Pappy said, sadly, "that won't be hard. All my life, I've never know there to be a shortage of chains."

# Chapter Fifteen

# Forgive us all

Mr. Nunn,

*Forgive me for taking so long to write. I have not forgotten you or the day of my visit. I've read the book you leant me and so have other neighboring plantation owners. I found it most informative. Still, as you know, a book can only help so much.*

*As per our last conversation, if I am to be so bold, we would like to take you up on your offer to teach us the art of peanut farming. A small group of plantation owners have formed a brotherhood to help one another get through this war. We discussed adding you as a member. I'm sure you will find it beneficial. No one can have enough friends.*

*If it is convenient, we would like to visit you this Saturday at three. We can discuss the brotherhood and peanut farming. Please, send word with my boy. There will be five of us. Don't bother about being a gracious host; it would be our pleasure to bring the refreshments.*

*Yours Truly,*

*Tom Garrett*

"Who is this *Tom Garrett?*" Uncle Aaron asked.

"He's a thorn in our side," Josh replied. He turned to Caleb. "We need to warn the family to make ready for this Saturday's visit. When they're here, I want you out of sight."

"Me?" Caleb said, pointing to his chest. "Why me? What did I do?"

"Nothing," Josh said, "and I want to keep it that way. It'd be just like you to sass one of them, and we'd have a mess on our hands. I'll just give them a quick tour, some words on how to grow peanuts and send them on their way."

"We need to make sure they don't look in the barn. We've all those new wagons and chains we bought."

Josh shook his head and sighed. "Oh, I hate this."

"Well, there's one good thing about it," Pappy said.

"What's that?"

"The children will be glad they don't need to wash until Saturday night."

\*\*\*\*\*\*\*\*

They rode on the Bush plantation like a band of desperadoes, waving their pistols in the air, firing potshots at low flying birds. They halted in front of the main house with a blur of powder and dirt. They laughed at everything. It was clear they'd been drinking.

"Gentlemen, let me introduce to you Mr. Josh Nunn, peanut farmer par excellence," Tom Garrett said.

"You can just call me Josh."

Garrett made the introductions. "Josh, I'm sure you know these other gentlemen: Jim Buchman, Rusty Wilson, Mack Harris, and Greg Cutter."

Josh put out his hand; but instead of receiving a handshake, he got a jug of moonshine.

"You're a few steps behind, Nunn," Mack Harris said. "I make it myself. It's good for what ails you; and whatever's left over you can use to strip the paint off your barn."

Not wanting to cause a scene, Josh twisted the jug into place, put it to his lips and took a long pull. It burned going down in his throat and in his nose. It choked him that he had to cough.

"It'll put hair on your chest, that's for sure," Rusty Wilson laughed. "If ya already got some there, it'll take it off."

They passed the jug around a few times more. Josh pressed it to his lips, but never opened his mouth.

"Well, gentlemen, if you'll follow me out to the fields, I'd be glad to answer any of your questions about raising peanuts." Josh was the only one walking a straight line; they followed slowly, laughing.

Josh knelt down on one knee, scooped up a handful of soil and held it for all to see. "We're blessed in this part of the world with the perfect environment for growing peanuts." He tilted his hand, letting the soil blow away; he clapped his hands to remove the excess. "Our soil is light and sandy and we have hot dry weather most of the year." He held up a peanut shell. "Contrary to popular belief and its name, the peanut is not a nut it's a legume – a bean. It's good for human and animal consumption. Archeologists have found evidence the people of Peru grew and used peanuts as far back as 7,600 years ago. It needs lots of water. I'd suggest you work up an irrigation system. You plant the seeds two inches deep and about five to ten inches apart. Plants will take one hundred twenty to one hundred fifty days from planting to reach maturity, which is between one to one and a half feet in height."

"Sounds easy," Tom Garrett said. "What's the downside?"

"It takes a lot of effort just to yield a sizable crop," Josh replied.

"Thank God for slavery," was Rusty Wilson's answer to that.

"Mold…mold is your number one enemy. Peanuts need a lot of water, but too much rain and dampness can lead to mold. You can't sell moldy peanuts even for cattle feed."

"So what do you think, gentlemen?" Tom Garrett asked.

"I've got to do something," Mark Harris said. "With this war on, I'm not doing half my business. I can at least get by with selling peanuts locally." The others agreed.

"I've already took the liberty of having my boys attach a few young plants to all of your horses," Josh said. "Call on me at anytime; I'm at your disposal."

There was lots of handshaking and backslapping. They passed the jug around several times to make it official.

"So, Mr. Nunn," Tom Garrett said. "Why don't you show us the rest of your operation? I'm sure they'll be impressed."

"Of course," Josh said. "Right this way."

They walked through the slave quarters. All the workers kept their eyes to the ground, looking their worst in the manner of most plantation slaves.

"You seem to have more slaves than the last I was here," Tom Garrett said.

"A few," Josh said, trying to make it sound like not much had changed.

"Some of them ain't bad on the eye," Rusty Wilson said as he watched a young fourteen year old girl carrying two buckets of water from the well to the cabin.

"That ain't nothin'," Tom Garrett said. "You should see the two Josh here keeps for himself at the main house. He's got a mother and daughter up there, one as sweet looking as the other, only the daughter's light skinned, which makes me wonder." Tom laughed, and the others followed.

"It's not like that," Josh said. "It's not like that at all."

"Here, cutie, let me give you a hand with that," Rusty Wilson said, trying to take the two buckets away from the girl.

"Stop it, Rusty, that's so wrong," Mark Harris said. Josh looked at Harris, hoping he'd found a sympathetic comrade, but he hadn't. "That's so wrong, Rusty. The idea of blacks and whites together makes me sick. They ain't no better than farm animals."

"No ones makin' you do nothin'," Rusty said. He turned his attention back to the young girl. "Come on, cutie, we'll use this water to wash you down, get you smellin' half human; and then we can have some fun." He pulled the water buckets from her hands, the water splashed everywhere. She looked through teary eyes at Josh, who nodded for her to leave. She ran off.

"Say, where ya goin'?" Rusty asked. He turned to Josh. "Where's she goin'?"

"Just let her go," Josh said.

Rusty laughed. "What are talking about? I ain't gonna hurt the merchandise."

"Just forget it," Josh said. "We don't do those kinds of things here."

"Well, that's not very neighborly of ya." Rusty smiled. "It's all right when Massa Josh wants to play house with his mother and daughter darkies; but when a friend wants a taste, no can do."

The first thought that went through everyone's mind was that Rusty Wilson was dead. Josh round-housed him from the right, hitting his fist square on his jaw. Now, Rusty Wilson is not a large man, boy-like in stature. Still, it took great force to lift him off the ground as high as he went. He landed with a thud and did not move. The others rushed to his side. Mark Harrison placed his ear against Rusty's chest.

"He's alive," he said, sounding relieved.

"What he needs is a drink," Greg Cutter said, placing the jug to Rusty's lips and tilting it.

Rusty coughed and choked to consciousness. "Greg, ya idiot, what ya are trying to do, kill me?" He jumped to his feet and looked Josh square in the eye. "So, what was that all about? I thought we was friends."

"It seemed like the only way to stop you. I told you, we don't do those kinds of things here."

Rusty pointed his finger in Josh's face. "Listen here, Nunn. We came here in good faith, our hands extended in friendship; and this is the way ya repay us? Boy, ya not only lost some good friends, you've made some enemies. If I were ya, I wouldn't be so glad about it right now." He turned and marched off. The others followed.

Tom Garrett walked a few steps backwards, staring Josh down. "That was a big mistake, Nunn, a big mistake."

When they were gone, Josh entered the cabin the girl had run inside.

"Melinda, it's me, Uncle Josh!"

He found her hiding behind her parents' bed. Her eyes went wide and full of tears. She ran into his arms.

"Oh, Uncle Josh, that man scared me so bad."

"Don't fear, child, I won't let anything bad ever happen to you."

"Uncle Josh, Lord forgive me; but sometimes I thinks I don't likes white folk."

Josh held her close. "God forgive us both, child, forgive us all."

# Chapter Sixteen

# Deals and Promises

To avoid suspicion from the neighbors about what the folks at the Bush Plantation were up to, Pappy had Josh buy their needs for the upcoming journey outside the county. Needs being: wagons, horses, tents, and a chuck wagon fully stocked with enough food to feed everyone for a month. Of course, shackles and chains, miles of chain.

Inside the wagons they fitted with shackles and chains for the women and children. Long lines of chain with connecting shackles they attached to the backs of the wagons where the men would be walk behind. Hand shackles for all the men to wear. The trick was to devise a way of making the shackles look as if locked, but they could open at a moment's notice. Uncle Aaron solved this problem with small pieces of thin wire that held the shackles in place, but opened with a good hard tug.

Again, personal hygiene needed to be at a minimum, to give the appearance of poorly kept slaves, an inconvenience for parents and a joyous holiday for the children. As the day of the Exodus approached, they held daily meetings in the barn. It was on one particular hot day, as the adults met in the barn, the unexpected happened.

"There are a few loose ends we need to tighten," Pappy said, standing in front of the family. "I'd suggest we construct false bottoms under the wagons to hold changes of clothing, so no one has to live in one pair of clothing, though it may appear that they are. Also, it would be a perfect place to hide guns. I'm not one to promote violence, but we need to be prepared. It's better to have a gun and not use it, then to need a gun and not have it."

All agreed.

"Cousin Bartholomew, you're good with such things. How long will it take to make this happen?"

"Three days on the outside..." Cousin Bartholomew said with confidence.

"Fine," Pappy said. "Once Bartholomew finishes, there's nothing to keep us. We leave."

A thrill unfolded over them. After hoping, praying, and preparing, it was actually going to happen.

Just then the barn door opened, the sunlight blinding everyone for a moment. When it closed, their eyes adjusted and they could see once more. There stood Caleb and an older white man.

"I found this fellow walking around outside," Caleb announced.

Pappy recognized him immediately. "Judd Taylor, what are ya doing here?"

Judd shot an indignant look at Caleb and then looked about as if taking inventory.

"I was in the area; I thought I'd stop by and see if there's anything I can help ya with, track down a family member or something."

Pappy thought fast. "It's good ya came today. We was just talking about getting in touch with ya. Do ya remember the slave, Jasper Brow?"

"Of course, I remember him. He's the property of Eli Sihon. Eli refused to sell him at any price."

"Well, things have changed," Pappy said. "We're willing to pay twice as much as we offered before."

"Twice as much!" Judd echoed. "He must be a pretty important darkie?"

Pappy ignored the derogatory remark. "Yes, he's the last of our family members that we need to collect."

Jasper Brown kept his head low, not that Judd Taylor would recognize him. Just the talk about him made him uncomfortable.

"Very well. I'll be in touch," Judd said, walking out of the barn. Caleb kept the door ajar, watching him walk away.

"I don't trust that man," Caleb said.

"Rightfully so," Pappy said. "How much do ya think he heard?"

"It's hard to say," Caleb said. "I don't know how long he was out there."

"We need to act fast," Pappy said. He waited a few moments. "This meeting is adjourned."

Outside, Judd mounted his horse and galloped off the plantation. Under the coverage of some trees, he came upon his brother, Tobias.

"They're planning to make a run for it. They gave me some cock-and-bull story about wanting me to buy one of their family members. It was just something to throw me off."

Tobias smiled, his gold tooth gleaming. "I know the slave trade better than anyone. I tell ye, Brother Judd, there's money to be made here."

"How?" Judd asked.

"We need to visit the nearest plantation owner. Just let me do the talking."

\*\*\*\*\*\*\*\*

97

Tom Garrett owned the neighboring plantation. Judd and Tobias stopped in front of the main house; but before they could dismount, a black man, a house servant, came running out waving his arms.

"We don't give handouts to no saddle tramps here. So ya might as well keep a movin' down the road."

"We're not saddle tramps, you ole fool," Tobias growled.

"Massa say he got everything he need. He ain't got no uses to buys anything, if ya is sellin'."

"You tell your Massa we ain't sellin' anything. You tell him we want to give him something. You tell him if he wants to be rich, he needs to see us."

"Massa already rich."

"Well if he wants to get richer, and he's got half a brain, he'll see us," Judd said as he dismounted. "Well, just don't stand there with your mouth open catchin' skeeters; tell your Massa the Taylor Brothers are here."

They were ushered into an office. Tom Garrett stood before a paper cluttered desk. He held a gold watch in one hand. He glanced up at them and then looked at the watch.

"My time is precious, gentlemen...?"

"My name's Judd Taylor, this here is my brother Tobias."

"Well, Mr. Taylor, this better be good. You have exactly three minutes to make your point before I have you thrown off my property."

Judd stepped forward. "In this county, if a plantation owner commits an act of treason against the Confederacy or breaks any of its major laws concerning Slavery, he is subject to prison or possible execution. He looses ownership of his plantation, and it becomes the property of the Confederacy. In these times, when the South is in need of funds, the property is sold for half of its true value. The edict also states that any neighboring plantation get first dibs on purchasing the property, with the stipulation that the new owner continues to farm it."

"Go on," Garrett said. He closed his watch and put it in his pocket. "Are you saying one of my neighbors has broken the law and is a criminal of the Confederacy?"

"Not yet, but he's about to."

"And might I ask his name?"

"His name is Josh Nunn."

"And how do you know he's about to commit a criminal act?"

"Trade secrets, I have my ways."

"I see," Garrett said, "but now that I have this information, what do I need you gentlemen for?"

"Do you mind if we sat down?"

Garrett walked to the doorway and shouted down the hall. "Benjamin, bring whiskey and three glasses."

Seated, Judd told Garrett everything he knew about the Bush plantation, about the true owner, the family, and their plans to escape to the North.

"Then why don't we call the authorities on him now?" Garrett asked.

"Because he's not doing anything wrong; and it would be our word against his."

"So, we need to catch him when he leaves with all his slaves," Garrett said.

"He'll just say he's taking them to auction them off."

"Sellin' all his slaves, isn't that suspicious?"

"Suspicious, yes; but there's no law against it. A man has a right to sell his own property, some or all. No, we need to catch them as they're leaving Confederate territory and heading into Yankee territory. Then his intentions will be clear."

Garrett sipped his whiskey, smiling. "Again I ask you, gentlemen; what do I need you for?"

"I think it best my brother, Tobias, explains."

Tobias leaned forward, his gold tooth grin widened. "I been in the Slavin' Business since I was knee-high to a tadpole. I learns it from me father who learns from his father. Three generations of buying and selling slaves. I can smell a darkie under a mountain of horse dung. They can'ts hide from me. I can track a trail better than any redskin. I tell ye, I wouldn't want to be my enemies, being tracked down by ole Tobias. I'd soon give it up at the start than put me-self through such misery."

Garrett's smile grew as large as Tobias'. "Again, I ask, why do I need you gentlemen? I may not be a great tracker, but I can track nearly a hundred darkies being pulled by mules. I've got friends."

Tobias laughed, slapping his knee with delight. "Friends? You mean a militia of your drinkin' buddies who don't know their vital parts from a hole in the ground. These are men who expect payment for their efforts, for a piece of the action."

Garrett took offense to this. "I suppose you want only to do this to further the cause of the South or out of the kindness of you heart."

"I have no kindness in my heart for anything or anyone," Tobias said in a cold and disturbing way. "Yes we do this for profit; but it will be no skin off your nose. The ability to buy Nunn's property at a fraction of the cost is all yours. The slaves are part of the property. My brother Judd and I walk away with full ownership of every runaway slave from the Bush Plantation. In exchange, we will see Josh Nunn comes to justice; and you are the proud owner of the Bush Plantation. Is it a deal?" Tobias held out his hand.

Garrett thought about it long and hard. He shot his whiskey to the back of his throat and coughed long and hard. "It's a deal," he said, offering his hand in friendship to both Judd and Tobias, "but I want to be in on the chase."

"Ye will have a front-row seat," Tobias laughed.

********

Benjamin rushed inside the small, one-room shack down the road from the Garrett's main house. His wife, Wisteria, stood hunched over the hearth cooking. Their infant son, Jonathan, sat on a blanket at her feet. She turned and smiled.

"Why, Benjamin, ya is early. Dinner won't be for another hour. Sit down and keep me company."

"Never ya mind any of that, Wisteria. Sit down; I got something important to say."

She sat down in the rocking chair, picked up little Jonathan and held him in her arms. She looked woefully at her husband.

"What is it, Benjamin? Is it trouble?" She said the word "trouble" like it was a well-known, much-hated, unwanted family member who came to visit now and then without warning and staying far too long.

"I loves ya, Wisteria," he said as he paced the floor. "I loves our son, too; but we is slaves. If Massa wanted to sell me or sell ya away from here, we'd never see each other again. If he had a mind to sell our son away from us, there'd be nothing we could do."

He stopped pacing and looked at her. There were tears streaming down her face.

"Oh no, Massa gonna sell one of us," she moaned.

He fell to his knees and held his family in his arms. "Oh no, honey, Massa ain't gonna sell nobody. I was just makin' a 'for instance'. I'm just sayin' we is slaves, and we ain't got no say."

She stopped her crying and looked at him. "Then what is ya sayin'?"

"I'm just sayin' if we was free, we wouldn't have to live ascared."

"No, Benjamin, I ain't runnin' away. We'd be caught for sure, and then we'd be done for."

"Ya know the old Bush Plantation down the road?"

"Yeah, what about it?"

"Ain't none of them slaves, really slaves."

"What ya talkin' 'bout, Benjamin. They skin is as black as ours. I ain't never seen a black man who ain't a slave. If they ain't slaves then what is they?"

"They is free! They're all one big family and they is free; and they is gonna make a run for it. I heard Massa talkin' 'bout it today."

"So they is makin' a run for it. What's the difference if one slave runs for it or a hundred? The man will hunt them down and bring them back and make them wish they was dead."

"This is different, Wisteria. These folks ain't just runnin' away; they is runnin' *to* something."

********

After dinner, Pappy and Uncle Aaron sat silently on the veranda smoking their pipes. Uncle Aaron pointed the bit of his pipe in the direction of the front gate.

"Look yonder, Brother Moses, a wagon be comin'."

The wagon was old and rickety, drawn by one old swayback mare. Moses strained his eyes for a better look. "It's a man drivin' with a women sittin' next to him." Moses tilted his head so he could keep an eye on the oncoming wagon and hollered into the house through the open front door. "Josh, ya best get yourself out here and take a look at this."

Josh walked out on the veranda. He'd left his jacket inside, his shirt collar was open, and his sleeves rolled up.

"What's all the...?" He stopped midsentence when he saw the wagon.

When they were closer, Uncle Aaron stood up. "That woman's got a baby in her arms."

Pappy stood also. "I recognize the driver. That's that sassy young boy from the Garrett place, the one that gave me lip the last time he was here."

The wagon stopped in front, Josh stepped forward.

"Can I help you folks?"

"Good evening, Massa Nunn, my name is Benjamin; and this here's my wife, Wisteria. We is from the Garrett Plantation."

"I know who you are," said Josh. "Now state your business."

"We know ya people are gonna make a Freedom Run to the North. We was hopin' ya could find it in your heart to take me and my family with ya."

"Freedom Run, where'd you get an idea like that?" Josh asked.

"I hears two men talkin' with Massa Garrett, tellin' him all about it."

Pappy stepped closer. "Those two men, was one of them a tall, skinny white man dressed in black?"

*101*

"They both be lookin' like that," Benjamin said.

"Sounds like Judd Taylor," Josh said to Pappy.

"That's the name, Taylor," Benjamin said. "They is the Taylor brothers."

"What we gonna do?" Uncle Aaron asked.

"Nothing we can do," Pappy said, "but get out of here as soon as possible."

"Please, Massa Nunn, take us with ya," Benjamin pleaded.

"We're not ready to leave yet," Josh said. "If you stay here, they'll come looking for you and then no one will get to leave. Besides, if you go back to the Garrett Plantation, you might be able to learn more important information. Don't worry; when it's time to leave, I'll get word to you."

Benjamin looked regretfully at Pappy. "Forgive me, sir. I'm sorry I called ya a house monkey. Please, sir, you've got to let me and my family goes with ya."

"That's water under the bridge, son." Pappy smiled. "Don't ya go frettin'. Ya go back home and keep your eyes and ears peeled. I swear by the life of my grandchild, ya will come with us to the Promised Land."

"Please, sir..."

Wisteria placed her hand on her husbands. "It's all right, Benjamin. When a man promises on the head of his grandchild, ya can trust him." She looked at Josh. "If we learns anything new, we'll send word. Thank ya, gentlemen, and bless ya."

Benjamin slapped the horse gently; they started back the way they came. The three men watched as they trotted out of site.

"Get Caleb out here," Pappy said to Josh. "We need to make plans to skedaddle, and soon."

# Chapter Seventeen

# A Little Faith

Outwardly, the everyday goings-on at the Bush Plantation looked like any other day, but inwardly, there was an under current of preparation for the journey ahead. Now, change touched everything; there was an enemy watching their every move. Caution was foremost. It was Benjamin who discovered this and sent a warning.

Pappy, Uncle Aaron, and Josh were in the barn checking on the wagons the men recently worked on. The false bottoms were almost complete. Stepping out of the barn, they saw a horse galloping at full speed onto the property.

"Look, a runaway horse," Aaron said, pointing.

At first it did look like there was no rider, but as it approached they could see a small black boy hunkering down in the saddle. The horse stopped in front of them, kicking up a cloud of dust. The boy sat up in the saddle.

"Mister Benjamin told me to tell ya that there are ten bad men over in them woods over yonder," the boy said, pointing at the wooded hills east of the plantation.

"Don't point, boy," Pappy said, as kindly as he could. "We don't want them knowing we know they're there. What else did Mister Benjamin say?"

"He say they is looking at ya through a 'Terrible Soap'."

"You mean 'telescope'?" Aaron asked.

"Yeah, that what he say."

"Anything else?"

"No, sir, that is all he say for me to say. I gotta go, sir. If Massa find me gone, he gonna whip my hide."

"What's your name, boy?" Pappy asked.

"Gabriel, sir, my name's Gabriel."

"Well, Gabriel, we thank ya for what you've done; when ya get back, you tell Mister Benjamin 'thank ya', too."

"I will, sir."

The boy pulled the reins till the horse turned around. He kicked his heels in the side of the beast; it took off flying. He hunched down low in the saddle till again he was barely visible.

"That worries me," Pappy said, once they were alone.

"I'll say," Josh said. "Being watched from afar like that."

"That's not what worries me," Pappy said. "I expected that. What worries me is we promised Benjamin we'd take him and his family with us. Now this boy knows something is up. I wonder how many more folk at Garrett Farm know about this."

********

Just then, the front door of the barn opened; out walked Julius Babcock. He'd married into the family.

"I couldn't help overhearing," he said. "I think I can help."

"How?" Pappy asked.

"My Granddaddy was a full-blooded Cherokee."

The three men stared at Julius with questioning looks, wondering how this applied to their problem. They waited for the other shoe to drop.

"Don't ya see? I've got Injun blood runnin' through my veins. I can sneak up on 'em without them knowin'. I can find out what they is up to and keep an eye on them. If they watchin' us, then we need be watchin' them."

"I don't know if that's such a good idea," Pappy said. "If they catch ya, they'll kill ya."

"That's just it; they won't catch me. I move silent like a fox, and I blend in like a snake. I got Injun blood in me."

"You know, it's not a bad idea. It would be good to know what we're up against," Josh said.

Pappy thought long and hard before he spoke. He looked at Julius. "Ya promise ya won't take any unnecessary risks."

"I promise."

"Then ya have my permission; but I want ya to report to me and only me."

"I understand. Don't worry, Pappy; I won't let ya down."

"I want ya to..."

Before Pappy could finish, Julius, in his excitement, was off and running.

Aaron laughed, watching him. "The boy didn't mention anything about being quick as a jackrabbit."

********

It was when the sun is just about to surrender the day to the moon. A golden crescent dipped into the western horizon. The eastern sky became a dark curtain, showing off the stars like diamonds on black velvet. In the middle of it all, a slow-appearing moon hung like a lantern in the firmament. Julius kept low as he swiftly moved from tree to tree.

In a tight clearing, there was a large tent. A man stood in front, peering into a telescope, never once looking up. Julius sneaked behind the tent and pressed his right eye against a small slit in the canvas. He counted nine men sitting on the ground around a lantern. Nine plus the one man outside made ten, as he heard earlier that day.

"These beans taste bad enough when they're hot, but they're worse cold like this. Can't we make just a small fire to heat 'em up?" said one of the more grubby men seated in the circle.

Another man who was standing...the leader, Julius suspected...kicked the tin plate out of the man's hand.

"If ye don't like it, ye can go without," he shouted into their faces. "I tell ye, no fires!"

"Oh, what are we waitin' for?" said another man sitting on the ground. "Why don't we just go in and kill the lot of 'em?"

Julius recognized Judd Taylor standing with the other man. "Because, ya jackass," said Judd. "If we go in and kill 'em now, it's a massacre; the law would be after us. If we wait till they leave the South, then the law is on our side; then we can kill 'em."

The other man standing with Judd continued. "And I tell ye, when the shootin' starts, I wants ye to kill every white man there is. If I catch ye shootin' any slaves, I'll shoot ye me self. That's our profit in all this."

The flap of the tent opened; in walked the man who had been looking through the telescope.

"What do ya want?" Judd demanded.

"I came to get my grub."

Judd kicked him in the rump and out of the tent. "Ya can eat later! Don't ever leave your watch again! That goes for the rest of ya. We can't afford to miss them leaving. If you're on watch, ya stay on watch!"

An hour later, a different man took his place at the telescope; the other entered the tent and ate his supper. Another hour later, they turned down the lantern. The men lay down on their sides and went to sleep. Julius decided he'd seen enough. He silently and swiftly slipped away.

********

Julius made his report like a soldier giving account to his general. His story was short, precise, and to the point, leaving no detail out. Yet the story he told the others on the plantation was just a might shy of being as accurate.

Understand, Julius was a likable fellow; a person would find it uncomfortable to call him a liar. Still, anyone who knew him would admit he was prone to talk big. Late that night, after all the children were asleep, seated around the community fire, Julius retold the story with some slight embellishments.

He told them of the men who were hiding in the woods. He'd seen ten, but there was no telling how many there actually were. He told them how mean and ornery they looked. How well armed they were, and how they talked about riding in and killing everyone on the plantation.

They listened, wide-eyed and shivering with fear, hanging on his every word. That night no one slept. Men sat up all night keeping watch while women folk prayed over their children.

Not surprising, the following morning, they formed a committee of elders and asked to speak with Pappy. He met them in front of the barn. Josh, Aaron, and Caleb were at his side.

"What can I do for you good folks?" Pappy asked.

The group chose Cora Brown to be the spokesperson. She was as old as Pappy and could hold her own with man or beast. She was a gossip, a bit snooty, and a might headstrong for Pappy's liking.

"We were discussing the predicament we are in..."

"What predicament is that?" Pappy interrupted.

"Having all those bounty hunters at our front door, watchin' our every move, and waitin' to pounce on us as soon as we make a move is a like the sword of Damocles hangin' over our heads."

"Where did you get this idea?" Pappy asked.

"I'd rather not say," Cora replied.

"His initials wouldn't be Julius Babcock, now, would they?" Aaron said sarcastically.

Cora ignored the remark and continued. "As I was saying, with bounty hunters ready to pounce, perhaps we should rethink leaving."

"Are ya saying we remain in the South and continue to be slaves?" Pappy asked.

"That's not what I'm saying," Cora replied. "I'm just saying we should wait. Now's not a good time."

Pappy felt the anger rise in him, but he swore he wouldn't act on it. He took in a deep breath and let out a long sigh. "When ya say it's 'Not a good time', I suppose ya mean it ain't safe. Cora, we've both lived long enough to know there ain't ever a good time. It never was safe to turn your back on injustice and walk away from slavery; but I learned there is a right time, and that time is always right now. Cora, ya need to have a little faith."

"Faith!" she huffed. "Faith in what…in who?"

"Cora, that's something you gonna have to answer for ya. I tell ya, ya better find it soon 'cos as soon as we can, we is gonna skedaddle to freedom."

# Chapter Eighteen

# A Blessing in disguise

No matter how old the person, no one in the county held a memory of there ever being such a day. It would go down on record as the day of the Big Storm.

Pappy liked to get up early in the morning before sunrise. He'd wash, dress, and spend some quiet time in his bedroom reading his Bible. He'd sit by the window, reading by the first light of the new day. This day was different. Pappy pulled back the curtains; it looked like nighttime. A black blanket of clouds blocked the sun.

Everyone on the plantation gathered in front of the main house and stared up at the sky. Pappy went down to meet them.

"What are we to do?" shouted someone.

The wind started kicking up; flashes of lightning were off in the distance. The people huddled in fear. Ellie clung to Josh; Becky held on tight to Caleb. Miriam and Aaron stood alongside their brother.

"I've never seen anything like this," Miriam said. "We're in for one heck of a storm."

"The storm will be the easy part," Aaron said, pointing to the horizon. "I seen this before. You see the way those clouds are moving? We're in for a twister."

Pappy held his arms up to the crowd. "Everybody, listen up. We all need to stay calm. I suspect the safest place would be here in the main house. Go get food, blankets, and anything else ya think we might need, and meet back here at the house."

Aaron stepped forward. "It'd be safer if everyone stayed on the first floor in the middle of the building, away from the windows."

"Ain't gonna do no good. When your time's up, your time is up," Cora Brown said. Pappy gave her a slight glance, but ignored her for the most part.

Once everyone returned, they hunkered down on the floors of the dining room, library, and hallway. Ellie, Becky, Miriam, and some of the women went into the kitchen to prepare food and plenty of coffee. The wind became so strong the windows began to rattle. They heard an ear-piercing whistle from outside. The flashes of the now-closer lightning lit the rooms up for a moment and then plunged them back into darkness. The building shook as if hit with cannonballs with each crack of thunder. The children clung to their parents.

The babies and the younger ones burst into tears, crying without ceasing. Pellets of thumb-sized hail beat against the windowpanes like a drum. Then the rain came, sheets of large droplets, so strong and thick you couldn't see farther than a few feet.

"It's the curse of Noah," one of the old women cried. "We're all gonna die."

"Hush up, you old fool," Caleb shouted. "Don't talk like that in front of the children."

Hours passed; the strength of the storm stayed the same. No one moved from their spot, some prayed silently, others out loud. Suddenly there was a thunderous pounding on the front door. All eyes fixed on the door. The pounding stopped for a moment and then started again, even louder.

"It's the devil himself knocking at our door!" another of the women cried. The children began to screech. Josh went to the door, opening it; in stepped a very wet Julius Babcock. He stood drenched from head to toe, shivering and wide-eyed.

"Where's Pappy?" he asked, trembling like a scared rabbit.

"Here I am," Pappy said, walking over. "What are you doin' out in this weather?"

"They gone," Julius said.

"Who gone?"

"Them men, they all gone. I went out a spying. The wind done ripped their tent to rags. The lighting and thunder is got their horses kickin' and howlin'. They took a-runnin'. They is all soaked to the bone."

"They've probably gone to seek shelter," Josh said. "With this storm, they figure we ain't going anywhere."

"Then now's the time to leave," Pappy said. He turned and spoke as loud as he could. "Listen to me, everybody. The men who've been watchin us are gone; the storm scared 'em off. We need to leave today."

"Ya crazy old man," Cora said. "Ya gonna get us all killed."

"Cora, I swear," Pappy said. "If ya don't want to go, ya can just stay here. If anyone else is a scared to go, they can stay, too. Listen, we may never get another chance like this. If we're gonna skedaddle, now's the time."

"I'm with you," Julius said.

"Me, too," Percy shouted.

"We're all with ya," others yelled.

"Good," Pappy said. "Now ya all know what to do; so let's do it."

Cora shook her head. "Ya all crazy."

Pappy took Caleb off to one side. "We promised Benjamin that he and his family could go with us. I want ya to take one of the horses, ride out to the Garrett place, and bring them here as soon as ya can; and be careful."

"Will do," Caleb said, rushing out the door. He turned, standing in the rain. "Pappy, tell Becky not to worry. I'll be right back."

Two hours later, all was ready. They lined the wagons on the road leading to the front gate. They filled the chuck wagon with as much food as it could hold. The false bottoms of the wagons they filled with firearms, ammunition, extra clothing and food. The young white overseers were on horseback, each holding a rifle. The storm had not let up. The rain soaked everyone. Its pounding made it hard to see. With each crack of thunder and lighting, the children and horses wailed loudly. When the women and children got into the wagons, the wheels sunk deep into the mud. The men stood behind the wagons waiting for the others to chain and shackle them. Pappy and Josh stood in the front of the caravan, staring at the road ahead.

"Where's Caleb?" Pappy asked. "What's takin' him so long?"

Suddenly, Caleb, on his horse, appeared down the road.

"Oh, no," Pappy said. "That's just what I was afraid would happen."

Behind Caleb's horse walked twenty to thirty people, men, women, and children, every slave from the Garrett Plantation. They halted facing Pappy and Josh.

"They found out about it," Caleb said. "I didn't have the heart to leave them."

"I just don't know," Pappy said.

They all looked so pitiful, the rain pounding on them, standing up to their ankles in the mud.

"Please take us with ya," Wisteria with her baby in her arms and Benjamin at her side begged. "We can't go back; if we go back now, he'll beat us all to death."

"We don't have enough supplies, and there's not enough room in the wagons," Pappy said.

Ellie stood up in the wagon, shouting over the pouring rain. "We can put the old folk and the children in the wagons, and we woman can walk in the back with the men."

"Bless ya," Wisteria said.

"We don't have enough chain and shackles," said Josh.

"Then hog-tie us to the back of the wagons with rope," Ellie hollered.

"Do we have enough rope?" Pappy asked Josh.

"We have quite a bit in the barn."

"Very well, you can come," Pappy said.

"Thank ya, thank ya," they cried.

Pappy looked at Wisteria and Benjamin. "Get your children and old folk in the wagons and line up the men and women in the back of the wagons. Josh, Caleb, get the rope from the barn."

As Pappy walked back to the wagons, he noticed Cora seated in the front wagon. "Why, Cora, I thought ya were gonna stay?" She ignored him. He laughed as he walked away.

It was difficult moving about in the storm; but in time, everyone was in position. Josh mounted his horse and rode to the front; Caleb mounted his horse and moved up behind him. Pappy walked over and looked up at Caleb.

"Caleb, son, ya need to get down and walk behind the wagons with the rest. We need to look like a bunch of slaves being taken to market. It defeats the purpose. A black man on horseback looks suspicious."

Without words, the two men communicated their feelings with their eyes. It was clear to see how hurt Caleb's feelings were; but he knew it was the right thing to do. There was sadness and sympathy in Pappy's eyes.

"I understand," Caleb said as he dismounted.

Pappy placed his hand on the young man's shoulder. "You're a good man, Caleb, don't ya forget it."

To have an older man show such respect for him took some of the edge off. He took his place next to Becky behind one of the wagons. Pappy hopped up into the lead wagon and gave Josh the signal to move forward.

It was slow going at first. The wagon wheels were deep in the mud. As they approached the front gate, they heard a loud sound like a runaway freight train coming up from behind. The earth shook. Everyone turned to see a twister spinning toward them. It was a dark whirling mass, from the sky to the ground and as wide as it was tall. It tore the barn apart, sucking it into itself. It did the same with the main house only slower, one plank of wood at a time. The howl of the twister muffled the people's screams. The horses moved forward, pulling the people behind the wagons. Everything was moving at top speed; still the twister was at their heels.

Some folks call it the Hand of God, others call it a Twist of Fate, and still others call it just Dumb Luck. Whatever the case may be, what happened next was shear puzzlement. Just when the twister was about to overtake them, it veered to the right and went past. Then it veered to left and got before them. It moved forward, as if blazing the trail before them. It moved like it had a mind of its own. The horses calmed down and moved forward.

*111*

Then the children stopped crying, people became peaceful and quiet. They kept their eyes fixed on the twister. It was a strange feeling, as if an impenetrable protection surrounded them.

The twister moved down the road, and they followed. When they came to the crossroads, the twister stood still for a longtime, like it was trying to make up its mind about which way to go. It turned north, the direction they needed to go. They followed close, unafraid. When they got to the border of the county, the twister began to slow down. As its spinning slowed, it began to loose its hold on the rubbish it held. Bits and pieces of the farm began falling to the ground. The barn door, windowpanes from the main house, farm equipment, came hurling from the sky. They gradually maneuvered around it all. Finally, the twister became smaller and smaller till it disappeared as quickly as it had appeared.

They followed the road north. With nightfall, the rain stopped and the sky cleared. The stars showed the way.

Josh moved his horse next to the front wagon that held Pappy.

"Pappy, everyone is exhausted. Shouldn't we stop and make camp?"

"No, we've been blessed with such a great lead. I want to take full advantage of it. We need to keep goin'."

Josh told the others. The people took turns sleeping in the wagons. The white boys on horseback slept in the saddle. They passed around bread and salted meat so as not to stop even to eat. After two days of hard traveling, they set up camp. No one bothered to eat, they were so tired. They laid blankets on the ground, falling asleep as soon as they closed their eyes.

Pappy lay on the ground, staring at the stars, thinking. Josh came and sat on the ground next to him.

"If you don't mind me asking," Josh said. "Where are we going?"

Pappy got up on his elbows. "I been thinkin' about that. Things have changed since we took on the folks from the Garrett place. We don't have enough supplies. We're gonna need help. The Southern Seminary has always been good to us, sending these good boys to help out. Tomorrow, let's get with Lester; he should know the way. We need to get to Newberry, South Carolina."

# Chapter Nineteen

# What the other side saw

Judd woke to the sound of canvas tearing all around him. Blurred figures of men ran past his slowly waking eyes.

His brother, Tobias, stood over him, kicking him. "Wake up! The world's coming to an end, and ye be sleepin' like a pig in a trough. Get up!"

The others were running about aimlessly, gathering their gear, running after clothing the wind blew away.

Tobias kept his head. "Everyone get your gear and make for the horses."

Just then the lookout came in holding the telescope. "I ain't stayin' out there all by my lonesome." He dropped the telescope on top of some bedrolls.

Tobias wacked him off the side of his head with an open hand. "There's a wooden case over there, put it away. It be worth more than ye ever will be."

Just then, the wind ripped the top of the tent, exposing them. The center pole flew up into the sky, pulling the tent pegs out of the ground. The men frantically tried to get control of the horses. They untied the horses from the trees and pulled at their reins. Two of the beasts managed to break free and ran off. It was difficult loading the gear and mounting, the horses kicked and reared. Two of the men doubled up on the horses. At first, they ran in circles and were hard to control.

"Blast your hide," one of the men said as he tried to whip his horse into submission.

Tobias wheeled his riding crop across the side of the man's face. Blood shot from the wound in his cheek.

"Don't ye dare hit my animals. If ye want a horse to beat, buy your own!"

"Where we going?" asked one of the men.

"Anywhere's from here," Tobias replied. "The closest safe haven would be the Garrett place. I say we head for it."

"What about watching the Bush Plantation?" Judd asked.

"I wouldn't worry too much 'bout them. They won't be goin' anywhere's, not in this weather."

"Follow me, boys!" Judd cried as loud as he could. He kicked his boot heels into the side of his horse. The others did the same, and they were off.

It took a long time just to get to the road. The wind and rain came into their faces at high-speed, making it difficult to see. When they made it onto the road, it was near impossible to stay on it; the wind blew them into the gullies and ditches. Branches tore from trees and flew about like birds of prey.

The dark world would suddenly light up when lightning struck. The thunderclaps, like explosions, sent the horses into a panic. They'd rear up, nearly throwing the rider. If the lighting and thunder came from behind, the horses would race forward trying to get away. If it came from in front of them, they'd try to make an about-face. If it came from the right or the left, the poor confused animals stood still, fearful to move and hard to control.

"We're halfway there," Judd proclaimed when they came to a crossroad. There was a loud rumbling sound coming from behind. They stopped at the crossroad, turning to see what it was. Off in the distance was a mountain-sized twister.

"Look, it's over the Bush place, and it's workin' its way towards us," one of the men shrieked.

"What are ye so frightened of?" asked Tobias. "I've seen more wind come from a bagpipe."

"Quit your yappin'," Judd hollered. "We need to get to the Garrett place, pronto!"

With the twister behind them howling and rumbling, it wasn't hard to get the horses to rally forward. In time, they were at the Garrett Plantation. There was not a soul in sight. They galloped to the main house, tied their horses, and entered the building. The main hallway was empty.

"Is anyone here?" Judd shouted. There was no answer. The sound of the storm was so loud; it was possible his cries went unheard or that they couldn't hear any response. They entered the sitting room. There was a large piano near the fireplace. Under it were Tom Garrett and his wife, Harriet. Garrett came out of cover and stood before them.

"What are you idiots doing here? You're supposed to be watching the Bush Plantation!"

"There's a killer storm out there, Mr. Garrett, if ya haven't noticed. I guess you're just hidin' under the piano because the lights better down there," Judd said. "Our camp was blown away, and instead of being blown away with it, we came here for shelter. As for the folk at the Bush Plantation, I wouldn't worry about them. They're not goin' anywhere's in this storm."

His wife came out from under the piano. "Tom, I'm so frightened. Where's Jack?"

"Jack, who's Jack?" Judd asked.

"He's our son, he helps manage the plantation. We haven't seen him since the storm started." Garrett walked to the doorway and shouted down the hallway and up the stairs. "Benjamin! Benjamin!" He walked back in. "Where is that fool? I ain't seen any of the servants for hours. They're probably hiddin' under the house like a bunch of scared rabbits."

"Runnin' like a bunch of scared rabbits is more like it." They turned to see a young man, short and muscular, with a square jaw, dark eyes, and a stern look. He wore a cowboy hat, boots, jeans and shirt. Tight, black leather gloves covered his hands.

"Jack, you're all right!" Harriet cried.

"What do you mean, 'runnin''?" Garrett asked.

"They've all run off," Jack said. "There ain't a darkie left on the plantation. They're all gone."

"It's that Benjamin; I wouldn't put it past him!" Garrett screamed. He looked Judd in the eye. "They've all run off to the Bush Plantation; I'd bet on it. I need you and your boys to go check it out."

"We ain't makin' enough money on this to go back out there in that storm," Judd said.

"I'll pay you a thousand dollars, if you do. Besides, if you lose them darkies, there goes your profit."

"What's the matter; ya scared?" Jack laughed.

Tobias pushed his brother aside and stood before Garrett. "A thousand dollars it is; and I'm gonna hold ye to it." Then he turned to Jack and pointed his finger in his face. "Tobias Taylor ain't never been afraid of nothin', mamma's boy."

"Let's just see." Jack smiled. "I'll show you who's a mamma's boy; I'm goin' wit'cha."

"No, Jack, no!" his mother pleaded.

"You be careful out there, son," Garrett said.

"Ye comin' or not, momma's boy?" Tobias asked.

Jack pushed the Taylor brothers out of his way, and he marched to the front door. Judd, Tobias, and the rest of the gang followed.

They found two fresh horses in the barn for the men who'd lost their mounts. They galloped off the property and onto the main road. From the start, there was an unfriendly competition between Jack and Tobias about who would ride up front. They pushed their horses to the limit, making it difficult for the others to keep pace. Finally, it came to blows. Tobias whipped Jack with his riding crop, and Jack flogged Tobias with his lariat; each tried to knock the other off their mount. In the confusion, neither one of them took notice of the twister up ahead, coming right at them; but the horses noticed. They stopped dead in their tracks, the entire group of them, at the crossroads. A twister the size of all outdoors whirled before them. Like a giant titan from Greek mythology, it blocked their way.

Tobias laughed at Jack. "So what'cha gonna do, cowboy? Are ye afraid?"

"Quit pushing the boy," Judd warned.

"Just ye shut up," Tobias spat at his brother. He turned his attention once more to Jack. "So what's it gonna be, momma's boy! Are ye afraid?"

Jack sat up high in his saddle and stared toward the twister. "I ain't afraid of nothin'."

"That a boy," Tobias said. "When you call the devil out, he always backs down."

As if in angry response, the twister began spitting out bits and pieces of debris it swallowed on its journey across the county (wooden planks, bricks, wagon wheels, and the like).

"What's it gonna be, momma's boy? Go around it, and we'll follow ye."

Jack prodded his horse to go forward, but the horse knew better. It whinnied and kicked, refusing to move. Jack dug his boot heels hard and deep into the side of the poor beast. It reared up on its hind legs and came down with a thud, but would not move. Finally, Jack took his lariat and whipped the animal till there were welts on its rump. The horse ran forward; but after a few yards, tripped over the rubble, falling to the ground. Jack went flying out of the saddle and tumbled forward a few more feet. The twister snatched him up. He let out a long, horrific scream. They watched him do one complete rotation in the twister; and then it sucked him into the darkness of its belly, never to be seen again.

Like a beast that devoured its kill and was now full and content, the twister started to move from the crossroads north up the road.

"This is crazy!" Judd shouted. "We'll all be killed. We need to head back to the Garrett place." He turned his horse around; the others did the same. He looked to his brother. "I'm not tellin' the Garretts about their son; ya are."

Tobias smiled. "It will be my pleasure."

********

Folks talk about the calm before and after a storm, rightfully so. The next morning the sky was clear, blue, and cloudless. No sight or sound of a bird. A silence hung over the earth so thick you could cut it with a knife. The Garrett Plantation was mostly worse for wear. The roads were torn up, cluttered with pieces of man-made structures and uprooted trees. The going was slow as they road around each obstacle.

The Bush Plantation looked like a war zone after a great battle. There were large holes in the ground where once stood great trees. Little evidence remained that there ever had been a barn or a house on the property. There wasn't a soul to be seen.

"Maybe they ran for cover into the woods?" one of the men said.

Tobias slapped the man on the side of his head. "If I want your advice, I'll ask ye for it. Look here." He pointed to the ground. There were deep furrows in the mud, left by the wagon wheels. "They be long gone. It was a desperate act but a cleaver one. We should never underestimate them again."

"It won't be a hard trail to follow," the man said, pointing to the deep grooves in the mud. Tobias struck the back of the man's head.

"They've got a good head start on us," Judd said. "We need to head back to the Garrett place, get supplies, and get after them as soon as possible."

Within the hour, they'd gathered supplies and were on fresh mounts heading north up the road from the crossroad.

Against his wife's wishes, Tom Garrett rode with them. She'd pleaded with him to remain home and morn the loss of their son; but that was the very reason he insisted on going. Somehow he now blamed the death of his son on the slaves of the Bush Plantation, and he wanted revenge.

The only thing more dangerous than a hungry animal is a wounded one.

# Chapter Twenty

# Silver and Peppermint

The going was slow, mostly because of the folks that walked behind the wagons; they set the pace. Folks would take turns riding and walking; no one could walk an entire day.

Josh sat proud in the saddle, riding up front. Pappy sat in the front wagon on the buckboard. His word was law, of what direction they would take. Aaron was at Pappy's side as first consul. Caleb was Josh's liaison between him and the people, dictating what Pappy decreed. Miriam and Ellie, with Becky at their sides, saw to the care of the women and children. Lester headed the overseers, the White Boys, as they were affectionately called.

Then there was Cora, the thorn in everyone's side, always with a complaint. It was becoming difficult to discount her, as more folks in their uneasiness began to agree with her grumbling. They looked to her as a leader who thought and suffered as they did, to make their grievances known to the unyielding leaders. Knowing they were being followed added to the uneasiness they felt. If the Taylor brothers and their men caught up with them, what could they do? They knew nothing of guns and fighting. They were farmhands and seminarians, no match for ruthless killers. At the slow pace they traveled, it would be no time before the men on horseback were upon them, it was inevitable. Silently and secretly, many folks began having second thoughts.

Each day as the sun set, they camped near water whenever possible. The women would take turns preparing dinner from the chuck wagon. There was plenty of food. Still they rationed it, knowing they needed to make it last. After their meal, the children would play and then collect firewood. Folks would gather around campfires, singing hymns and folk songs. Once the children were asleep, the adults huddled and talked among themselves.

"Blessings on ole Pappy," someone would say. "If it weren't for him, we'd still be slaves."

"Slaves...when were you a slave. We was all livin' free on the plantation," others said.

"Livin' free 'cos we was bought from 'slaver' by Pappy."

"Now we's runaways with a price on our heads and bounty hunters wantin' to claim it."

"We'll be free up north before they catch us."

"Ya don't know that; we may all be dead before tomorrow."

"Ya know ya ain't nothin' but ignorant."

"Ya be the one who's ignorant."

"I says we should have stayed on the farm and waited the war out."

"What makes you think the abolitionists will have their way. Now who is ignorant?"

"Well, I say we made the right choice; I trust Pappy and his folk to get us through."

"Ya say that now, but wait till the food is gone and the chillin' is starving."

"Ya is ignorant, for sure."

Away from the glow of the campfires, standing in the dark, Pappy stood, listening, his brother Aaron by his side.

"Aren't you gonna say anything?" Aaron asked.

"What can I say? Only action changes a person's opinion. I must deliver these people to freedom."

Also listening – not in the darkness but in the center of it all – was Cora, keeping silent, biding her time.

********

In the mornings, before sunup, some of the women prepared biscuits and coffee for everyone. They ate and drank as they marched forward, not wanting to lose a minute of daylight.

The road was mostly empty; they met few folks along the way. Every so often, they'd pass a farm. The slaves working these farms would either ignore the caravan or shake their heads in dismay. It was such common sight in the South. White folks would stare with curiosity. Farm owners and plantation owners who needed slaves would call out bids.

"I'll give you one hundred dollars for the big one, there."

"Sorry, they're all spoken for. I'm just delivering them," was Josh's response, which seemingly settled the matter without any trouble.

One day, Lester rode his horse to the front of the procession next to Josh.

"I recognize this place," he said. "We're close; it won't be long, now."

Josh slowed his horse to ride alongside the front wagon where Pappy sat.

"Lester just told me we're coming up on the seminary."

"That's good," Pappy said. "I've been worryin' how long we can keep up this lead. I guess it's safe to tell ya now; but our food supply is getting mighty low. This couldn't come at a better time."

********

119

The Southern Seminary in Newberry was a forty-acre compound, a city to itself. Fifteen hundred seminarians housed there at a time. Lester rode up front with Josh, pointing to each building, telling him what each was. When they came to the end of the main road, there was a large white building. They stopped; Lester dismounted.

"Reverend McGuire is head of the seminary. Give me a minute to announce you." He turned and disappeared into the building. Josh dismounted and walked to speak with Pappy.

"Pappy, why are we here?"

"Josh, we need all the help we can get. These folks have always been kind to us."

Lester came out and walked to them. He was smiling.

"I spoke with Reverend McGuire. I told him everything. He's willing to see you." Lester pointed to the building and started to walk back. "Just follow me."

Inside, the halls were long and painted white; the floors were polished dark cherry wood. They came to a beautiful hand carved mahogany door. Lester knocked.

"Come in," the shaky voice of an elderly man said.

The office was oval and two stories high. The top tier was nothing but shelves of books, hundreds of dark, leather bound, well-worn books. Below was a semicircle of windows with a large desk in front of them. Standing next to a deep-blue globe of the world was a bent-over, gray-haired old man. Smiling, he walked to Pappy, took his hand, and shook it.

"You must be Moses Brown. We finally get to met."

"It's a pleasure to meet ya, sir," Pappy said. "Lester's told me so much about ya; I feel like I knows ya."

"I'll just leave you to it," Lester said, making for the door.

"No, Lester, please stay," the Reverend said. "This concerns you as much as everyone else here." He let go of Pappy's hand and looked into his eyes. "So, Mr. Brown, how can I help you?"

"Sir, ya have been so kind for so long, I feel ashamed to ask ya for anything; but I must."

"Don't feel that way; ask away."

"I'm sure Lester told ya we're on the run. We plan to get north to freedom and a new life. We are low on supplies. We need a place to rest and hide for a few days; and if there is any way else ya can help, we'd appreciate it."

"Mr. Brown, now it is I who feels ashamed. Most certainly we will help you, but I'm afraid it will not be in the capacity that you've hoped for. As for provisions, the war has hit us hard; we have very little. We can spare enough for two or three days. I wish it could be more, but there isn't any more to give. As for a few days asylum, I'm afraid I have to ask you to leave immediately. We help so many other people, in our own way and secretively. If the authorities knew you were even here, and we helped you in any way, they'd shut us down. Then there would be no more help for anyone. Please understand."

"Of course, we understand," Pappy said.

Reverend McGuire looked at Lester. "You, my boy, have a decision to make, as well as the other seminarians with you. You can say goodbye to these good people and return to your studies here. Or you can continue helping them; but understand if you're caught, you can never return to Southern Seminary. Still, I want you to know that no matter what you and the others decide, I am very proud of all of you."

"I think I can speak for the others as well as myself," Lester said. "We'd like to continue and see this through."

"I thought that's what you'd say; I'm glad you did." He shook Pappy's hand again. "Farewell, Mr. Brown. I'll have some of the boys load your wagons with what food we can spare. If I can think of any other way to help, you will hear from me. You will be in our prayers, sir."

"As ya be in ours, sir," Pappy said. "It's been a honor."

Outside, Pappy took Lester by the arm, pulling him aside.

"The Reverend is right. If we get caught and don't make it...and there's a good chance that will happen...ya and the other boys will be in big trouble. Not being able to return to the seminary will be the lesser of it. Running an underground railroad, especially one this size, is a serious offense. It might even get ya hanged."

"I realize that," Lester said. "We've talked it over; me and the boys are willin' to take that chance. We believe in what we're doing. If a man ain't willin' to die for what he believes in, then he probably don't believe in it too deeply and ain't got the right to believe in it in the first place." A thoughtful look came over Lester's face. "I want to thank you, Pappy, for all you've done. It may sound strange, me being white and all; but you've been like a granddaddy to me."

"I don't think that sounds strange at all. Any man, no matter what color he be, would be proud to have a grandson like ya." The two men hugged. "Now get yourself back with the others. We need to skedaddle."

Pappy and Josh watched as a small group of seminarians loaded the donated food onto the chuck wagon.

"Two ten pound bags of flour, a can of lard, and a bag of beans. That won't last us two days." They turned to see Cora standing behind them, watching. She wasn't alone; three others stood at her side, wearing the same sour look on their faces.

"There'll be food," Pappy said.

"Where from, the sky?" Cora laughed. "You know it's not too late. We can head back home, and nobody would be the wiser."

Pappy looked at Josh. "Get the people back to the wagons. We head north."

********

The Taylor brothers and their gang trotted slowly through the compound. They stopped a young seminarian carrying an armful of books.

"Say schoolboy, what kind of place is this here?" Tobias asked, looking down on the young man.

"This is the Southern Seminary, sir."

"Seminary? What be a seminary?"

"We're here to learn to be preachers."

Tobias laughed. "Ye don't need no schoolin' to learn how to do that. It ain't something ye learn. Ye either got the spirit or ye don't."

"Who's in charge of this rat hole?" Judd asked.

"That would be the Reverend McGuire. Just keep heading down this road till you come to the last building. You can't miss it. His name is on the office door."

"Much obliged," Judd said as he started onward.

"Kind of old to still be in school," one of the men said. They all laughed.

When they got to the last building, Judd and Tobias dismounted. "You boys wait here," Judd said.

Tom Garrett remained on his horse, quietly staring. He normally was a take-charge sort, but now he let the Taylor brothers do all the thinking and ordering. It was as if he was a stewpot simmering, building up pressure and would one day blow. He was saving it all for when he would have his revenge on those he blamed for his son's death. Till then, he'd bide his time in silence.

Inside, Judd pounded hard on the office door.

"Come in," a frail voice said.

The brothers entered and began pacing and examining the room like a pair of bloodhounds sniffing for clues.

"Ya the headman here?" Judd asked.

"Yes I am. How can I help you?"

"We've been trackin' a group of darkies disguised as a bunch heading for auction. They're actually workin' their way up North. We believe they may have stopped here."

"Yes they did. They were here less than an hour ago."

Both brothers stopped and starred, surprised at how easily the old man offered the information.

"Then ya admit they were here?"

"Why would I deny it?"

"Did they tell ya their plans?"

"Not in detail; only that they were heading north. They stayed long enough for us to give them some food to take with them."

"Ya gave them aid?"

"Just enough to be a Good Samaritan. After all, they were hungry; and this is a seminary."

"Do you know which way they went?"

"Only that they left taking the road going north."

"You've been most kind; we thank ye."

"It's getting late. Won't you gentlemen stay the night as our guests?"

"Thank ye; but with them so close, we best be off."

The two brothers nodded and left the room. Walking down the hall, they whispered to each other.

"So, what do ya think?" Judd asked.

"I think it was all far too easy; the Reverend was far too obliging to be trusted."

When they came to the front door, they heard someone hiss to them from a dark corner. Out stepped a young student, short, with sandy blonde hair, bright blue eyes, and a beguiling smile that could woo the devil.

"So, what did the old man tell you?" he asked.

"Who be ye?"

"The names Rehab, Jericho Rehab; I think I can help you."

"Go to blazes," Judd said, turning to the door.

"The old man told you they went north, didn't he?"

This stopped both brothers in their tracks.

"Which is what we suspected," Judd replied.

"That's not true," Jericho said. "That's not the way they went."

"They're heading north; they want to go north. Why would they change the way they want to go?" Judd asked.

Tobias stepped forward. "If ye know differ, ye need to spit it out."

"What's in it for me?" Jericho asked.

"What do ya want?"

"One hundred dollars."

"You're dreaming. We'll give you ten," Judd countered.

"Fifty?"

"Twenty-five."

"Make it thirty."

"Fine, thirty it is."

"What currency, union or confederate?"

"Silver dollars."

"All the better." Jericho smiled.

"Well, spit it out, boy, spit it out!"

"They've gone east."

"East! What for?"

"They're makin' their way to the ocean, to Charleston. They've chartered a ship to take them north all the way to New York Harbor." He handed Judd a folded piece of paper. "That's the name of the ship and its captain.

Tobias took a pouch from his coat and gave it to Jericho. "Here's ye silver." He turned to his brother. "Let's go. Tell the boys we head east.

********

Jericho entered the Reverend McGuire's office without knocking. The old man sat behind his desk, rummaging through papers. Jericho marched up and stood at attention.

"So, Mr. Rehab, did you see our guests off safely?"

"Yes, sir, everything went as planned. They are heading east on their way to Charleston."

"Lovely city, Charleston. I'm sure they'll enjoy their stay," the Revered chuckled. "There was a pub on the pier that served a soft-shell crab in butter..."

Jericho produced the small pouch of coins and placed them on the desk. "They paid me thirty silver dollars for the information."

Reverend McGuire picked up the pouch, bouncing it in his palm. "Thirty pieces of silver, how ironic. I suppose we should put the money towards the Potter's Field." He stashed the pouch in his top drawer.

"I told them when they got to Charleston, they needed to find the ship *The Pequod* and ask for its captain, *Captain Ahab*."

Reverend McGuire stared blankly at Jericho for a moment and then burst into a fit of laughter. "It would seem our friends are not literary men. With the Taylor brothers heading eastward to Charleston, I'd say that should give the folks from the Bush Plantation a sizable lead." He took the lid off a round tin, offering it to Jericho.

"Peppermint stick?"

"Thanks, sir. Don't mind if I do," Jericho said, taking the peppermint stick and sitting down on the side of the desk.

# Chapter Twenty-one

# Beans, Barley, and Heroes

The going was slow and hard. There were some days they journeyed only a few miles. The only thing going fast was their food supply. Each night after eating only enough to sustain life from measured-out portions, everyone in their exhaustion fell fast asleep. So tired and malnourished were they that often they would wake far into the morning, way after sunrise.

One evening, they found themselves on a narrow road. The only thing to do was enter a field and camp for the night. In the morning, Josh woke, looking up he saw a group of five men on horseback hovering over him. Each man held a shotgun slung over his saddle, with their hands on the stocks and fingers on the triggers ready to start shooting in an instant. At first, he feared the Taylor brothers caught up with them; but he didn't recognize any of them.

"You know you're on private property," the oldest said. He was a squatty little man with a large stomach that covered the horn of his saddle. He was in bad need of a shave, and his teeth were in great need of a dentist.

"I'm sorry, I didn't know," Josh said, jumping to his feet.

The man couldn't help noticing that Josh had slept the night close to a black woman. He looked at Ellie; he looked at Josh, and then he smiled. "No harm done. How would you know? There ain't no signs. I can be mag…magnan…" He had a hard time pronouncing it, but in the end he let it out clear, "Magnanimous"

"Thank you," Josh said. "We'll just be on our way."

"What's your hurry? I don't recall hearin' of any slave auctions goin' on in the area. Tell ya what; I could use a few good hands. I'd take a few of these darkies off your hands, and buy one or two of them." The man was staring at Becky as he spoke. "My, my, what do we have here? She's a pretty little thing, ain't she? I don't recall ever seeing such a light-skinned colored girl in all my life."

"They're not for sale, mister," Josh said. "They're all bought and paid for. I'm just delivering them."

"The name's Barnabas Amnon. This here used to be my tobacco plantation, tobacco as far as the eye could see. When the war broke out, I saw the writing on the wall. I started planting beans and barley. We've done all right, but it ain't the same. How about you? What's your name?"

"Oh sorry, my name's Joshua Nunn, trader in slaves, taking this bunch to their new owners."

"That's a shame. You sure you couldn't part with one or two? I'd pay you handsomely." He was looking and smiling at Becky as he said this.

"Sorry, Mr. Amnon; but like I said, they're all paid for, and the owners are waiting."

"Call me, Barnabas; and I'll call you 'Josh', if you don't mind. Well, that's too bad, Josh. Say, my place is just over that ridge. The misses and I don't hardly ever get any visitors. These galoots ain't good for company." He pointed to his men. "None of them have the brains of a gnat. Be nice to have a new face to sit and jaw with. The wife is the best cook in the state."

"That's mighty kind of you, Barnabas; but we are on a schedule. To be honest, we only have so much supply to get to our destination."

"Heck, if that's all that's stoppin' ya? I got enough beans and barely to feed an army, literally. I guess we could spare some to feed your brood."

Josh needed to think fast. Fraternizing with strangers could be dangerous. Yet, he knew how hungry everyone was, especially the children.

"I suppose one day wouldn't hurt. Very well, Mr. Amnon, I mean Barnabas, I'd like to take you up on your offer. Just give us a few minutes; we'll be ready to pull out."

It was clear the Amnon Plantation must have been glorious in its day, but those days were gone. The barn leaned dangerously to the left, with poorly kept grounds and fields all around. The paint on the main house had faded to the point that it was impossible to guess what its original color was.

Besides having eyes for Becky, it was clear why Barnabas wanted to buy slaves; it was a desperately understaffed farm. There were no more than a half dozen hands working the field; three of them were local white farmers who were down on their luck.

The wagons parked near the barn. Everyone rested on the ground, finding what shade they could. Mr. Amnon invited only Josh and Lester into the main house.

"Wait here," Barnabas told Josh and Lester when they first entered. He walked to the back of the house. They could hear him giving orders in the kitchen. "I got a mess of black folk out by the barn. Put on a large pot of bean and barley and feed them; but don't put any meat in it; not even a bone, ya hear!" He came back into the hallway, wiping his dirty hands on a towel. "Sorry 'bout that. Shall we step into the parlor for a brandy?" He motioned with his hand to a room off the hall.

Once he'd poured the brandy, Barnabas raised his glass in a toast. "To the Confederacy..."

"To the Confederacy..." Josh and Lester echoed in unison.

The rustling sound of crinolines made them turn to see at a woman entering the room.

"Gentlemen, this is my wife, Mable Amnon."

"It's a pleasure to meet you, ma'am."

"Gentlemen..."

"Mable, darling, I've invited Mr. Nunn and his top hand here for some vittles. Why don't you go into the kitchen and whip up one of your miracles, like a good little wife?"

"Yes, dear." She nodded slightly to Josh and Lester, turned and was gone.

It was obvious the story of Mrs. Amnon was similar to that of the Amnon Plantation. She must have been a true beauty in her day, a true Southern Belle, but those days were now gone. She was lean and frail, downright boney. Her hair was graying, becoming thin and stiff like straw. She had the look of someone distracted, distant; her eyes were empty with a vacancy seldom found in the living.

"Drink up, gentlemen, this bottle is only one of many. Sit and tell me all about your travels."

It was a long dining table set for eight. Barnabas sat at the head, his wife at the far end. Josh and Lester sat in the center, on opposite sides facing each other. There were more dumplings than chicken, but Josh and Lester fought the urge to woof it down.

"Mr. Nunn, I think a man should always shoot straight from the shoulder; so I'm goin' to come right out and say what's on my mind," Barnabas said. "I know you told me that all your slaves are spoken for. Now, we both know that when you transport slaves they all don't always make it to the destination. Some are shot trying to escape; some die from all sorts of diseases; and of course, there are always unfortunate and unforeseen accidents. If you were to tell your client that one of your slaves died during delivery, I'd make it worth your while. To be honest, I'd sure like to get my hands on that cute little filly of yours. You know the one, that light skin colored girl I saw this morning."

Josh turned to see if Barnabas' statement would get a rise out of his wife. She continued eating as if she hadn't heard a single word. Either she approved of her husbands philandering with slaves, which he doubted, or she didn't mind, which was unlikely; or she had just given up, which from the look of her was the case.

The seemingly inexhaustible hospitality of Barnabas Amnon suddenly stopped. Once he realized he wasn't going to get what he wanted, a cloud of unfriendliness blotted out the sunshine of kindness. Josh and Lester found themselves on the porch of the main house with the front door slammed behind them. Thankfully, everyone had been fed. It was a strange ordeal; but Josh felt it worth the cost, as everyone now had a full belly.

After a long day's march, the caravan found a shady grove to spend the night. Since everyone enjoyed such a large meal earlier that day, they decided to just bake a few biscuits for the children; the adults would go without. Later, everyone settled down for a night's sleep. Becky and Caleb laid a blanket on the ground a few feet into the darkness that surrounded the camp, for some privacy. Once everyone was asleep, all was quiet; till in the middle of the night, shouts shattered the silence, shouts from Caleb.

"Becky! Beck!" he cried in every direction, standing in the center of camp. Once everyone was awake, they crowed around him.

"Caleb, what's wrong?" Josh asked.

"Becky, she's missing."

"She's probably off in one of the bushes."

Caleb took hold of Josh's hand, placing it on the crown of his head.

"That's good size bump you got there."

"Someone hit me on the head while I slept. When I came to, Becky was gone. Someone's taken her."

"That Mr. Amnon sure had eyes for Becky. He was angry when you wouldn't sell her to him. I bet ya he took her," Lester said.

"I bet you're right," Josh said. "Lester, saddle up the horses and take a couple of rifles. You and I are going back to the Amnon place."

"I'm goin' with you," Caleb added.

"No, Caleb, you stay here. She's my daughter; I need to go get her."

"She's my wife!" Caleb shouted. "She's my responsibility now, not yours."

He tried to force himself past Josh.

"Hold him down, boys," Josh said.

Many of the men grabbed hold of Caleb. He fought them as hard as he could. Finally, someone brought out a rope; they tied him to the wheel of one of the wagons.

"She's my wife!" he screamed over and over.

Pappy came and placed his hand on Caleb's shoulder. "Listen to me, son. I know how ya feel; but if Josh goes back, legally he has the right to reclaim his property. If ya so-much as step on that man's property, legally he has the right to shoot ya and Becky, too. I know this is hard; but you're gonna have to trust us."

"No! Becky! Becky!"

Josh and Lester had ridden nearly two miles before they could no longer hear Caleb's cries.

********

Josh and Lester tied their horses to the fence surrounding the Amnon property. They walked the rest of the way slowly and silently carrying their rifles. Everything was quiet and dark, save for a faint glow seeping through the cracks in the run-down barn. They looked through the cracks. There they saw Becky tied to one of the horse stalls. There was no sign of Barnabas. They rushed in and up to Becky. Her head hung down; her bare shoulder showed through rips in her dress.

"Are you all right, Baby?" Josh asked, grapping her.

Lester took out his pocketknife and began cutting her free.

She looked up. "Daddy, you came."

"Where's Barnabas?" Josh asked.

"He went to get something to drink."

Lester nearly had her cut free when the click of a gun hammer being pulled back made them all stop in their tracks. Josh turned to see Barnabas standing a few feet away, a bottle of whiskey in one hand and a six-gun in the other, pointed straight at him.

"'Daddy, you came'," Barnabas said, mocking Becky. "So it's 'Daddy', is it? I should have known from the look of that fair skin. She even looks like that black wench I saw you lying next to last morning. She's probably the mother, ain't she?"

"Barnabas, you don't want to do this," Josh said, stepping forward.

"That's close enough, Nunn. Why should I not want to do this? You probably don't have any papers on the girl. I'll just tell the authorities you came to rob *my* property, so I shot you and your friend, here." He aimed the gun at Josh, then at Lester, and then at Josh again. "So who wants to go first? I know, let's send Daddy to the hereafter."

He straightened his arm and pointed the barrel of the gun at Josh's forehead.

"No!" Becky shouted.

A gun blast rang out, but it wasn't the sound of a six-gun, it was much louder. Barnabas fell to the ground; behind him stood his wife, Mable, holding a smoking shotgun.

"Cut her loose and get out of here," Mable said.

Lester freed Becky. They started for the barn door.

"Come with us," Josh said. "They'll try you for murder."

"Murder," Mabel laughed. "There ain't no murder. He was drunk; he's always drunk. He came in the barn carrying a lantern." She walked over to the lantern and picked it up. "He dropped the lantern; the barn caught fire, and in his drunken stupor couldn't get out in time." She threw the lantern to the ground at Barnabas' feet. It shattered; the straw on the ground immediately caught fire. "See, there ain't no murder. Now you good folks get yourselves out of here."

They ran out of the barn and into the night, heading for the horses. Josh nearly had to carry Becky all the way. When they got to the horses, Josh mounted and lifted Becky up behind him.

"Look," said Lester, pointing back to the barn engulfed in flames, the sky was glowing orange from the fire.

"Are you ready?" Josh asked.

"Josh," Lester said. "All the time we were running, I kept looking back. I don't think that old woman ever came out of the barn."

*********

Becky held on tight to her father as they rode through the night, the side of her head pressed up against his back, every word he spoke rumbled in her ear.

"Caleb wanted to come, but I wouldn't let him. I thought it best. Barnabas would have surely killed him, and probably you, too."

"Oh, Daddy, I wish you hadn't done that. He has his pride like any other man. Think of how you'd feel if it was momma, and they wouldn't let you go. I wish you hadn't done that. It's going to take me a long time to restore in him what you've taken away."

At that moment, Josh felt the full weight of his actions. He had somehow disrupted the balance of nature. He was in awe of the wisdom of his daughter, far beyond her years.

When they arrived at the camp, Becky jumped off the horse and ran to Caleb, still tied to the wagon wheel.

"Caleb!"

"Becky, are you all right?"

"I'm fine, but it was close. Daddy and Lester got there just in time."

Caleb turned his head from her. "I'm so ashamed."

"Oh, my love, you must never say that. You had no choice. Caleb, look at me." He turned his head to her. "Caleb, you are my husband. You will always be my hero."

# Chapter Twenty-two

# The Light in the Lighthouse

Tom Garrett always took up the rear as they rode. He remained silent for so long that it caught everyone by surprise when he spoke up.

"Hold up, you idiots!"

They all stopped and turned in their saddles.

"What do you want, old man?" one of the men said.

Judd rode up alongside and slapped the man on the side of his head so hard he fell off his horse. He nodded to Garrett.

"Sorry about that, Mr. Garrett. What seems to be the problem?"

"I would think the problem was obvious. We left the seminary days ago, headin' for Charleston on the word of one man. You ever stop to think he may have lied to us?"

"What makes you say that?" Judd asked. Tobias was next to his brother, listening.

"They're in wagons, and we're on horseback. Wouldn't you think by now we'd catch up with them?"

They remained silent.

"All those people; and we ain't seen one track, not one bent blade of grass. Don't you think that's strange?"

"I understand what you're sayin', Mr. Garrett; but we might have somehow missed the trail. What do ya suggest we do, head back? We're so close to Charleston. We'd kick ourselves if we didn't at least check it out."

"Maybe we should split up," Garrett said. "Some of us can go on to Charleston, the other half can start headin' north."

"They is sure to have guns," Tobias added. "We'll need every gun when we catch them. If they ain't in Charleston, we can always catch up with them with some heavy ridin'."

"I think you're all a bunch of idiots."

"I say this once and only once, Mr. Garrett." Tobias smiled. "Ye is only along for the ride. We make money on the slaves whether ye is here or not, whether ye is livin' or dead. Ye understand me, Mr. Garrett?"

Garrett went silent.

"Good. Now we is all in accordance. Now just take up the rear nice and quiet like ye been doin' and be a good boy."

Tobias turned his horse and started east once again with his brother by his side; the others rode behind with Tom Garrett taking up the rear.

********

Charleston, South Carolina, an inlet harbor leading to the ocean, is one of the rarest and most beautiful of jewels of the Confederacy. Even though much of it the Yankees destroyed, its splendor was undeniable. They rode passed Saint Michael's Church on Broad Street, down East Bay Street, till they came onto the waterfront on the Battery. They found a welcoming-looking tavern called the Forty Days, Forty Nights at the water's edge.

It was dark inside. There were a few sailors playing skittles (Six ball Westbury). A plump barkeep wearing a tablecloth for an apron smiled as they entered. They moved two tables together and sat down. The bartender came to take their order.

"So what will it be, gents?"

"A bottle and glasses all around," Tobias said, placing a silver coin on the table, "and some information."

"Be glad to, if I can."

"We're looking for a boat that should be in this harbor," Judd said.

"We call them ships, mate. What's her name?"

"The 'Pequod'; the captain's name is 'Ahab'."

The barkeep scratched his head. "Don't rightly know a 'Pequod'. Since the war, things ain't been regular." He turned to the group at the skittle table. "Mick, you know of a ship named 'Pequod'?"

The sailor took a few steps forward. "'The Pequod'...let me think."

"The captain's name is Ahab, if that be of any help to ye," Tobias added.

The sailor smiled. "You have the speech of a man of the sea, sir."

"Never ye mind where I get me talk. Do ye know the ship?" Tobias insisted.

The smile left the sailor's face. Judd knew his brother's lack of tact was the wrong approach. He tried to intervene. "Can we buy you a drink, sir? Barkeep, fetch another glass."

"That's mighty kind of you, gents. Don't mind if I do." The smile returned. "The 'Pequod', 'Ahab', sounds familiar but I just can't place it." He turned to his shipmates. "Any of you heard of the 'Pequod'?"

They all shook their heads. One sailor stepped forward. "They need to talk to Daniel. He knows every ship that ever sailed these waters and then some. I bet ya Daniel would know."

"Who's this Daniel?" Judd asked.

"He's a retired sailor who works the lighthouse."

"Where is this lighthouse?"

"Just follow the water's edge; it's on the south mouth of the harbor. Ya can't miss it."

"I'd have me a few drinks before I'd go see Daniel. I find the experience hard on the nerves," one sailor said. They all laughed.

One young man shook his head. "I can't get enough whiskey in me to be able to be in the same room with the man."

"What are you all talking about?" Judd asked.

"You'll see. Just don't shake hands with him; the man's got a grip like a vice." Again, there was laughter.

Judd stared at Tom Garrett, looking for a sign that he might want to go with him and his brother. Garrett just sat, pouring himself glass after glass of whiskey.

"You boys wait here while Tobias and I go see this Daniel fellow," Judd ordered.

"What if we run out of whiskey?" one of the men asked.

If looks could kill, Tobias would be a murderer…again.

*********

The lighthouse was a lone, tall monolith on a high hill on the edge of a rocky cliff, a whitewashed Cyclopes staring out at the ocean. From the roadside to the front door was a gray slate walkway, lined on both sides with Sweet Williams of various colors. A few feet from the building was a small, well-kept vegetable garden. All around the structure were more flowers; under each of the windows was a window box overflowing with even more flowers. At the front door, Judd wrapped his fist hard on the door three times.

"Coming," a man's voice from within said. The door opened as if under the power of some unseen phantom. They stood there staring into the house, not seeing anyone.

"Down here," a voice announced.

"Their eyes followed the sound. There, on the ground at their feet, was a man. A man like no man they had ever laid eyes on.

He was no higher than three feet. He was without legs, cutoff at the hips. He had only his right arm, the left missing up to the shoulder. His right eye was a deep-sea green; a black eye patch covered his left. His head was bald, there were no more than five teeth in his mouth, and on his right check was a long and deep scar.

"How can I help you, gents?"

The sight of him took them off guard. Finally, Tobias spoke up.

"Would ye be Daniel?"

"That's me, none other. How can I help you?"

"My name's Tobias Taylor; this here's me brother, Judd. Some folks at the tavern say ye know your boats...I mean, ships. We're looking for a particular ship."

"Come in, gentlemen," Daniel said. "Close the door and have a seat."

The sight of the way Daniel moved about captivated them. He'd place his fist on the floor, and with his mighty arm scoot himself across the room. He moved with surprising speed. When he got to a rocking chair, he placed the palm of his hand on the seat and with one swift motion was sitting in the chair. He pointed to a window seat in front of him.

"Sit down, gentlemen, please sit down. Now, what is the name of this ship?"

Slowly Tobias and Judd sat down facing him. Judd looked clearly shaken.

"Forgive me, I've forgotten you brother's name," Daniel addressed Tobias.

"Judd be his name."

"Judd, Judd, listen to me." Daniel snapped his fingers to get Judd's attention. "Judd, if you're having a hard time with this, you can leave if you want or you can look out the window if it'd make you feel comfortable. I won't be offended. I'm used to it."

"He'll be all right. Jus' give him a minute," Tobias said.

"You don't seem to have a problem with it, Mr. Taylor," Daniel said to Tobias.

"On the contrary," Tobias replied. "Beggin' your pardon, but I can't help starin'. I find it fascinatin' to just look at ye. What happened to ye?"

"You have the speech of a sailor. You wouldn't be an ole salt, now would you, Mr. Taylor?"

"I hates the water," Tobias declared.

"That's a shame," Daniel responded. "I fell in love with the sea when I was a boy. I couldn't wait to sign aboard a ship. I was twelve when I did. I've spent more of my life on the water than on land. I've sailed all over the world. A few years back, I was aloft when I lost my footing and fell overboard. A school of sharks decided to have lunch; I was the main course. By the time my mates got to me, this is all that was left, what you see of me now. The good people of Charleston, out of the kindness of their hearts, gave me this post as lighthouse keeper, and here I've been ever since. Feeling better, Mr. Taylor?" he asked Judd who nodded. "Back to business; you said you're looking for a ship. What's her name?"

"The Pequod," Tobias replied.

"'The Pequod'; you say."

"Aye, the captain's name is 'Ahab'."

Daniels face went thoughtful for a moment. "Do you gentlemen read?"

"Of course, we can read," said Tobias, sounding offended.

"No, I don't mean *can* you read. I meant *do* you read. You know...books. I think someone's been having you on."

"Say what?"

"I'll show you."

With one graceful flowing motion after another, Daniel was out of his chair and scooting across the floor. A far wall was a bookshelf from floor to ceiling. He reached up, grabbed the third rung, and pulled himself up. With his chin he pulled one of the books loose; it fell to the floor. He let go, hit the floor, grabbed the book, and moved to Tobias.

"Here, look at this.

Tobias held the book and read the cover out loud. "*Moby-Dick; or, The Whale* by Herman Melville." He opened the book. There was an engraving of a longboat full of men, and a great whale crashing down on them. Harpoons and ropes covered the whale's body. He thumbed a little further. "My name is Ishmael..."

"Skip a few more chapters," Daniel said.

Over and over Tobias read the name "*Pequod*" and "*Ahab*".

"The ship and the captain don't exist," Daniel said. "Someone's been having you on."

"Thank ye," Tobias said, handing back the book. "Excuse us, but we must be goin'. We have to make up some lost time."

He stood up and took hold of his brother's arm and guided him toward the door.

Daniel reached up and tugged at Judd's pant let. "Mr. Taylor, don't feel ashamed. I have this effect on some people; and I take no offense. You need to know I'm happy with my life. I do feel blessed. I have many blessings to be thankful for. I should be dead, but I'm alive. I have a place to live and a job to do."

Just then, a woman wearing a green bonnet with a matching ribbon tied under her chin and carrying a basket entered.

"Gentlemen, this is my greatest blessings of them all, my wife, Biddy. Biddy, this is the Taylor brothers."

Her skin, tan from working the garden. Her smile was straight and white. Her hands were long and boney; her eyes were pale with a touch of sadness. She was an ordinary looking woman; still Judd and Tobias couldn't help staring.

"Good day, gentlemen. I was just about to prepare dinner. Won't you please stay and join us?"

Tobias tipped his hat. "Thank ye, ma'am; but we must be goin'. Thank ye, both."

"Blessings on you both," Daniel said as he closed the door of the lighthouse.

Once outside in the fresh sea air, Judd returned to normal.

"You gonna be all right?" Tobias asked as they mounted their horses.

"That was the strangest thing I ever seen in my life," Judd said.

"That it be," Tobias replied.

They rode back the way they came. The sun was setting. The colors of the world were fading into a solid gray.

Tobias rode in silence, lost in his thoughts; and then he spoke. "If I ever get me hands on that little weasel that steered us wrong, he'll wish he'd never been born."

Later down the road, Judd spoke softly. "Do you really think he's happy?"

"Who's happy?" Tobias asked.

"Daniel, he says he's blessed, and why would any woman stay with a man like that?"

"Judd, Sometimes ye say the stupidest things. I honestly couldn't care less. He gave me what I wanted, and that's all I care about."

"What if he hadn't?" Judd asked.

"Then there'd be one less freak in the world."

Outside the tavern, while they tied up their horses, Tobias took hold of Judd's arm. He pointed at the door of the tavern.

"If Garrett even looks like he's gonna say 'I told ye so', I'll kill him. I'll kill him with my bare hands, I swear."

# Chapter Twenty-three

# A Band of Renegades

Travel was so hard and slow that Josh could look back and still see where they had camped the past three days. The folks were all tired and hungry; the children cried themselves into silence. The old folks moaned whenever the wagons went over a bump. The younger ones walking behind the wagons contended with sore and tired muscles and swollen, blistered feet. Even Lester and his men, who compared to the others had it better, suffered from exhaustion and saddle-sores. The food stock was dwindling. They rationed the food mostly to the children, but no one ever felt full or strong. Ellie, Miriam, and Becky did their best to keep the women and children's spirits up; but it was getting harder with each passing day. Caleb set an example for the other young men. He never complained or failed to do his part. As long as he continued in such a manner, rather than look less in the eyes of the others, the other young men did the same. Pappy and Aaron spent time with each person, listening, sympathizing, and encouraging.

Cora never stopped opposing them. She formed a committee that would daily make their complaints to Pappy. He did what he could to sooth their grumbling, but it was difficult, and their numbers were growing.

"It's not too late to turn back," was Cora's battle cry. "Think of the children. We'll all die out here. When we get up north, what makes you think things will be any better? At least when we was slaves, we ate everyday."

Late at night, when his joints ached and his stomach rumbled, even Pappy felt tempted to agree with Cora; but something in his soul knew better.

********

There was a loud crash and the sound of screams. One of the wagons had lost a wheel. The passengers franticly staggered to their feet.

"Is anybody hurt?" Josh asked, jumping off his horse.

"It doesn't look like it," Benjamin said, trying to calm the horses.

"Does anyone know how to fix a wagon wheel?" Josh shouted. A few hands went up.

"Good, see what you can do. Everyone else, find some shade and rest while you can."

Pappy stood looking over the worker's shoulders. "How long's it gonna take?"

"Longer than we'd like. We need to make another pin to hold the wheel on; this one's broke. I guess we make one out of wood and hope it holds. It's gonna take the rest of the day and part of the night. We should have it ready by morning."

Pappy sighed. "We camp here tonight," he told Josh. "Becky, tell your mother to get all able body folk to gather wood for a fire and start preparing dinner." Josh was just about to walk away when Pappy placed his hand on his shoulder. "Don't look now, but we're being watched. I jus' saw someone move in those bushes. Turn around slowly."

Josh turned. "I don't see anything. No, wait, yeah I see him."

Josh slowly walked backwards to his horse. He was just about to take hold of his rifle when the sound of a gun hammer clicking into place stopped him cold. He felt the muzzle of a pistol pressed against the back of his head.

"Don't move a muscle," the voice said, low and gruff.

In a flash, no less then twenty men surrounded them, each holding a rifle or a pistol. One of them stepped forward. He was lean and dark with a full head of black hair and a close cropped beard. He wore a tall cowboy hat and a full-length duster. His eyes were aflame as he spoke.

"Everyone stay where you are; don't make a move or a sound. I'll shoot the first person that does otherwise. Now, who's in charge here? Raise your hand." Josh raised his hand. The man walked up and looked deep into Josh's eyes. "Tell your men to step down and place their guns on the ground."

"Do as he says," Josh shouted.

"Now tell them to unchain and untie these slaves."

"Lester, you and the boys untie everyone."

When they had freed everyone, the man moved to the center of the crowd. "I want everyone to place their hands on their heads, even the children. I want two groups, white folks in the front and black folks in the back. We're going for a little walk."

"Sir, we have some old folks that can't walk; and some women have infants and small children," Josh said as softly as he could and yet still be heard.

"Very well, we'll take one wagon, put them in it." He ordered one of his men to drive the wagon. "We best take the chuck wagon, too. We can use the food," he said to another man who got up on the chuck wagon and took the reins. When everyone was in place, the man stepped to the front. His men were all around, pointing their guns into the crowd. "Listen up! Stay close to one another, don't speak or try anything funny. My men have orders to shoot to kill, and I mean that for everybody and anybody. I don't care if you're white, black, old, or young. You hear? Now march!"

He walked slowly enough that everyone could keep up. After some time, many found it difficult to keep their hands over their heads. They dropped them; no one cared. They walked through a field. Josh slowly worked his way toward Pappy.

"These aren't Judd Taylor's men," Josh whispered. "What could they want?"

"Probably the same thing Judd Taylor wants," Pappy said. "A group of slaves this large can fetch a pretty penny. I'm afraid the future doesn't look too good for any of us. We'll all be sold at some slave auction; and ya, my dear boy, ya, Lester, and the boys, are sure to be killed."

"Quit talking," shouted one of the men, pointing his gun at them. "No talking; move away from each other."

They walked through fields and then came to a dense forest and entered. It was difficult to stay together, walking around so many trees. Walking onward, the forest became darker. Up ahead, they could see light; it was a clearing. They entered the lit, treeless ground, a round area just large enough to fit them all.

The leader took a revolver from his holster, pointing it at Josh, Lester, and the boys. "You, you, and you, put your hands back on top of your heads and move to the center." He waited till they were in the center of the clearing, surrounded by the others. "Now, get down on your knees." He walked in a circle around the kneeling men, always pointing his gun at one of them. "My name is Captain John Brenham. I am, or should I say was, an officer in the Confederate Army; and these are my men. We are a band of renegades. They call us deserters, but I say we are a handful of men who've decided to follow our own destiny." He moved in closer to those kneeling, pointing the muzzle of his gun in their faces. "You men, one day, men like you will be forced to give up your evil laws. No man is greater than another man. No man should own another man. For your crimes I sentence you to death." He placed his revolver against Josh's temple.

"No!" Ellie shouted, falling to her knees.

"No wait!" Pappy shouted, stepping forward. "You mustn't do this! Don't kill them!"

Captain Brenham lunged forward, grabbed Pappy and forced him next to Josh. He put the revolver in Pappy's hand and placed the muzzle again to Josh's head.

"Go ahead, old man. It is more fitting that you strike the first blow. Go on, old man, proclaim your freedom."

"I can't," Pappy cried.

"You'd plead for the life of the man who says he owns you, the man who would sell you to another man? Kill him!"

"I can't because he's my son-in-law!"

A silence fell over the area. No one took a breath. It was as if time had stopped for that moment.

"What are you saying?" Captain Brenham asked.

"I can't kill him because he's my son-in-law." Pappy handed the gun back to Captain Brenham. "Ya are abolitionists, and I commend ya; but this is not what it seems. We are family. Most of us are black, and some of us are white; but nonetheless, we are a family. We travel under the flag of slavery, but we are all free. We are disguised as slave traders taking slaves to market only to move without suspicion. Our goal is the Promised Land; we travel north."

Captain Brenham placed his revolver in its holster. He knelt down on one knee next to Josh. He gently guided Josh's hands down from on top of his head. "Dear brother," Captain Brenham said. "Dear brother, forgive me."

All Captain Brenham's men raised their rifles high and cheered, "Hooray!" As if swept away by the wave of emotion, everyone cheered, "Hooray!"

********

"That's an amazing story, Mr. Brown," Captain Brenham said.

"Call me Pappy, everyone calls me Pappy."

"Very well, but you must call me John." He turned to Josh. "I hope you can forgive me. We live in desperate times. A man sometimes must do the unthinkable. More coffee, Mr. Nunn?"

Everyone, the folks from the Bush Plantation, the white boys, Captain Brenham, and his band of renegades settled back for an early meal, to break bread together in peace. Captain Brenham supplied all the food.

"Captain Brenham, I mean John, we've told ya how we've come to be here. Ya must tell us how a group of Confederate soldiers became abolitionists," Pappy asked, smiling.

"That's a good question, Mr. Brown, and not an easy one to answer." He stared into the campfire as he spoke, as if looking at the past unfolding in the flames. "I guess I've always been an abolitionist, somewhere in my heart. I come from a wealthy southern family. We owned a large tobacco farm. I was my father's pride. He raised me as his heir. One day I would own and run the farm. He taught me all about tobacco farming, and how to run a farm with an iron fist. This meant keeping his many slaves in constant fear. As kind

*141*

as he was to me, he was cruel to his slaves. I always felt this was wrong, but I never told him. I never spoke up."

He stopped for a moment, moving the red coal in the campfire with a stick.

"My mother was neither cruel nor kind; she was indifferent, especially to me. No matter how hard I fought for her attention, there were always other things more important. I, too, became indifferent. The only kindness and love I experienced when growing up was from my Mammy, a plump, round-faced, black woman named Phoebe who treated me like I was the center of the world. At least in her world, I was. I must admit, it was she who truly raised me; and if there is any good in me, I got it from her."

He sipped at his coffee, but it had grown cold. He tossed the last ounce into the fire. The fire hissed for a moment, sending up a small cloud of smoke. Using an old towel, he took up the coffeepot and poured a fresh hot cup.

"When war broke out, I enlisted. My father was so proud. My mother seemed to care less. Only Phoebe cried the day I left. Through my father's influence, I flew up the ranks quickly and easily. I fought, but my heart wasn't in it. More than that, it was my heart that tortured me. I knew within my heart I was on the wrong side.

"It was late in sixty-one, at the Battle of Greenbrier River in Virginia…that was my last battle. It wasn't much of a battle for most; but for me, it was a turning pointed. I was wounded, nothing serious, just a shot in the arm; but it was enough to be relieved of duty for a month. I took the time to visit home. I found it the same as when I left it: my father proud of his son and angry at the world, my mother cold and distant. What I learn when I arrived home, what my father had failed to write me in his letters, was that Phoebe was ill and dying. She lay on her bed in her small room near the kitchen. I stayed with her night and day. For three days she suffered, till on the third day calm came over her. The pain disappeared. Her eyes were clear in her last moments. With her last breath she told something that changed the course of my life. She said, 'I am your true Mammy. Your father is your father, but I am your true Mammy. Ya are my true son, bone of my bone and flesh of my flesh. I love ya as my son now, and I will love ya even more in heaven.' With that, she closed her eyes and gave up the ghost."

He looked up from the campfire, smiling into the staring faces around him. "You wouldn't know it to look at me. I have dark hair, but my skin is as white as parchment, but I'm a black man. I confronted my father about it. He neither confirmed nor discredited what Phoebe told me. As they say, actions do speak louder than words. He shouted at and cursed me, and disowned me, saying he no longer had a son, and that I was dead in his eyes. That told me that Phoebe's last words were true.

"It was a true dilemma. What was I to do? All my feelings of being on the wrong side were no longer feelings but facts. I could no longer comfortably serve in the Confederate Army. A black man couldn't serve in the Confederacy as a soldier, let alone as a Captain in charge of men. So, I never returned to duty. I wandered around the countryside without purpose. Then providence played its hand. In my travels, I met others who felt the same way I did. We formed a coalition, with me as the leader. We've lived in these woods doing whatever we can in our own way to fight against slavery."

"That's an amazing story," Pappy said.

Josh looked at Captain Brenham. "John, you seem a gentle man. Before, when you put your gun to my head, would you have really killed me?"

Captain Brenham's face went cold and stern. "This is a conflict for men's souls; war where evil is pitted against righteousness. There will always be casualties in any warfare, like it or not. It is for the better good. Yes, Josh, I would have killed you."

A shiver ran up Josh's spine.

"So, now we are friends," Captain Brenham laughed, slapping Josh on the back. "Fate deals the cards, and no one knows what will be dealt next."

"Unless you cheat," Josh said.

"Not if Fate is dealing. No one can cheat Fate." Again Captain Brenham's coffee had turn cold. He tossed it into the fire. "Gentlemen, I have something to share with you in confidence, and I have a favor to ask of you."

"What is that?" Pappy asked.

"Come, I'll show you."

He rose, turned, and began to walk away from the campfire light into the forest. Pappy and Josh followed closely. The trees blocked the last light of day; it was as dark as night.

"Do you know where we're going?" asked Josh. "I can hardly see a thing."

"I've walked this way hundreds of times. Don't worry, it's not far."

Up ahead, tiny yellow lights flickered like dozens of fireflies. As they got closer it was clear to see they were lanterns and campfires. They came to another clearing, a small village of tents, occupied by runaway slaves. It was clear they had been slaves, not just by their dark skin but by the scars many of them wore on their faces and arms from whippings and on their wrists and ankles from chains and shackles.

"Good evening, John," an old man said, walking by. "Good evening, John," a woman said, holding a child in her arms. "Good to see you, John," another said. "Bless you, John," still another said. They smiled and greeted him with respect.

"Who are these people?" Josh asked.

"Mostly runaways, slaves who'd been pushed so far over the edge they felt it worth the risk of being caught and hung than stay where they were. Most were half dead when we found them. They stay with us, we hide them, protect them, and feed them, and now and then, sneak them up north to other abolitionists. It's difficult and we do it so seldom. Now there's you, you have come up with a plan so outrageous it has to work."

"Wait a minute! Hold your horses!" Pappy said. "I see where this is leading. I don't want to sound cruel, but we're already pushed to the limit. I have my doubts we may make it. If we add one more mouth to feed, I don't think we can make it. It's not a question of do we want to take any more on. I have to think of the folks in my care. Their chances are slim, but they still have a chance. I can't take the chance. Sorry, John, we can't take these folks with us."

"You must!" There was urgency in Captains Brenham's voice. "The war has been closing in on us. Hardly a day goes by we don't hear gunfire off in the distance; each day the sound gets nearer. Soon these woods won't be safe. We'll have no place to hide. Besides, food is getting harder to come by. We won't be able to feed and shelter these people much longer. If you don't take these people with you, there're doomed."

Pappy's face went long as he fell into deep thought to consider what he'd just heard.

"How many folks are there?" Pappy asked.

"Thirty-two, three of them are grown men; the others are women, children, and old folks."

Pappy let out a long sigh. "John, ya make it hard for a body to say no. Very well, they can come; and may heaven help us."

A bright smile lit up on Captain Brenham's face. "Thank you. You won't regret this, I promise. Come, let's tell them together." He walked to the center of the makeshift village. "Everyone gather around. I've something important to tell you all."

********

Later, back at the camp, Pappy and Josh explained what they agreed to with Captain Brenham. There were concerns and questions, of course; but most folks felt it was the right thing to do. Still, there were a few who found cause to complain. Cora was their leader.

"The more people we take on, the harder it is to move about unnoticed. Are ya trying to get us all killed? What about food? How are we to feed all these new folks when we can't even feed our own people?"

"Cora, have a little faith," Pappy said as he walked away, shaking his head.

********

That night, while everyone slept, Becky woke to the sound of a voice coming from outside the camp perimeter. She listened carefully. She couldn't make out the words, but she recognized the voice as that of her grandfather. She gently managed to release herself from Caleb's strong arms without waking him. She followed the sound of Pappy's voice. She found him in a small clearing among the trees, standing in the ray of a full moon. He stretched out his arms to heaven as he spoke. Becky hid behind a tree, listening in secret.

"Zipporah…Zipporah, it's me, Moses. Can you see me? I'm over here in the moonlight."

Becky's mind raced for a moment; the name finally rang a bell. It was the name of her long-dead grandmother. Pappy was calling on his late wife, Zipporah.

"Zipporah, I miss ya, Darlin'. I'm sure ya been watchin' and know the dangers we face. I been prayin' to the Boss up there; I know we're in good hands, and I shouldn't worry. If only ya could put in a good word for us, I'm sure it wouldn't hurt. There never was a time when that pretty face of yours couldn't sway a body. Thank ya, Darlin'.

"Oh, by the way, if ya see Bernie Bush, I say 'if' because I was never sure if he'd ever get his wings. If ya see Bernie, tell him to set up the checkerboard. I suppose I won't be much longer in comin' home. I miss ya, and I love ya. I'll see ya when I see ya."

He lowered his arms and stepped out of the moonlight. Becky spun around and ran back to the camp. She fell to the ground and into Caleb's arms, waking him.

"Are you all right?" he mumbled.

"Caleb, promise me that if I die before you that you won't stop talking to me."

"I promise," he murmured without question. He filed the incident somewhere in the back of his mind where he kept all the out of the ordinary requests his wife had made or ever will make. He knew he'd never understand them. Still, he treasured them because they meant the world to her. A minute later, he was sleeping again.

*******

The sun was only moments from rising. They let the children sleep. It would be another long hard day. The women made coffee for everyone and biscuits for the children. They decided that none of the adults would eat, since they'd eaten their fill the night before. The thirty-two lost souls from the makeshift village came, some with bundles over their shoulders holding what little possessions they owned; others came empty-handed.

After the children were feed and the fires put out, everyone took their places, lining up to move out. Three of Captain Brenham's men volunteered to go with them and drive the additional wagons. The chuck wagon they loaded with what supplies they could spare. The sun was fully up when Captain Brenham and Pappy said their goodbyes.

"Ya sure ya won't come with us?" Pappy asked.

"You'll have your hands full trying to feed the mouths you have. We can live on roots and berries, if we have to; we've done it before."

"What will you do?" Josh asked.

"What we've always done. It isn't much; but if everyone did a little…pulled their share… this war would be over much sooner, and slavery will become a memory."

"When I hear it coming from ya, I tend to believe it," Pappy said. "Heaven's blessing upon ya and your men, Captain Brenham."

"Godspeed to you and your people, Mr. Brown."

With that Pappy hoisted up onto the buckboard of the front wagon; Josh mounted his horse, taking his place at the front of the caravan. Without looking back, they marched forward.

Pappy looked down from his seat to see Becky running along side the wagon.

"Why, Pumpkin, what are ya doin'?" he asked.

She smiled up at him. "I want you to be the second person to know. I'm gonna have a child."

"Why, Sweetheart, I haven't heard such good news since your mother told me she was havin' ya."

"I discussed it with Caleb. If it's a boy, we're gonna name him 'Moses'; and if it's a girl she'll be called 'Zipporah'."

Pappy took out his handkerchief and wiped the tears from his eyes. "What ya doin' gappin' up at me? Go tell your momma."

# Chapter Twenty-four

# You Have No Power Here

None of the men asked any questions. From the time the brothers fetched them from the tavern and for miles up the road, none of them so much as looked at Tobias. His scowl and fiery eyes made it clear the first man to say one word would regret it. Only Tom Garrett dared to look. He rode behind Tobias, staring a hole in the back of his head. Tobias could feel Garrett's eyeballs pressing on him. Finally, Tobias turned in his saddle and confronted Garrett.

"Ye have something to say to me?" Tobias spouted.

"Do I need to say it?" Garrett laughed.

"Yeah, ye need to say it. I'm stupid as a house monkey. I need it spelled out for me. I need to hear it."

"Very well, I told you that you were on a goose chase."

"I knew ye would say that."

"You demanded me to tell you. You are as stupid as a house monkey."

Tobias took his revolver from his holster, pulled back the hammer, and pointed it at Garrett.

"I said that ye ain't more than a guest on this trip. We make the same profit whether ye are with us or nay, and whether ye are dead or alive."

"I see your point," Garrett said. "I'll make a deal with you. I'll give you five thousand dollars if you let me continue with you."

"Scared of dying, Mr. Garrett?"

"Let's get one thing straight. I couldn't care less. I will give you five thousand when we return for the privilege of personally killing each and every person responsible for the death of my son."

Tobias slowly clicked the hammer of his revolver in place and returned it to his holster. A smile swept across his face. "That's what I like to hear: good solid, honest hatred. If at all possible, ye will have your wish, Mr. Garrett."

Tobias turned in his saddle, and they continued.

Farther up the road, they came to a fork. One lane continued going west; the other headed north, the logical path for them to take. Tobias continued the straight trail.

"Brother, where ya going? We need to head north," Judd said.

"Mr. Garrett has got me thinkin'," Tobias answered. "Revenge is a sweet dish that I ain't had a taste for in a long time. I got the hankerin' for it right now. I want to get my hands on that little weasel that steered us wrong; and when I do, I'll squeeze the life out of him. This here is the road that takes us back to that there seminary place. Nobody does that to Tobias Taylor and lives."

"We're so far behind; we need to keep on if we're gonna catch-up with them. Think of the profit! Revenge...? Brother, ya talkin' like a fool, like a little child."

Tobias looked solemnly at his brother. "Judd, ye be my brother. No man talks to me like that and lives. I'll let it slide just this once. One more word, and I'll kill ye; and that goes for the rest of ya. Anybody else got something to complain about?"

They all stared silently at the ground.

"I thought not," Tobias said. "What about ye, Mr. Garrett? Ye got anything to say?"

Garrett smiled. "I understand revenge. Do what you want. I'm not worried. I've known men like you before in my life. When they say they're gonna do something, they're gonna do it; and ain't nothing in the world gonna stop them. I don't like you, Mr. Taylor; but I do believe you. I know you'll get the job done. No, Mr. Taylor, I got nothing to say."

"Good! Now follow me."

Taking the western trail, they rode on.

They stopped at the crest of the hill, looking down at the seminary below. Tobias checked his revolver and rifle to be sure they were fully loaded.

"We're not gonna shoot any of these people, are we?" Sully, one of the younger men in the gang, asked.

"I don't remember ye ever havin' second thoughts about killin', Sully," Tobias said.

"I usually don't, but these here are holy people. These here are God's people."

"So, ye fear God more than ye fear me, do ye now?"

Sully took a moment to answer. "Yes, I do."

"Well maybe ye would be happier workin' for him."

It all happened so quickly, no one was sure exactly how or what happened next. Tobias drew a six-inch blade from out of his boot. In the blink of an eye, he tossed it at Sully. In the next blink, the blade was deep in Sully's chest to its hilt, only the handle protruding in front of him. Sully looked at the knife in his chest, and then he looked for a moment wide-eyes at Tobias. The next moment, his eyelids closed; and he toppled out of his saddle to the ground.

Tobias dismounted, pulled the knife from Sully's chest, and wiped the blood off the blade onto his pant leg.

"I want to make one thing perfectly clear; I liked Sully. I killed him for a reason. I killed because of thee. Since we formed this crew, there's been lots of sassin' back, not followin' orders, and downright disrespect. That's all gonna change, ain't it, boys? Now, I'd like to put this here blade in Mr. Garrett's chest even more than Sully's; but he's payin' us five thousand dollars to be his own man. Now if any of ye have five thousand, then put it up or shut up, and start doin' what you're told. Ye, take the reins of Sully's horse."

As they slowly rode down to the seminary, Judd pulled his horse next to his brother. "Momma always said ya were ornery," Judd whispered.

"If I'm any judge of character, I'd say she was burnin' in hell right now alongside Daddy."

********

It was getting dark. Nearly deserted were the streets of the seminary. What few students were out, stared at the small band of ruffians who obviously didn't fit in, standing out like a sore thumb.

"What are ye looking at, peckerwood?" Tobias snarled from on top of his horse. Most students dropped their gaze to the ground and walked on faster. One young man stopped and smiled up at him. "What ye smilin' for?"

"I'm just smiling."

"Only a village idiot just smiles. Do ye know Jericho?"

"Sure do. It's in the Middle East. Joshua and his army marched around it, blowing trumpets till *the walls came a-tumbling down*." He sang the last part

Tobias drew his pistol and pointed it at the lad. "Are ye havin' sport with me, boy?"

"No, sir," he said nervously. "I was just telling you about the city of Jericho."

"I don't know nothin' about no city. I'm lookin' for a man by that name."

"Sorry, mister, I never heard of anyone by that name."

"Ye certainly are sorry. I tell ye what: I'm feelin' benevolent. I'm goin' to count to ten. When I get to ten, if I see thy ugly face, I'm gonna shoot it. One..."

The other men laughed as by the count of eight, the young man was gone. They rode on till they came to the great, white building that housed Reverend McGuire's office. They entered the building. This time Tobias and Judd took the other men with them.

Tobias pointed to a space in the hallway. "That's where we met that weasel. I'm gonna kill him with my bare hands."

Tobias kicked in Reverend McGuire's office door and entered.

An old woman was waxing the Reverend's desk. She stopped and looked up. "What do you think you're doin'?"

"Where's the Reverend?"

"He's gone home; it's past six o'clock."

"Where's his home?"

"Who are you?" she asked.

"Missionaries, come to see the Reverend."

"You don't look like missionaries."

"We come from a very poor parish. Now where is his home?"

"Go back the way you came; follow the road left till you get to a large green house. You can't miss it; but the Reverend and his wife are havin' a party tonight."

"We were invited." Tobias turned and started down the hall. "Come on, boys. We don't want to be late for the party."

*********

It was dark when they arrived. Brightly lit was the large two-story home of Reverend McGuire and his wife. Music and the smell of barbecue filled the air. There were many empty carriages on the property.

The front door opened when they walked onto the front porch. A short, elderly black man wearing black tie and tails stood in the doorway.

"May I help you, gentlemen? Are you expected?"

"No! Let's just say this here done turned into a surprise party and we're the surprise," said Judd, pushing the old man aside as he entered, his brother and the others followed.

The guests wore their finest attire. They all stepped aside and stared at the men as they walked passed and entered the main hall. A string ensemble sat in the far corner playing softly. A long table stood against a wall of windows; on it were plates of finger foods and cups of crystal around a large crystal punch bowl. Tobias dipped one of the cups into the punch, took a sip, swirled the liquid in his mouth, and then spit it out into the punch bowl.

"Lemonade!" he announced in disgust.

"Excuse me; may I help you?" a voice said. Tobias turned to see Reverend McGuire.

"Why, Reverend, good to see ye again. Do ye remember me?"

"Yes I do. What is it you want?"

"I want to know where Jericho is."

"It's in the Middle East."

Tobias drew his gun and pointed it at the Reverend.

"What is with these holier-than-thou folks with their sassiness?"

The music stopped, the room went silent; all eyes focused on the two men.

"Ye lied to us," Tobias said.

"No. I didn't," said Reverend McGuire. "I told you that the last I saw of the people you are looking for they were heading up the north road. That was the truth. It's not my fault you didn't believe me."

"Once again, without the sassiness...where is this fellow Jericho?"

"He's not here. He's gone. I sent him on a mission."

"You're lying."

"I must admit I have not always told the truth in my life; but I've tried hard these days not to lie. I can assure you I'm not telling a lie, now; but then, I could be lying about not lying."

"There's that sassiness again," Tobias said. "What if I blew that head of yours clean off your shoulders?"

"Then you'd never get any information from me, be it the truth or a lie."

There was a charming older woman standing next to Reverend McGuire. Tobias turned his aim on her.

"Is this your wife, Reverend?"

"Yes, this is my wife."

"What if I blew her head off?"

Reverend McGuire remained surprisingly calm. "I do wish you wouldn't. Besides, I've always hoped I'd be the first to go."

"Oh, Darling," Mrs. McGuire said. "I know it sounds hopelessly romantic, but I've always had this vision we'd die together."

"Ye all are crazy! Now tell me where is Jericho."

"I told you he's on a mission; that's the truth." Reverend McGuire pointed his finger in the air. "You know what might be the problem? I would suspect you and your men are hungry." He turned to the elderly black man who'd opened the front door. "Douglas, see that these men have something to eat."

"Where's this mission?" Tobias demanded.

"Oh, I can't tell you that."

Tobias moved in closer and pointed his gun between Reverend McGuire's eyes.

"Listen, my good man," Reverend McGuire said, still cool and composed. "You're barking up the wrong tree, figuratively speaking. Yes, you have guns, but what can they do? You can kill our bodies, but you can't touch the true self. Kill me, and you send me to a far better place. In short, you have no power here, sir, so be gone."

No one made a sound or a move.

"Forget it. These holier-than-thou ain't worth the price of a bullet," Judd whispered to his brother.

Tobias still held his gun to the Reverend's head; neither one of them blinked.

"Forget it, Tobias; this distraction blows us off course and far behind," Judd said.

Tobias reset the hammer of his pistol and tucked it back into his holster.

"You're lucky I'm feeling benevolent, tonight," Tobias said.

"There's no such thing as luck," Reverend McGuire said. "We have something much greater. Go in peace."

Tobias pushed his way to the front door with his brother and the other men following close behind. Standing outside on the porch, Judd took hold of his brother's arm. Tobias pulled himself free of his grasp.

"Don't say a word," Tobias spouted. "Just get back on your horses. We've got some hard ridin' to do."

Just then the front door opened. Douglas, the elderly black servant, walked out onto the porch holding a large sack. He handed it to Tobias.

"What be this?" Tobias said.

"Here, sir, you forgot your food. The Reverend and his wife want you to have it."

Tobias ignored him and refused the sack.

Once on their horses, they rode off into the darkness. None of the men said a word. Tobias could feel Tom Garrett's stare.

"You got something to say, Garrett?"

"Me, no, not me, I got nothing to say."

"Good, `cos if ye say one word, five thousand dollars or not…it would be worth it to shoot a hole between your eyes."

# Chapter Twenty-five

# New and Old Friends

Only the horses ate regularly; they grazed each night on the grass and straw in the fields where they camped. Water was scarce but not a problem. When they found a spring or a stream they filled the water barrels. It was food that was the problem. There was wild game in the fields and pastures and fish in ponds; but the fear of dangerous men hunting them kept them going, never stopping long enough to gather or hunt. Those who could walk took turns riding in the wagons; but with the old, sick, and children, there was little room for that. As rations became less, the weaker they became, which meant the slower they traveled. It seemed like a losing battle with no solution in sight.

During the day, the young men and the older boys spread out in all directions as far as a half mile from the others, but always moving north. Their job was to gather as much food as possible. On good days, they came back with turkey eggs, blackberries, chestnuts, wild yams, frogs, turtles, snakes, and locust. On bad days, it was just roots and water lilies. There were plenty of mushrooms; but no one knew how to tell the poison from the clean so they never touched them.

Each of them carried a large gathering sack, the kind they use for picking cotton. At the end of the day, they'd bring back their finds to the camp. The women would skin and clean the frogs, turtles, and snakes; they'd boil the eggs till they were hard. They'd have the children peel the hard-boiled eggs and pull away the shells from the scored and roasted chestnuts; their small hands and fingers made for such work. Then with the locust, berries, roots, and water lilies, they'd throw it all in a hot boiling caldron. Some nights, the combination didn't taste half bad; or perhaps their hunger affected their taste buds. There was never enough food, never enough to ever feel really full. Just by the nature of the fare, never enough to build up their strength.

As bad as that was, there were days when they found nothing, absolutely nothing. On those days, the lines around the parents' eyes would deepen as they rocked their crying children to sleep.

Without fail, every night, a group gathered around Pappy and Josh to voice their concerns and disapprovals. The leader and most vocal of the group was always Cora.

"Do we have to wait till one of our children dies before we wake up?" Cora protested. "We were better off as slaves with a roof over our heads and full bellies than wandering aimlessly without food or hope. I say we head back before it's too late and wait out this war."

Pappy stood front and center, staring them down coldly.

"I will shoot the first person who turns to leave, man or woman; I'll shot 'em, even if I have to shoot 'em in the back as they run away."

"Who made you Massa?" Cora cried. "Ya talk all high and mighty about being free, yet ya take that freedom away. Everybody should be free to come and go as they please."

"Cora, I've had it up to here with ya. We is a family; and family sticks together. This is for the good of all of us. If we split apart now, none of us will make it. Ya want to go back, back to what? You'd never make it on your own; and those of us who continue to head north won't make it either. We've got to stick together, like it or not. We're at the point of no return. We can only move forward. Now get back to your places, and let's get on with it."

Cora stepped up, raised her finger and pointed it under Pappy's nose. "Very well, Moses Brown, just keep in mind that it's all gonna be on your head. Whatever happens is on your head."

"Get back to the wagons, Cora."

********

On a lonely road, they came to a crossroad. At the northeast corner was a broken-down old wooden fence. Behind that were tall, long rows of yellow corn. No one said a word. They ran for the fence and hopped it. Men, women, young and old, and children began tearing the ears of corn from the stalks. They shucked them and bit into the raw sweet corn. Only the sound of teeth ripping and chewing could be heard. They pushed and shoved one another as they grabbed franticly at the ears.

"Stop it! Stop it!" Pappy hollered from the fence. "You're acting like animals! Look at the corn; it's not wild corn. Those are straight furrows. Someone planted that corn; someone worked hard; someone owns that corn. What you're doin' is robbin'."

"We're hungry!" someone shouted.

"I understand that; but bein' hungry don't make it right. Now drop those ears. I'm ashamed of all of ya."

It was something in the way he spoke, like a preacher on Sunday. They dropped the ears and stood still. Pappy looked across the field. There was small shack on the other side of the field, made of the same wood as the fence and just as broken-down.

"All you men pick up those ears of corn and follow me," Pappy ordered.

He bent low and worked his way through the slits in the fence. He started toward the old shack; the men with arms loaded down with ears of corn followed. Standing in front of the shack, Pappy ordered them to drop the corn on the porch. He turned to Josh. "It would be best if ya do the talkin'."

Josh knocked on the front door. A thin woman dressed in worn clothes with two small youngsters clinging to her side answered the door.

"Yes?" she asked.

A man's voice called from within. "Tessie, who is it?"

"There are some people out here," she cried back into the house.

A slender fellow dressed in overalls with windblown hair and reddish suntanned skin came to the door.

"Can I help ya?" he asked.

Josh took off his hat in respect, holding it as he spoke. "Sir, we're here to apologize. We've been on the road for sometime now. Food's been scarce. When my people saw your corn, I guess their hunger got the best of them. They started picking your corn. I've made them put them here on your porch." He pointed to the pile of corn at his feet. "I'm afraid they ate some, too. I don't have much, but I'd like to pay you for what they ate."

The man walked out onto the porch. "Well, that's all right. I know what hunger is; I know what it can do to a body. No harm done. Let's just forgive and forget."

"Well, I am sorry; and I thank you," Josh said stepping off the porch.

The man took a few steps forward into the sunlight. "Say, wait a minute." Josh turned and listened. "That corn is ripe and ready for harvest. With the war on, it's hard to find men who can work. I'll tell ya what. Ya and your folks help me get that crop in, stack it in the barn; and I'll share it with ya. How does one tenth, a tithe, sound to ya?"

"Just give me one minute," Josh said, pulling Pappy aside. He whispered low to Pappy. "What do you think? We've got the Taylor brothers on our tail. Can we afford to waste a couple of days?"

Pappy shook his head. "I don't know if we have a choice. Look at the way our folks are acting and looking like. We can't afford to say 'no'."

"It's a deal," Josh called up to the man.

"Good. Just give me a minute and meet me by the barn; I'll get ya started."

********

The man's name was Chester. Call it a strange coincidence, his last name was Brown – Chester Brown. His wife's name was Tess; they called their children *Brother* and *Sissy* – the boy being no more than five and the oldest by a year.

Chester had them bring the wagons alongside the cornfield. He handed out old sacks to put the ears in and then dump them into the wagons. When a wagon was full, they drove it to the barn and unloaded. Everyone worked; even the elderly and children. Every little bit helped. Even Chester's family…his wife and children…worked alongside the others.

It was a long hard day. When the sun set, they built bonfires and roasted the ears of corn. The ears were sweet and everyone had their fill and felt satisfied.

Late in the evening, after they put the children to bed, Josh and Lester sat on the edge of the Brown's shack as Chester rocked in his rocking chair. He went into the house and came out with a jug. He handed it to Josh.

"Here ya go, gentlemen; there are more uses for corn than meal."

They all took turns swigging on the jug. It burned going down, but was reassuring and warming.

"So, Mr. Nunn, what is your business, if I may be so bold as to ask?"

"These slaves have been bought by various men of distinction. We are just delivering them to their rightful owners."

Chester took the jug, took a long hard pull, and burst into laughter. "Mr. Nunn, ya seem like a fine young gentleman, but you're lying has much to be desired."

"What do you mean?" Josh said.

"What I mean is, I never seen a trader in slaves act like you do. Ya treat them like they were family. The one you call Pappy; ya don't make a move without consulting him. That pretty little black woman…what was her name…Ellie? Ya watch over her like she was made of gold. No, Mr. Nunn, I don't know what your game is; but you're no slave trader."

Josh remained silent for a long time, and then he spoke. "We're family. That woman you spoke of is my wife, Ellie. The old man, Pappy, is my father-in-law. Except for the white boys like Lester here, everyone is related one way or another. We're hiding behind the guise of being a slave caravan. We're working our way north to Yankee territory."

Chester nearly rolled to the floor with laugher. "Dang, boy, I ain't never heard a story so dang sideways in my life. It's one to beat the band; I tell ya." His face went serious. "Ya know you're takin' you life in your hands when ya go 'round tellin' strangers your business. Don't worry; your secret is safe with me." He took a long pull from the jug and handed it to Lester. "Well, gentlemen, we got another long day ahead of us in the morning. I bid ya goodnight."

The next day started early. It was more of the same; a long, hard day of harvesting corn. That night, Chester's wife gave the women a side of bacon to go with their dinner of corn.

It wasn't much, but it was a nice change in the flavor of things. The following morning they lined up to head out. Chester and his family stood by the fence to see them off.

"Dang, if ya don't look like slave traders takin' a mess of slaves to market," Chester laughed, pointing to the folks chained and tied to the back of the wagon. "It's been nice doin' business with ya folks, ya got enough corn for another day or so. I wish it was more, but that's all there is."

"You've been more than kind, sir," Pappy said. "We thank ya."

Chester looked Pappy up and down. "So you're really the leader of this here bunch, ain't ya?"

"I'm afraid so," Pappy said.

"Dang, I never would have believed it. A darkie boss over a bunch of white boys, I never thought I'd live to see the day. Well, ya folks take care."

Chester Brown, Tessie, Brother and Sissy waved till they were out of sight.

********

With full bellies, the next day they traveled a little faster. The territory was a series of hills and valleys. After drudging up one very tall and steep hill, they stopped to rest. Everyone who had walked lay on the ground, out of breath. The horses had worked up lather and needed a breather as well. Pappy sprawled out under a tree with his eyes close.

"Pappy, are you asleep?"

He opened one eye to see Josh standing over him.

"What's wrong?" Pappy asked.

"I need to show you something. Get up and walk with me. Act like we're just stretching our legs. I don't want anyone to catch wind of this."

They nonchalantly walked to the crest of the hill, looking back on the way they came.

"What am I looking for?" Pappy asked.

"Out there," Josh said. "Four valleys back, what do you see?"

Pappy strained his aging eyes. "Is that smoke? But it's red."

"It not smoke; it's dust."

"Riders!" Pappy said. "Ya think it's the Taylor brothers?"

"I can't think of who else it would be."

"How soon before they catch up to us?"

"It's hard to say. Remember they're on horseback. We're no match for them. I'd say if we keep moving and don't stop, not even to sleep, then they'll be on us in two days."

"Maybe we should stay where we are; at least we have the high ground."

To their surprise, they heard Lester's voice behind them. "I've got a plan."

*157*

They turned to look at Lester.

"What's that?" Pappy asked.

"Let me take the white boys; we can ambush them somewhere between here and where they are."

"No good," Pappy said. "If ya fail, we'll be stuck on this hill completely helpless."

"At least let me go out and take a few potshots at 'em from afar. Maybe I can get their numbers down."

Pappy thought long and hard. "Ya promise me ya won't take any foolish chances, a few potshots and come right back?"

"I promise," Lester said.

"Wait," Josh said. "What do we tell the others when they see Lester riding off back the way we came?"

"Tell them I lost my reading glasses, and Lester's gone back to get them," Pappy said.

"You're kidding," Josh said.

"You'd be surprised what folks will believe. It sounds so ridiculous, it has to be true." He turned to Lester. "You be careful, son."

"I will, Pappy."

In an instant he was on his horse, riding swiftly back south. Becky came up, wondering what was happening.

"Where's Lester going?" she asked.

"Pappy can't find his reading glasses. He thinks he left them at our last camp. Lester's gone back to fetch them."

She looked at her grandfather with scolding eyes. "You need to be more careful, Pappy. They're your only pair."

\*\*\*\*\*\*\*\*

Pappy told Josh to pass the word along they would camp where they were that night at the top of the hill. They said the reason being was that most folks looked worn out by the day's journey and the terrain up ahead looked even more difficult than where they'd come. They said everyone needed to rest and build up their strength for the following day's march.

"Are we going to lie around in the sun while everyday brings the Taylor brothers closer?" Cora complained.

"We'll be just fine," Pappy said. "Besides, it's not your problem, Cora; it's mine; and I'll take care of it."

The atmosphere in the camp was calm, relaxing, and jovial. They built fires and roasted ears of corn. Some folks began complaining about only having corn to eat; but it was nothing the others couldn't easily ignore.

After sunset, they sat around the fires. They played with the children, sang songs, and told jokes. There was laughter; and just for a moment, things felt normal again. Pappy and Josh went off alone to discuss their options.

"I don't like this," Josh said. "Something's not right. Lester rode off to take potshots at the Taylor gang, and we haven't heard a shot, yet."

"They were a long way off," Pappy said. "He might not have come up on them until nightfall. He's probably waiting for daylight."

"That's possible," Josh replied, "but it just doesn't feel right."

"I've been thinking this whole thing out," Pappy said. "If we're goin' to make our stand here against the Taylors, there's no reason why everyone should be here. I think we should get up early, explain to everyone what's goin' on. We take the guns and ammo out from the false bottoms of the wagons. Then we put the elderly, sick, and the women and children in the wagons and send them on ahead. All the able-bodied men stay here to fight."

"Makes sense," Josh replied. "Well, let's get some shut-eye; it's going to be a long busy day."

\*\*\*\*\*\*\*\*

Just before dawn, Pappy roused everyone; and like a loving father, he explained their predicament. Everyone kept calm as they went about their assigned duties, but the scent of fear was in the air. They took the guns and ammo out from the false bottoms of the wagons and laid them all in a pile. Not knowing how long they may have to hold up on that hilltop, they took a third of the food from the chuck wagon.

Cora came with a small delegation to Pappy, to voice her concerns and disappointment. Pappy gave them such a stern look that none of them said a word, but silently went about their business.

With the first rays of sunlight, Pappy and Josh stood on the edge of the hill, keeping a look out.

"I don't understand; something's not right," Josh echoed his sentiments of the night before. "See the dust they're kicking up; you see how faraway they still are. They won't be here till later in the day. If they're on horseback, why are they moving so slowly?"

"Maybe Lester slowed them down?" Pappy remarked.

"We haven't heard any gunshots. I'm worried about Lester."

They stood watching the oncoming red dust.

"You know, Pappy," Josh said. "In theory, you're an old man and should go on with the others."

"In theory, you're right," Pappy answered, "but I'm still the head of this family; my place is at the front. One day when I'm gone, you'll be the head of the family; then you'll understand."

"I think I do already."

********

At times such as these, there are no easy ways to say goodbye. Men held their women and children tightly in their arms. Tears ran freely. Just the thought that you might not see each other again was a terrible weight to carry. Finally, they parted ways. The men stood on the hilltop watching their families ride off. When they could no longer see them, they turned to the other side of the hilltop and the task at hand.

They divided the guns and ammo as equally as they could. Those who'd used firearms before did what they could to teach those who hadn't. They each took their places on the ground behind rocks facing south. They watched and waited.

Every so often, a red puff of dust shot up over the tops of the trees, showing them where the riders were. Each hour, the dust rose closer; till late in the day it floated above treetops at the bottom of the hill. Soon the riders would appear.

Each man tensed his body, keeping his aim down the barrel of his rifle. Suddenly, a wagon with a sole driver appeared at the foot of the hill, not the Taylor brother's gang.

"Hold your fire!" Josh ordered as he stood up, the wagon driver halted his horses. "Who are you?" Josh shouted down at the man.

He stood up in the wagon, cupped his hands around his mouth, and shouted back. "The name's Rehab, Jericho Rehab. I'm from The Southern Seminary out of Newberry. If your name is Moses Brown, I've got a wagon load of food for you, a gift from Reverend McGuire, the head of the seminary!"

Some of the men ran down the hill and helped guide the wagon up the hill. At the top, Jericho jumped off the wagon, smiling back at the smiling faces surrounding him.

"I'm Moses Brown," Pappy said, stepping forward and shaking Jericho's hand. "Ya couldn't have come at a better time; we're mighty low on food. Last time we saw the Reverend McGuire, he was kind enough to give what little food he could spare, but it was very little. How do we come to be so blessed?"

"It's true, what the Reverend gave you was all we could spare," Jericho said. "He felt bad about that. So bad that he got in touch with some of his wealthier friends in the county and asked for donations; he even threw a fund-raising party at his own home. We took the money and bought some supplies, and I volunteered to bring it to you. It's only bags of flour, oats, and barely, but it's all yours."

"We're grateful to have it," Pappy said, wrapping his arms around Jericho. "Young man, ya is heaven-sent. I'm so happy, I don't know if I should cry or spit." Then he addressed the other men standing around them. "Someone, get on a horse and catch up with the others. Tell them what's happened. Tell them we're safe and to wait for us; we'll be there soon...and with food!" He shouted this last part and all the men cheered. "We need to unload this man's wagon and put the food in one of ours."

"I rather you didn't," Jericho said. "I believe in what you're doing. I'd feel privileged if you'd allow me to be part of your family. I've driven that wagon this far, I wouldn't mind being a part of all this and driving it a few more miles."

"Listen, son, we don't know for sure if we're gonna make it," Pappy said softly. "We may never make it."

"I understand, sir; but I'd still like to come."

"Very well," Pappy said. "You're more than welcome to come, on one condition: that ya consider yourself a member of our family."

The men cheered again and patted Jericho on the back.

Just then, Caleb stepped forward and stood before Jericho.

"In your travels," Caleb asked, "you didn't happen to meet a tall, slender, white boy by the name of Lester?"

"Sorry, I haven't seen a soul since the day I rode out from the seminary."

Caleb turned to Pappy. "I need a horse, Pappy. I need to go back and try to find Lester."

"Caleb, I know he's your best friend and ya love him; but...but ya got a wife and comin' child waitin' for ya a few miles north; and ya want to ride south to find Lester. I admire ya for that but..." Pappy looked at Caleb and realized his plea fell on deaf ears. He placed his hand on Caleb's shoulder. "Very well, son; ya take one of the horses. I'll try to square it with Becky, but I don't know. Ya got to promise me that if ya don't find Lester in three days, you'll turn around and hightail it back to us."

"I promise," Caleb said, rushing to one of the horses, mounting it, and galloping south.

"What's the matter with the rest of ya?" Pappy shouted. "Quit standin' around. We got hungry family to go feed!"

# Chapter Twenty-six

# What Happened to Lester?

As Lester galloped southward, his mind remained preoccupied. They agreed he would head south and take potshots at the Taylor brother's gang. Exactly what did that entail? Was it just to try to slow them down...which may or may not be enough... or was he expected to stop them? He'd never shot another man, let alone kill one. Both prospects left him feeling uneasy. He could try to shoot the horses out from under them; but that thought left a bad taste in his mouth, also. Whatever he was to decide, he needed to do it soon. He was galloping south at a fast pace; the road dust kicked up by whoever was ahead of him drew closer.

He came up on a small lake; he stared at it as he rode by. Perhaps because neither he nor his horse was watching where they were going, they stumbled over a rock and fell. His horse rolled over several times; luckily, Lester flew out of the way. He soared into a tree and was knocked unconscious.

When he woke, it was dark. He was lying at the foot of the tree; his horse was standing nearby. When he got up, the world spun for a moment; the top of his head pounded with pain. He reached up and felt a lump on the top of his head the size of a silver dollar. He checked his horse; thankfully, there were no bones broken. He looked out on the lake. There on the opposite shore was the flicker of a campfire. He tied his horse to a tree, took his rifle, and went to investigate.

Coming up slowly and quietly on the campsite, Lester hid behind a tree, watching and listened. It was the Taylor brother's gang, for sure. He tried to think of what to do. Should he start shooting, should he rush them? It all sounded so foolish. Picking them off like sitting ducks did not sit well with Lester, and there were too many of them to rush. He decided the time was not right. He snuck back to the other side of the lake, sat on the ground with his back against a tree, pulled his hat over his eyes, and caught a few hours of shut-eye.

With the first rays of the morning sun, Judd woke to the sound of water splashing. He opened his eyes to find he was looking up at a rifle aimed at his head. The others woke in a daze.

"Nobody move," Lester ordered, standing over them, moving the aim of his rifle from one face to the next.

Each man scurried to find his weapon but they were unable to find them.

"Me gun, what have ye done with me gun?" Tobias shouted.

"They're all at the bottom of the lake," Lester announced. "Just this here rifle; and I guess that makes me king over ya all."

"What do ya aim to do?" Judd asked.

"Well, guess I could kill ya all," Lester said, "but that ain't my way. Not that I'd be against shootin' any of ya, if ya were to make any false moves. I could take your horses and leave ya here. Ya may or may not get back on the trail in due course, but I have a better idea. We're all goin' to mount up and start headin' south. When I feel you're far enough from my people, I'll let ya go."

"'Your people'," Tobias smirked. "You must be color blind."

Lester laughed. "You're right. I am color blind. That's how I'm able to call them my family." He shook his head." Ya just don't get it, do ya? Well, ya can't get blood from a turnip. Everybody, get up on your horses. We're headin' south."

They road together slowly southbound with Lester taking up the rear, holding his rifle pointed at the backs of their heads.

Tobias started to laugh.

"What's so funny?" Lester asked.

"Ye be; that's what so funny. How long do ye think you can do this?"

"This rifle says I can do it as long as I want," Lester said, aiming the rifle at Tobias.

"What if we rushed ya?" Judd asked.

"I guess ya could. That would be one way of stoppin' me. I'd probably only get two or three of ya. The question is: who wants to be one of the three?"

"What happens when ya gotta eat, or wash, or do your business?" Judd smirked.

"I can eat as well as the next man with one hand," Lester replied. "As for washin', like most folks, I don't mind my own stink. When I do my business, ya all can sit on your hands with your backs to me. Ya got any other bright ideas?"

"Just one," Tobias hissed through tight gripped teeth. "Ye gotta sleep, sometime." He addressed the other gang members. "From now on, boys, we sleep in shifts." He smiled at Lester. "Ye gonna sleep, sometime. Ye can't watch us sleep every night. Maybe one or two nights, maybe even three; but as soon as ye closes your eyes, I will get that gun from ye and blast what little brains ye must have in that ugly skull of yours." The men laughed with Tobias; Lester's face went stone-cold.

********

They stopped for the night in a clearing; Lester was able to watch them. He ordered them to gather wood for a fire. One of the men wandered to the far end of the clearing. Lester took a potshot just inches from the man's feet.

"What'd ya do that for?" the man complained. "I wasn't goin' anywhere."

"No, but ya were thinkin' about it," Lester said. "Jus' stay close."

Honestly, Lester didn't think the man would have done anything; but he wanted to put some fear into them.

After a dinner of dried beef and cold biscuits, half the men stretched out by the fire to sleep. The other half sat crossed legged staring at Lester.

"Get some sleep," Lester ordered.

"We're not tired," one of the men protested.

So that was how it was going to be. In the middle of the night, the group that stayed up woke the sleeping group. They went to sleep while the rested men took to staring down Lester.

The next morning, the men felt tired, but not half as tired as Lester. As they rode south, Lester made an announcement.

"Last night was the last time ya all are gonna pull that game on me. From now on, we don't stop. No sleep for anyone, you hear? I'll shoot the first man who falls asleep."

They rode the entire day slowly, only stopping whenever they came on water to allow the horses to drink and rest, and to fill their canteens. When the sun set, they continued. Luckily for Lester, it was a full moon; and he was able to keep an eye on them.

At sunrise, every man slumped in his saddle. One or two leaned forward, trusting their horses knew which way to go. Lester rode next to them, nudged them with the butt of his rifle.

"Wake up! I told ya I'll shoot the first man who falls asleep."

"Go ahead, shoot me," one of the men said. "At least I'd get some sleep."

Lester kept them going south. Everyday that he kept them going away from his folks was another day closer to their freedom.

Another night of riding, the moon was still bright enough to watch their every move. They stopped once or twice, to eat and to rest the horses. Lester kept his aim on them, forcing them to stand. He knew that if any of them sat, they'd fall asleep.

The next morning, the sun burned into Lester's eyes. He strained not to see double. Twice they stopped because one of the men fell from his horse. If that were to happen to him, Lester knew they'd be on him in seconds; he'd be a goner.

The west glowed orange and purple as the sun fell below the horizon. It would be dark, soon. Lester was unsure if he could continue staying awake and alert.

"There ain't no reason to make these horses suffer," said Tobias. "They'll fall over dead if ye don't let them get a night's rest."

As much as Lester didn't want to admit it, Tobias was right. The breathing of the horses began to sound labored. At a clearing, Lester ordered them to stop. After building a fire, the men spread out on the ground and fell fast asleep, save for Tobias and Lester.

"It just be the two of us," Tobias said, his smile glowing in the firelight. "A battle of wills, ye might say. Let's see who goes to sleep first. I tell ye, if I see ye sleepin' I'll take that gun and kill ye."

Hours passed, Tobias closed his eyes, but every so often he'd open them to see what Lester was doing. Even with his eyes open, there were moments when Lester wasn't sure if he'd dozed off or not. He felt as if floating in and out of consciousness. What seemed like a blink might have been hours. The next thing he knew, Tobias was standing over him. He was smiling, holding the rifle to Lester's head.

"All of ye, wake up!" Tobias shouted. "I want ye all to see me shoot this dog." The men woke and stood, watching. "Do ye know any one-minute prayers, boy? Because that's all ye have left."

"Don't anybody move!" a voice cried. They turned to see Caleb standing before the campfire, holding a rifle on them. It took Tobias off-guard; in that second, Lester grabbed his rifle and held it on Tobias.

"I suppose ye plan to kill us," Tobias said.

"We don't do things like that," Caleb replied.

"I wasn't talking to ye, boy," Tobias snapped. He looked directly into Lester's eyes. "I'd kill us, if I were ye."

"Shut up, Tobias," Judd growled. "Don't give 'em any ideas."

"Don't worry," Tobias laughed. "They don't have enough guts betwixt the two of them. I'll tell ye one thing; we'll hunt ye two down and shoot ye like the dogs ye are."

"Not without your horses," Caleb said. "Lester, get the horses."

"I can't believe my ears," Tobias said. "A darkie givin' a white man orders, what's this world comin' to?"

Both Caleb and Lester ignored him. They mounted their horses, took hold of the reins of the other horses, and rode off, kicking dust in the faces behind them.

Once they were out of sight, Tobias hauled off and punched Tom Garrett square on the chin. The man fell to the ground; he came up shaking his head and holding his chin.

"What you go do that for?" Garrett complained. "I didn't say anything."

"No, but ye were thinkin' it." He looked at the others. "Come on, we got lots of walkin' to do before the day is done."

********

Caleb and Lester rode hard and long. Every few miles they switched to a fresh horse so they could go nonstop. They camped that night without a fire or anything to eat. They got a few hours sleep and were on the road again. The next day, in the late afternoon, they caught up with the caravan.

"Look, it's Caleb and Lester," someone hollered. They all stopped and ran to greet them. Caleb and Lester dismounted. Folks were hugging and kissing them, and patting them on the back. Becky pushed her way forward and threw her arms around Lester.

"Oh, Lester, thank heavens you're back safe."

"Lester? Lester?" Caleb shouted. "What about me?"

"I'm not talkin' to you, runnin' off like that without even a word," she huffed at her husband.

"I don't get it," Caleb said. "You're glad Lester's safe; but if I didn't go after him, he wouldn't be safe!"

"I'm not talkin' to you," Becky announced as she walked away.

"I don't get it; I just don't get it!"

Pappy smiled into Caleb's face. "Ya don't get it, and ya never will. So just stop tryin' and go on." The crowd burst into laughter. "Come on, everybody," Pappy proclaimed, "let's camp here tonight and celebrate the return of our two prodigal sons!"

# Chapter Twenty-seven

# Barbwire, Beans, and Birds

Pappy declared a celebration for the return of Lester and Caleb, and celebrate they did. Everyone got a double portion of food. They built one large bonfire, and sang and danced around it into the night. Once the children were asleep, they sat around the fire singing softly together. As the flames began to wane so did their strength. Many fell asleep where they lay. Pappy sat surrounded by his immediate family. He was just about to call it a night when Cora and a few of her lackeys walked by.

"I jus' thought you'd like to know that the people are complaining about the food. Fried dough and corn is becoming monotonous. People need their meat; I just thought you'd like to know."

"Thank ya, Cora; I'll keep that in mind," Pappy said.

"I jus' thought you'd want to know," she repeated as she moved on followed by her group of complainers.

When she was out of earshot, Caleb whispered to Pappy.

"Tell me," Caleb asked. "What did her husband die of?"

"I think it was from relief?" Pappy answered. They all laughed, exchanged kisses, and settled down for a long night's sleep."

********

The morning was fresh and new. The sky was blue and cloudless with visibility to the horizons in all directions.

"We need ta press on harder and faster than ever," Pappy told Josh.

"Why? Caleb and Lester sent the Taylor boys running with their tails between their knees," Josh replied.

"That's just it," Pappy said. "They're probably madder than wet hens; they're sure to be more determined than ever; they'll find a way. I wouldn't count them out, jus' yet. We need ta push."

They reached flat ground, cattle grazing land, which made traveling easy. Up ahead, they saw a small group of men on horseback, standing and waiting.

"What do you think they want?" Josh asked Pappy.

"We could never outrun `em; so I guess we'll jus' has to find out."

As they got closer, they saw a barbwire fence in front of the group of men; it ran east to west as far as the eye could see. They stopped just short of the fence. One of the men rode up to the fence. "My name's Shannon Highborn, and this here's my spread." He pointed left and then right. "East to west, as far a one can see is mine. I don't want anyone crossing it, especially your kind. You'll just have to go around."

"What do you mean by *your kind*?" Josh asked.

"What I mean is that we're in the South but only by a few miles. The Mason Dixon line is north of here, Yankee territory. We live under the noses of the confederacy and the union; and don't think they don't take notice of what goes on here. What makes me suspicious of you is that we ain't never seen slave traders this here far north. Them there chains don't mean nothin' to me. I've got a good mind to believe you're really abolitionists trying to sneak north. Then again, you might really be slave traders. Either way, I don't need you crossin' my land. The war's gonna come to a head real soon. If the north wins, which I suspect, and they knew I was partial to slave traders, they'd come down on me hard. If the south wins, which I doubt, and they get wind I helped abolitionists, I'll lose my property for sure. So ya see, your only choice is to go the long way around, west or east, ain't none of my business. I'm gonna have my men follow ya with orders to shoot the first man who touches this fence. Have I made myself clear, sir?"

"Yes, sir, you have," Josh replied.

"Good, then there'll be no trouble. Ya have a good day, sir." With that, Shannon Highborn rode off, leaving his gun-toting men staring down the caravan.

"Well, that's that," Pappy said. "Which way should we go?"

"Your guess is as good as mine," Josh said.

One of Highborn's men rode up to the fence and shouted over. "If ya want to avoid Yankee territory, I'd go east. If you're looking to get to Yankee territory, west is the best route."

"Thank you, much obliged," Josh said. He turned to Pappy. "Talk about laying your cards on the table, I guess we're heading west." He rose in his saddle. "Everybody, we're taking a turn left; we're going west. I need everybody to stay close together and stay clear of the fence."

*******

Meanwhile, farther south, the Taylor brothers were rethinking their strategy. There was no alternative other than to walk back to the nearest town. By midday, their feet were swollen; they cursed the world with each step.

It was nearing sundown when they came to the small lazy town of Silver City. They felt tired, hungry, and were ragged-looking from a full day's hike. The town's folk stared and stepped aside as they walked through the center of town to the only hotel, The Mayfield.

Heads turned as the dusty band walked through the lobby to the front desk.

The clerk was a tall lanky young man of no more than twenty with a full head of red hair and a face full of matching red freckles.

Judd stepped to the front of everyone and made everything clear. "We'd like five rooms with double beds in each, hot baths for everyone, and something to eat."

"All too happy to oblige," the clerk smiled. "Now, let's see," he said, working the numbers with a pencil and paper. "That will be ten dollars for the rooms at two dollars a room, five dollars for the baths at fifty cents per bath; and I guess we can add the price of your meals, depending on what you order."

"Just bill us; we'll pay in the mornin'," Judd said.

"Sorry, sir, hotel policy is cash on the barrelhead."

Judd pointed to Tom Garrett. "Do ya know who this is? This here is Tom Garrett, owner of the Garrett Plantation, one of the riches men in three states. In the mornin' when the wire office opens, he'll wire for money, and we'll pay, then."

"I am sorry, sir; but like I said, hotel policy is cash up-front."

Tobias pushed his brother aside, reached over and grabbed the clerk by the shirt and pulled him halfway over the front desk. "Listen, ye carrot-top prairie chicken, jus' do what ye are told."

"Is there a problem here?" a soft voice spoke. They turned to see a tall, broad-shouldered, middle-aged, man dressed in western attire, from his boots up to his cowboy hat. He wore a six-gun holster; his right hand rested on the hilt of the gun.

"Ain't none of your business, mister," Tobias hissed.

"I'm afraid it is my business. My name is Victory Fuller. I'm the sheriff here in Silver City. My advice to you is to let go of the boy." Tobias let go of the clerk. "That's good; thank you. Are you all right, Billy?"

"Fine, Sheriff; there's no harm done."

"How's Sarah doin'?" Sheriff Fuller asked.

"She's fine, Sheriff. She's as big as a watermelon, only got two more weeks till the baby."

"Well, you give her my best."

"Do we have to listen to this drivel?" Tobias growled.

"Listen, mister," Sheriff Fuller said in a kind but firm manner. "You already started out on the wrong foot. If I were you, I'd try to get on my good side. Now, Billy, tell me what this is all about."

Tobias pointed at the clerk. "This here kid is tellin' us that we..."

"I'm talkin' to Billy; I didn't ask you anything. Your best bet right now is to just hush up. Go ahead, Billy."

"Well, Sheriff, these here men inquired about rooms, baths, and food. When I told them the prices, they said they wanted to pay in the morning. I told them hotel policy is cash on the barrelhead, no credit. I guess they got a little upset. No harm done, Sheriff."

"We'll be glad to pay the bill in the mornin'," Judd said. "We jus' need to have the money wired to us when the office opens tomorrow."

"I'm sure that's true," Sheriff Fuller said, "but this is an imperfect world, full of imperfect folk. Because of that, some folks have been known at times to not always tell the truth. For that reason, we have rules and laws, which even good folks like you must follow. So, if you don't have the money to pay, I'm afraid you're gonna have to leave."

"Sheriff, we've had a bad time of it," Judd pleaded. "We've had our guns and horses robbed from us; and we had to walk miles to get here. Can we jus'...?"

"I feel for you, son; I really do," Sheriff Fuller broke in. "I'll tell you what. It won't be the best but it'll better than sleepin' out in the wilderness. Since you men don't have any money, I can run you all in on a vagrancy charge. The jail ain't much; but at least you'll be covered; you'll each have a bunk and something to eat. What do you say?"

Judd looked to his brother for an answer. Tobias just rolled his eyes. "Very well, Sheriff; we plead vagrancy."

"That's a wise choice. Just follow me, gentlemen. You have a good night, Billy; and you say 'hello' to the misses for me."

"Thanks, Sheriff; I sure will."

The jail was directly across the street from the hotel. It was a dark, dank, dirty little room. At the far end were two large cells. A man seated in a chair slept with his feet up on the desk with his hands folded across his chest.

"Wake up, Tiny! We have guests," Sheriff Fuller announced. The man woke, his feet slamming down on the floor. He jumped from his chair, snapping to attention.

Tiny was not tiny. He was a mountain-sized man, six feet four and as wide as a church door. His hair and skin were dark; there was a touch of Spaniard to him. His eyes were close-set and his mouth cherub small. He moved slow, but was consistent and got the job done. Folks said his heart was as big as all outdoors.

"I've booked these men on vagrancy charges. I want to split them into two cells," Sheriff Fuller ordered. Tiny took a set of keys from the wall and marched the men into their cells, locking them in. "I promised these men something to eat. Why don't you rustle up something?"

Tiny's speech was a slow as his movements. "It's late; but I'm sure Dorothy has something on the stove. I'll go fetch some."

Sheriff Fuller addressed the men. "Gentlemen, I will be leaving town with the mornin' light. I have business in another county. Tiny, here, will take good care of you. Enjoy your stay." He gave some last minute instructions to Tiny and left.

"I'm gonna get ya some food, now," Tiny said. "I'll be right back. Don't go away, now, ya hear." He laughed to himself.

A half hour later, Tiny returned carrying a tray, which he placed on the desk. There was a coffeepot and cups, plates, a loaf of bread, and a large cooking pot with a ladle hanging from it.

"I hope coffee don't keep ya awake; it's all there was," Tiny said. He poured out the black coffee and handed it through the bars. He dished out a plate of beans for each of the men and placed a piece of bread on each. He passed the plates through a slit under the bars, and then handed out spoons.

"Beans, I hate beans!" Judd shouted.

"They ain't so bad," Tiny smiled. "Dorothy makes them with ham hocks. Ya get a piece of meat every once in a while, if you're lucky."

"Ya know what ya can do with your beans," Judd bellowed as he threw his plate at the bars.

Some of the beans splashed onto Tiny's shirt. He calmly wiped them off. "I'm sorry ya don't like beans, but that's all there was. I guess you're just gonna have to go hungry." He walked back to the desk. "By the way, you'll never guess what's for breakfast." He chuckled, sat down, put his feet up on the desk, and closed his eyes. "Well, goodnight, gents."

At first light, Tiny woke the men by running the ladle across the cell bars. "Good morning, gents. I got coffee, bread, and beans for all."

Judd jumped up and ran to the bars. "I told ya what ya can do with them beans."

Tobias threw in his two cents. "Listen, ye glandular freak, let us be on our way."

"Nothing would give me more pleasure," Tiny said, "but the penalty for vagrancy is three days in jail."

"Three days," Tobias echoed. "We've got to be here two more days?"

"There is one way," Tiny said.

"What's that?"

"Ya can pay the fine."

"Very well," Judd said. "Let Mr. Garrett out. He'll go down to the telegraph office, have the money wired in; and we'll pay the fine."

"Sorry," Tiny said. "He can't leave because he's serving a sentence for vagrancy and he doesn't have the money to pay the fine."

"What kind of business is that?" Tobias argued.

"It's not business," Tiny said. "It's rules and laws."

"If I ever get out of here," Judd growled.

"Oh, ya will; in two more days." Tiny smiled. "Beans, anyone?"

\*\*\*\*\*\*\*\*

The next two days dragged by slowly. The men paced their cells like wild animals confined in a zoo. They itched to get out. Tiny read away the hours, his nose buried in books and newspapers. He'd place a checkerboard on the desk; he'd sit in one chair and play the black pieces, and then switch to another chair and play the red. Desperately hungry, Judd ate his meals of beans without complaint. Tobias sat in his bunk, his back against the wall, biding his time.

On the third day, late-afternoon, Tiny opened the cells.

"I've a good mind to give ye what for," Tobias hissed.

Tiny smiled. "Officially, I should let ya out at sundown; but I'm givin' ya all time off for good behavior...bad attitudes, yes...but good behavior. Besides, this way ya have time to get to the telegraph office." Tiny looked at the clock on the wall. "It closes in five minutes. So ya see, ya don't have time to give me what for." Tiny laughed as the men ran out of the office and down the street.

They got to the telegraph office just as Old Man Tully was locking the door.

"What are ya doing?" Judd shouted, nearly out of breath.

"I'm going to get something to eat," Tully said. "I'll be back in an hour."

"We've got to get a wire out; it's an emergency," Tom Garrett said.

"My stomach growlin' is an emergency, too," Tully replied.

"I'll give you twenty dollars, if you get my wire out pronto," Garrett said.

Tully held out his hand waiting for payment.

"I don't have it, now," Garrett complained. "That's what the wire is for. You can deduct the twenty from the money my bank wires me.

Tully shrugged his shoulders, unimpressed and unconcerned. He continued to lock up.

Make it fifty," Garrett added.

Tully turned the key in the opposite direction and opened the door. They all flooded into the office.

Judd pointed to the safe in the corner of the room. "How much money ya got in that safe?"

"That's none of your business, young man," Tully replied. "If I don't have enough money to cover your wire, you're just out of luck, and you can have what there is."

Garrett filled out the form, and Tully wired it off.

"Well, that's gonna take a few hours," Tully said. "If you don't mind, I'm gonna get me something to eat. You fellers can stay here; just don't' burn the place down." He looked at Judd. "You, young man, keep your mitts off that safe."

"Jus' get back in time, ye old fool," Tobias said.

Tully returned two hours later, just in time to receive the response. He wrote it down and looked at Tom Garrett. "Your bank has approved your request for five thousand dollars. I only have thirty-six hundred in the safe."

"I'll take it," Garrett said.

"Minus my fifty, of course," Tully added as he spun the dial on the safe.

They immediately went to the Mayfair and registered for five rooms, cash on the barrelhead. They went to the Parker House (the only restaurant in town) and ordered everything on the menu except beans. That night, they slept on clean sheets, in beds without critters.

The next morning, after a large breakfast, they went to the livery stable and bought two horses for each man. Then to the dry goods store for supplies and lastly to the gun shop for all the firearms and ammo they could carry. The plan was to make up for lost time by riding the horses ragged. Then they'd switch to the spare horses and ride them till exhaustion, and then switch back.

"I'll kill the first man who stops for any reason!" Tobias announced as he dug his heels into his horse's side, galloping out of town, his brother at his side, the others following close behind with Tom Garrett taking up the rear.

********

After a long, hard day of heading west, the end to Shannon Highborn's property was nowhere in sight. The barbwire fence still stretched to the horizon. Josh ordered them to stop and make camp. Highborn's men dismounted and watched from the other side of the fence. After everyone finished eating, Pappy took a plate and walked over to the fence. The leader came walked over

"It ain't much," said Pappy. "Just fried dough, but you're welcome to some."

The man smiled. "No, that's all right. We're going to leave in a few minutes. You're at the point of no return. If you keep movin' west you'll be at the end of the property in no time. It would be a waste of time to go across Mr. Highborn's property, now." There was a moment of silence, and then the man spoke. "So, you're abolitionists?"

"I never thought of it that way," Pappy said. "I guess in a way we are; but actually, we're just a family tryin' to get north to freedom."

"A family?" the man said. "Ya mean, black folk and white folk in the same family?"

"Why not?" Pappy replied.

"I don't know; it just sounds strange," the man said. "I really couldn't say. I ain't ever known any black folks, really."

"We ain't no different than anybody else."

"Really?"

"If ya prick us, do we not bleed? If ya tickle us, do we not laugh? If ya poison us, do we not die? If ya wrong us, shall we not revenge?"

"How's that?" the man asked.

"It's just something some Englishman said a long time ago. I guess the easiest way is to show ya."

Pappy took a strip of barbwire and pressed his thumb against a barb. He held his thumb out to the man.

"What do you see," Pappy asked.

"Blood," the man said.

"What color is it?"

"It's red."

"Right, it's red, no redder than yours. It's all the same, flowing from the same fountain."

"I never thought of it that way," the man said. "I guess we all want to be happy."

"Now, you've got it," Pappy said. "I wish ya happiness."

"May it find ya, too," the man said. He returned to his horse and mounted it. The others did the same, and they rode off.

********

Later, Pappy lay on his blanket, looking up at the stars through half-closed eyes.

"Moses, Moses Brown, is you awake?"

Pappy didn't have to look to see who it was; he knew that voice.

"What is it, Cora?"

"If I told ya once, I told ya a thousand times. Folks is talking. They're getting tired of eatin' nothin' but fried dough. A body's got to have meat. What ya gonna do about it?"

"I'm gonna say a prayer and roll over and go to sleep, and that's what ya need to do."

"Ya gotta do something about it."

"I did; I just said a prayer. It's in bigger hands than mine, now. Goodnight, Cora."

"Yeah, but…"

"I said, 'Goodnight Cora'."

********

In the morning, everyone woke at the same time for the same reasons. The wind began blowing hard from all directions at once, filling the air with blinding dust. A rumbling sound came down from the sky, like the sound of rolling thunder. Above them was a large, black cloud that moved like a waving flag.

"What is that?" Lester shouted.

"It's the shadow of death!" someone screamed.

"No, look, it's a flock of birds, thousands of them," Benjamin said.

"They look like quail," Josh hollered.

"That can't be; quail can't fly," Benjamin replied.

"They don't like to, but they will when they have to," Caleb said. "They're flying for some reason."

"Who cares what the reason is," Pappy shouted, pointing to the sky. "Get your guns and let's get us some!"

Every gun, even the ones hidden under the wagons, they handed out. They shoot at the cloud. There was no need to aim. The flock was so thick that each bullet brought down two to three birds.

As suddenly as it all started, it finished. The black cloud moved across the sky and out of sight. Hundred of birds lay at their feet.

"Everybody start pickin' and pluckin'," Pappy ordered. "What we don't cook now, we can smoke and dry out and salt down." He turned to Cora. "Well, Cora, what do ya think?"

"Them be nasty birds," Cora said.

"Maybe, but they're meat. Ya asked for meat and ya got it," Pappy laughed.

# Chapter Twenty-eight

# Facing North

It took nearly a full day's travel to reach the edge of Highborn's property. They turned right, still with the barbwire fence alongside; only now they traveled north. The women made meat pies with flour and shortening for crust and quail meat combined with roots and herbs they found along the way for filling. The people seemed content; and thankfully the change of diet quieted Cora and her band. With full bellies, they traveled well and fast. Still, it took another full day to come to the most northern edge of Highborn's land.

As they left the barbwire fence behind, the land began to change. The flat lands gave way to rolling hills, which grew larger with every mile. Every so often, they nervously looked over their shoulders from where they just came, expecting to see red dust kicked up by the horses of the Taylor brothers and their men, always at their heels. They felt relieved to see no sign of them. They knew it would only be a matter of time before their pursuers caught up with them. What they would do then was a question that haunted them. Their only hope was to cross the Mason Dixon Line into the north before that day came. Yet even then, there was no guarantee the Taylor brothers would ignore that boundary and continue to hunt them down.

********

Meanwhile, farther south, the Taylor gang was running their horses ragged. They did whatever they could to make up for lost time. With each man having two horses, they galloped north, switching horses every few hours. As they rode, they ate beef jerky and biscuits.

They came face-to-face with a band of five armed horsemen behind a long barbed wire fence.

"Let me do the talkin'," Judd told his brother. "I'm better with folks than ya."

Tobias looked at Judd with a side-glance that was half-smile and half-smirk of contempt.

"Ya can stop right there," the older rider and obvious leader of the band said. "My name's Shannon Highborn and this here's my land as far as ya can see. Ya can go right, ya can go left, and ya can turn back, but ya ain't goin' ahead."

"Mr. Highborn," Judd said, sitting up on his mount. "We're looking for a group of blacks led by a handful of whites. They're abolitionist posing as slave traders. Have ya seen them?"

"Now I might like abolitionist and hate slave traders, but then again, I might like slave traders and hate abolitionist. Either way, it ain't none of your business. So ya can jus' get along."

"We'd be willin' to pay for any information about them," Judd said. Tobias shot his brother a look of disapproval.

"I don't need your money," Highborn said.

'I'll give ya one hundred dollars," Judd replied.

"Confederate or Yankee money?" Highborn asked.

"Neither," Judd said. "I got silver pieces."

"Toss 'em over," Highborn said.

Judd reached into his vest-pocket and tossed a handful of silver pieces over the fence. Highborn motioned for one of his men to dismount and pick them up. The man handed up the coins to Highborn who put them in his top pocket.

"There was a group just like ya described here two days ago. Bunch of blacks in wagons, some of 'em chained behind the wagons, a few whites on horseback with rifles. They didn't fool me. We don't see slave traders this far north. There ain't no place to sell 'em. They wanted to cross my land as a shortcut north; but I told 'em no way, they had to go around my property."

"Which way did they go?" Judd asked.

"They took the west route," one of the men said.

"We've been ridin' hard to catch 'em. I'd pay ya another hundred if ya let us cut through your land," Judd said.

"These must be important folks," Highborn said. "What do ya want them so bad for?"

"We have our reasons," Judd said.

"Well, ya can cross my property," Highborn said, "but it's gonna cost ya one thousand dollars."

"That be a might steep," Tobias said.

Highborn laughed. "It'd be worth it. You'll make a hundred times that with sales of them slaves."

"We ain't got anymore silver," Tobias said. There were two bags dangling from Tobias' saddle. He patted one and then the other. "I got both kinds of money, Confederate and Yankee. Which kind would ye prefer?"

"I'll take it in Yankee bills. Everyone knows the rebels won't hold another year."

Tobias reached into one of the saddlebags; he came out with a six-gun and began firing. The first shot hit Highborn in the chest; the next shot winged one of the men in his right arm, making him useless. He caught another man in the neck with a fatal blow. Judd responded by drawing his six-shooter; he plugged two men in the head. The others were riddled with bullets from the men of the Taylor brother's gang. Each fell from their horse.

Tobias dismounted and walked to the barbwire fence. He shook one of the fencepost till it came loose and fell to the ground. He walked onto Highborn's property. He stood over the bodies like a general surveying dead enemies. The others slowly rode over onto the property. Tobias reached down and retrieved the silver coins from Highborn's top pocket; he put it in his own pocket. He turned to his brother, Judd, "Don't ye ever be so free with money, again. Remember, bullets are cheaper."

They rode at breakneck speed. Using the Highborn property as a shortcut, they could make up for lost time, and within twenty-four hours close-in on their prey. They passed acres of grazing cattle. They thought of shooting one of the steers and butchering it. They could have used the meat, but that would take too long and sway them from their mission.

After twenty minutes of hard riding, they came on some open property, with a barn and an adjoining corral. Across from that was a large, two-story log cabin style home. A beautiful young woman in her late teens stepped out onto the porch. Her long chestnut hair covered her shoulders; her eyes were the same reddish-brown hue. She held a shotgun in her arms, pointed to the ground.

"Stay on your horses and don't come any closer." Her voice was sweet but firm.

"Excuse us, Ma'am," Judd said. "We got permission from your father; we're just passing through."

"My father!" she laughed. "If you mean Shannon, if that old buzzard was my father I would have ran away from home a long time ago. No, that cantankerous old coot is my husband. Don't judge me harshly for it, though. We all have to do what we have to do to get by." She lifted the shotgun and pointed it at them. "Now, ya can just keep riding. I want ya off this property."

"We have your husband's permission," Judd said. "We even paid him to let us ride through."

"I find that hard to believe," the young woman said. "I know my husband. Even if ya paid him, once your back was turned he'd have his men kill ya. He'd keep your money and horses and leave your hides for the buzzards. Since you are here, though, I can only believe that you've somehow outwitted him and that he and his men are dead. For that, I thank ya; but that still don't make us friends; and I certainly don't trust ya. Now, just move on; and I'll let ya keep your heads."

"You have a good day, Ma'am," Judd said, tipping the brim of his hat.

As they rode off, Tobias turned to his brother. "If I ever settle down, it would be with a woman just like that. Only I'm sure it would take a whole lot of beatings to knock the sassiness out of her."

Never slowing to less than a gallop, it took the rest of the day for them to approach the end of the Highborn property. They tore down the fence and rode off into the hill country.

********

Josh thought it best to camp on high ground, to keep an eye out for their pursuers. After everyone ate their fill and the sun set, they sat around campfires. Only now the atmosphere was different. They no longer sang or told jokes. Hardly anyone spoke. They silently stared into the flames and every so often looked to the south for signs of the Taylor brothers. Everyone was on edge, finding it hard to sleep. Josh looked to the edge of the hill. Pappy stood alone, staring out into the south from where they had come. He walked over and stood with him.

"What do ya think that there is?" Pappy asked, pointing south.

"I'm not sure I know what you're looking at," Josh said.

"There, on the horizon, that tiny speck of flickering light."

"It's a star or maybe a planet?"

"Or a campfire," Pappy said remorsefully. "If that's the Taylor brothers, they'll catch up with us sometime tomorrow."

"We don't know that for sure," Josh said.

"No, we don't; but then what does it matter; tomorrow or the next day? We move too slowly. They're on horseback; eventfully they'll catch up. Then what will we do?"

"There is a way to beat them," a voice said. They turned to see it was Jericho, Caleb and Lester stood with him.

"What do ya mean?" Pappy asked.

"Jericho has an idea," Caleb said. "Listen to him, Pappy."

"Go ahead, I'm listenin'."

"I know this part of the country like the back of my hand. I was raised in these parts," said Jericho. "We're not too far from the Mason Dixon Line; we can be in Yankee territory in less than twenty-four hours."

"How's that?" Pappy asked.

Jericho pointed out into the darkness. "Just east of here is a pass. It's called Whisper Canyon. It's a long canyon that cuts right through the mountain range, a shortcut into the next county. If we get through her, we can be in Yankee territory in less than an hour."

"What's the catch?" Josh asked. "There sounds like there's a catch."

"There is," Jericho said. "The walls of the pass are high with loose, red rock that the slightest noise will cause an avalanche; a person could get buried alive."

"Can it be done?" Lester asked.

"Sure it can," Jericho said, "but for everyone who's made it through, there are two who didn't."

Pappy scratched his head and then rubbed the whiskers on his chin. "I've got an idea," he said, smiling. "We carefully work our way through the pass. When we get to the other side, we cause an avalanche, blocking the Taylor brothers' way." Pappy looked at Lester. "Lester, you're the best shot we have with a rifle. Do ya think ya can shoot enough rocks down to block the pass?"

"I ain't ever tried to shoot rock; but I guess I can do it," Lester replied.

"Of course ya can, my boy," Pappy said.

"I don't know about this," Josh said. "It sounds...dangerous."

"What ya need is a little faith," Pappy said. "Now, all of ya turn in. You'll need your sleep. It's going to be a rough day, tomorrow."

"Little faith, or lots of faith, it's all the same," Josh said. "It sounds dangerous."

********

Tobias pointed into the darkness. "Ye see that?"

Judd strained his eyes. "See what?"

"On top of that hill at the farthest point of the horizon, what do ye see?"

"Stars, twinkling stars."

"They not be stars. Them be campfires. We be close, real close."

"We could sneak up on them in the dark," Judd said.

"Nay, they be farther than ye think. It be morning by the time we reach them. Best to get a night's sleep and go after them in the mornin'. Maybe tomorrow, we get 'em."

"I just want to get my hands on those white folks helping 'em," Judd said. "Nothing would give me more pleasure than to cut their throats."

"Ye will have ye chance, my brother, and soon."

********

Mornings come and mornings go, but this morning was different. Everyone felt it, they smelled it. A scent like it was the first day or the last day. Only Pappy understood that it was both.

They cooked biscuits over the still hot coals of last night's fires. They stirred the ashes and wet them down good. This day, they turned to face the sunrise and headed east. The only sounds were the clip-clop of horse hooves, the squeal of wagon wheels, and the rattle of chains. A cloud of gloom and foreboding hung low over them. The moment they had worked for and dreamed of for so long was approaching. It didn't seem real.

********

Tobias dismounted and knelt on the ground; he ran his hand through the ashes. "Warm," he announced. "They were here this mornin'. We be gainin' on 'em." He stood up and looked on the ground, reading the markings like some folks read a book. "That be strange," he said.

"What is?" Judd asked.

"They turned right," Tobias said. "They be headin' east. Why would they do that, if they want to go north into Yankee territory?"

"Maybe they're tryin' to loose us?" Judd said.

Tobias shook his head. "No way, they didn't even try to cover their tracks. It's as if they wants us to follow them."

"Maybe they're gonna lay in wait and try to ambush us?"

"Maybe, but that still don't explain why they be headin' east."

"If you girls are finished," Tom Garrett said. "The only way we're gonna find out is to follow them."

Tobias pointed at Garrett. "Ye be hangin' by a thin tread, ye know that mister?"

"The one they call Pappy, he's mine," Garrett said.

"The spoils is ours," Tobias said. "That were the agreement."

"Then I'm buying him in advance. I'll give you one thousand dollars for him," Garrett said.

"Sold to the man for one thousand dollars," Tobias declared.

********

"How ya feelin', pumpkin?" Pappy smiled up at Becky seated in one of the wagons.

"Pappy, what are you doin' walkin'?"

"Oh, I just had to stretch my legs. If I sits too long, I gotta walk; and if I walks too long, I gotta sits. This gettin' old ain't for the weak of heart, I tell ya. Promise me one thing, pumpkin: you'll never grow old."

Becky laughed. "I don't know, Pappy. I'll try. I'm gonna have me a child; folks say children give you gray hair and age you before your time."

"Hogwash!" Pappy said. "Why, it's the exact opposite. Chilin keeps ya young. Why, I didn't have a gray hair on my head till your mamma grew up and got married."

"Honest, Pappy?"

"Well, maybe one or two gray hairs, but it weren't your mamma that gave `em to me. It was your grandma that gave `em to me."

"Really?" Becky asked. "What did she do to give you gray hairs?"

"She died, child; she up and died. After that, everything started to go gray."

"You miss her, Pappy?"

"What do ya think would happen to ya if Caleb up and died on ya?"

Becky thought long and hard on the prospect. "I guess I'd turn gray."

Pappy started hobbling. "Well, I've reached the point of walkin' too much, now I gotta sits." He flagged down the next wagon. "Love ya, pumpkin."

"Love you too, Pappy."

*********

Judd allowed the band of men to slow down from a gallop so they could eat their lunch and still move forward. Tobias eased back and rode alongside Tom Garrett.

"A thousand dollars is a lot to pay for a run-down old black house-slave. What be between ye and this Pappy?"

Garrett's gaze remained forward as he spoke. "From what I've learned, he's the brains behind this whole business; he put this all together. If it weren't for him, my son would still be alive."

"What will ye do with him?"

"If I can keep my anger down, and not kill him the moment I see him, I'll take him back home with me. I'm going to put a leather collar around his neck and keep him chained up in my kennel with the rest of my dogs. I'll beat him every day till he begs for mercy and for me to kill him; but I won't. I'll keep him alive as long as I can; and I'll make him suffer."

Tobias laughed so hard, he nearly fell off his horse. "Ye certainly are a sentimental ole fool. I'd jus' shoot him on sight. Then again, it's your money; ye must do what makes ye happy."

*********

Pappy sat on the buckboard of the front wagon, Jericho sat next to him holding the reins. "Is that it?" asked Pappy, pointing to a mountain range with a v-shaped crack running down the center. "It don't look like much."

"That's because we're still a half day's ride from it," Jericho remarked. "It's wide enough to drive two wagons side by side through it."

"Have ya ever gone through it?" Pappy asked.

"No, but I've heard of folks who have. It's dangerous, but it can be done."

Pappy thought it best to change the mood by changing the subject. "So, tell me how ya got to be called Jericho?"

Jericho laughed under his breath. "It's not as romantic as you might think. Actually, it was more of a joke than a name. My father was a minister, a fine man. He was a Bible scholar and an expert in old Hebrew. Well, besides being a city in the Old Testament, the word Jericho means 'place of fragrance'. My father got the idea while changing my nappy, if you get my drift."

The two men laughed till they were leaning helplessly against each other.

"So your daddy was a preacher; that why ya in the seminary?"

"I guess so," Jericho said. "The apple didn't fall far from that tree."

Pappy's face went solemn. "I'm glad you're here, son; and we're thankful for your help; but tell me...why are ya here?"

Jericho's eyes watered up slightly as he looked to the sky. "Because my daddy taught me; he'd say, 'Jericho, if you're gonna be a man of the cloth, you gotta give your life to the church; and remember the church ain't just a building. It's everywhere you go and in everyone you meet'."

********

"For cryin' out loud, Tobias, we ain't gonna catch up with 'em on dead horses," Judd shouted to his brother. "We gotta stop for a spell."

Tobias raised his hand to halt the others. He pointed down at the ground.

"There, look there," he said.

He dismounted and fell to his knees. There was an indent of a wagon wheel in the dirt. Tobias placed his hand down on it.

"They were here only a few hours ago. We're only a few hours behind them."

One of the men turned to another and chuckled. "How could he know that? What is he, some kind of bloodhound?"

Tobias rushed over, pulled the man off his horse and dragged him across the dirt. He took the man's arms and placed his hand on the indent the wagon wheel had left.

"So, what do ye feel?" Tobias hollered.

"I don't know what to say," the man cried.

"I said 'what do ye feel?'" Tobias repeated.

"I don't know. What am I suppose to feel? I feel dirt, that's all."

"Do ye feel how tightly packed it be?" Tobias said. "Soon the soil will loosen up and then eventually blow away; but for now, it be tightly packed. Which means it be new, only a few hours old." Tobias pushed the man's face into the dirt. "If I didn't need every hand on deck, I'd kill ye, here and now; and I might do it after all is said and done. Now get on your horse and give thanks that I'm feelin' benevolent."

********

They stood silently staring into the gapping mouth of Whispering Canyon. It looked harmless enough, but then, so does a sleeping lion. The high walls were smooth and red, the color of berries. It was wide at the bottom and ever increasing toward the top, maybe two-hundred feet up. Josh rode to the front of the line, sat high in his saddle, and spoke.

"I'm sure by now you know what we're up against. The Taylor brothers and their men can't be far behind. On the other end of this canyon is Nebo county and a stream, which is the Mason Dixon Line. Once we cross that stream, we're in Yankee territory. The obstacle we face is that this canyon is prone to avalanches. Our plan is to make it through safely, and on the other side cause an avalanche that will block the Taylor brothers. What we need to do..."

"What we need to do is count ourselves lucky and head back home," a voice behind him said. Josh turned in his saddle to see who it was. All eyes focused on the small group standing behind Josh.

It was Cora and five of the men standing at the mouth of the canyon. They all held rifles.

Pappy got down off the wagon and stood next to Josh's horse. "Cora, what in tarnation do ya think you're doin'?"

"Savin' ya from yourself is what I is doin'."

"Listen, Cora..."

"Don't go preachin' to me, Moses Brown. Ya may have these other folk bamboozled, but not me. We is suffered, starved, and thirsted for so long just to get between a rock and a hard place. If the Taylor bothers don't get us, this here canyon will. Now, I say we cut our losses, head west and then back south. The Taylor brothers would never suspect it. We'd be home before they ever figure what happened."

"Yeah, but back there we was slaves, not even considered human beings!" Pappy pleaded. "I may die today; but by gum, I'm goin' to die a man."

Cora didn't answer. She just stared through him and pulled back on the hammer of her rifle till it clicked into the far back position.

"Listen to me, Cora," Pappy demanded. "We're goin' through with or without ya. We can go 'round ya or we can go over ya. It be your call."

Cora placed her rifle on her shoulder like a marching soldier, her thumb on the trigger. "Not if I close the gate," she said as she shot a round into the canyon.

At first, there was the sound of the ricocheting bullet. The echoes repeated for a long time and finally faded. There were a few seconds of silence, and then a rumble like storm clouds rolling in; the ground moved under their feet like an earthquake. A large slab of red rock tore away from the side of the canyon, hit the opposite wall, knocking smaller pieces off from that wall. It all came crashing down on Cora and her small band. It happened so fast they didn't have time to scream, let alone run out of the way. Only their arms and legs showed from under the pile of rocks.

Everyone stood dumfounded, watching the red dust cloud slowly settle. Close relatives of those just killed ran crying to the mound and began tossing the rocks from off the bodies, but it was a case of too-little too-late.

Pappy looked to his side to see Caleb standing next to him. "Caleb," said Pappy. "Round up all the able bodied folk and move them rocks off to the side."

"Yes sir, Pappy."

An hour later, Caleb reported to Pappy. "We've cleared the way. What should we do with the bodies?"

Pappy looked left and then right. He pointed to a not so far-off grassy area with a few trees. "We'll bury 'em there."

"Bury them?" Caleb questioned. "We've wasted so much time clearing the way. The Taylor brothers must be close by. We can't afford to waste any more time."

Pappy shook his head and placed his hand on Caleb's shoulder. "Respecting family members is never a waste of time." He pointed to the grassy area, again. "We'll bury 'em over there."

********

Judd pulled back on the reins to halt his horse. He raised his hand; the others stopped behind him.

"Did ya hear that? Sounds like a flurry of gun shoots," Judd said.

"That weren't any flurry," Tobias said. "It be a single gunshot echoin'. Can't ye tell? They all sounded the same and faded till they were no more."

Then they heard a rumble like far off thunder.

"I say the sound came from that there canyon in them mountains out yonder," Tobias

*185*

said. "Sounded like an avalanche, probably caused by that gunshot."

"What do ya think happened?" Judd asked.

"I don't know," Tobias replied. "I guess we'll find out. Still, it worries me. If they went through the canyon and caused an avalanche to block the way, we'll never catch 'em."

"What if the shot was an accident?" Judd said.

Tobias smiled. "If the shot were an accident, they got nowhere to go. They be sittin' ducks. Come on, let's ride."

********

Pappy stood before the graves, he eyed them slowly and looked at all gathered. "If two or more disagree, that be all it is, a disagreement; and that be all right. Loved ones can disagree, and it do not affect the love between 'em. These be family, they are loved, and they will be missed." Pappy bend down, grabbed some dirt, and sprinkled it over the graves. "Ashes to ashes, dust to dust…" He looked intently at the assembly. "These buried folk deserve more, but time is runnin' out. Take the chains and the ropes and place them in the wagons. We can sell 'em for food when we reach up north. We need to be as quiet as mice when we walks through this valley. Take whatever spare clothing we have and wrap 'em 'round the wagon wheels and 'round the horse's hooves. What cooking grease we have, splatter that over the axles of the wagon wheels. We don't want any loud squeals. Mothers…I can't tell ya how important it is to keep your chilin quiet. Our lives depend on us getting' to the other side. We can do this, we have to. Now quick, go about your business."

Everyone scattered like ants. Pappy stood alone at the graves. He looked down.

"Rest in peace, Cora, I'll miss ya. Ya and I, Miriam and Aaron, were the last of our generation in this family. Now we down to three, and it be feelin' so lonesome. By the way, when ya see Zipporah, give her all my love. I'll be seein' ya all soon."

In no time, what Pappy ordered they made true. They stood before the mouth of the canyon, the wagons filled with mothers and children and the old folk. The white boys were on their horses. Those that could walk got behind the wagons; only now, they were no longer shackled and chained or tethered with rope, and it felt good.

Josh sat on his horse in the front of the caravan. Instead of his usual loud command to go forward, he raised his arm, brought it down, pointing into the canyon. The march began. They moved quietly and slowly, keeping away from the canyon walls. It was an uncomfortable feeling, like being swallowed by some great monster, especially further in when they could no longer see the entrance behind them or the exit before them. The sky was no more than a snaky blue line above their heads. Mothers held their babies close, to soothe them and keep them quiet. The older children seemingly sensed the need to be silent. Even the horses gave the impression that they too were aware and willing to be part of this silent march. For as quiet as they were, there were still some noises. They would echo off the sides of the canyon. They held their breath and listened with caution till the echoes faded into silence. Jericho calculated it would take at least an hour to make it through the canyon. Ten minutes in, it felt like an eternity.

********

The horses halted in front of the mouth of Whisper Canyon. Tobias dismounted in a flash and began to survey the area.

"Tobias…" Judd said.

Tobias held up his hand to silence his brother. He looked to the left and right of the entrance. "Stay here," he ordered the others. He walked to the graves, knelt down to examine them. He grabbed a handful of dirt in his fist and slowly let the grains drizzle out to the ground. He stood up and walked back to the others.

"Ye see these rocks?" He pointed to both sides of the canyon's entrance. Then he pointed to the graves. "Ye see those graves. Well, they be fresh-dug. I think I got this all figured out. By accident or on purpose, the gunshot we heard caused the rocks to fall, killing some of their people. They buried 'em and then moved these rocks out of the way. Don't ye see? They plan to get to the other side of this here canyon and block our way with another avalanche. They must still be inside the canyon."

"What makes ya say that?" Judd asked.

"We haven't heard another gunshot. They won't cause an avalanche till they reach the other side. We got to move fast."

"It ain't worth it," Judd said. "If we go through the canyon, we may get buried alive. If they get to the other end before we get to them, they'll block the way out. If we catch up in the heart of the canyon, what can we do? We can't shoot 'em; we'll bury 'em and ourselves, as well."

"I ain't come this far to turn around and go back home empty-handed. We just keep our distance, and then rush them at the other side before they can do anything." Tobias smiled up at Tom Garrett. "What do ye say, ole man?"

"I say we go for it. I got nothing left to lose and everything to get."

"Ah, revenge," Tobias laughed. "It be more precious than gold."

********

With no wind, it became harder to breath, as they rode the canyon. The stifling air was heavy. Sweat poured from their bodies, dripping down their foreheads and burned their eyes. The walls began to close in till the wagons had to form a single line, with only a few feet on each side. Those on horseback rode two by two; every one of those walking huddled close together. With each few yards it was like a vise tightening around them. One accidental loud sound and the canyon would be their coffin.

Pappy and Jericho sat on the buckboard of the front wagon. Before them, all they saw was wall after wall of red rock, weaving like a snake (right and left, right and left). Jericho leaned over and whispered into Pappy's ear.

"Pappy, did you see it?"

Pappy looked up. "See what? I just see more of the same red rock."

"No, look, there it is again."

They were following the maze of the canyon. Pappy looked and waited. He saw it, but only for a split second, a fine blue line from the floor of the canyon to the top. It disappeared when they made another turn.

"We must be coming to the end," Jericho said.

"It would seem so," Pappy said. "Jus' don't get too excited. We've done good so far. Jus' keep doin' what your doin'."

With each turn, they saw it again. As they moved forward, it no longer was a fine blue line, but clearly the gapping end of the canyon opening to a clear blue sky. Like waking from a bad dream, the caravan was through the canyon. No one spoke till they were far from the mouth of the canyon. Then there was much sighing and nervous laughter. Josh galloped to the front of the line, stopping next to Pappy.

"Well, Pappy, what do we do, now?" Josh asked.

Before the mouth of the canyon was a large, high rocky hill; Pappy pointed to it.

"Before we seal off the canyon with an avalanche, I want our people some place safe. Jericho, I want ya to lead our folks 'round this hill and wait for us at its base. Josh, go get Lester and tell him to bring his rifle. Oh, and bring Caleb, too. We're gonna climb to the top of that there hill."

Once Jericho and the caravan were marching around the corner of the hill, Pappy and the others began to climb up the side of the hill. It was a hard, steep climb; Caleb and Josh had to help Pappy, his arms around them.

At the top, they turned and looked down. They were higher than the walls of the canyon and had a clear view of its mouth.

"Well, Lester," Pappy said. "Ya think ya could pull a rifle shot from here?"

"I can't see why not," Lester said, getting down on one knee and taking aim.

Lester squinted, taking careful aim, his finger on the trigger; he took in a deep breath and held it when...

"Hold it, don't shoot!" Pappy shouted.

Down below appeared the Taylor brothers and their men, still maybe thirty feet into the canyon.

"We've got them!" Caleb cried. "Shoot, Lester, shoot, now!"

Pappy grabbed the end of Lester's rifle and pulled it out of his hands. "No, don't. I was all for causing an avalanche to block their way; but I ain't for murderin' 'em. It ain't our way."

"If we don't get them now, we'll have to fight them!" Caleb said.

"Then we'll fight 'em," Pappy replied. "A fair fight is one thing; this would be murder."

"A fair fight!" Caleb argued. "It won't be a fair fight; they're professional killers. We won't stand a chance. I say get them, now. It's only self-defense."

Just then, Tobias looked up and saw the men on the top of the hill. He raised his hand to halt the group. They were still well into the mouth of the canyon. It was Tobias in front with his brother at his side; the other men followed with Tom Garrett taking up the rear. Tobias pointed; the others looked up.

Suddenly, Tom Garrett lifted in his saddle and brought his rifle up into position.

"This is for my son!" His voice echoed through the canyon.

"No!" Tobias shouted.

It was too late. Garrett got off three shots before anyone could move or say another word. The red rock broke away from the walls in large boulders. In the blink of an eye, all of them were buried alive, a red cloud of dust rose to the sky.

"Did you see that? Did you see that?" Lester said, nervously.

"Look!" Caleb cried, pointing to the ground behind them. The others turned to see Pappy lying there.

They fell to their knees. Josh lifted Pappy. He'd been shot in the stomach.

"Pappy, can you hear me?" Josh asked.

"Get me to my feet."

"Pappy..."

"Please, get me to my feet."

All three of them slowly and gently raised the old man up. Pappy buttoned the front of his jacket, covering the bloodstains.

"Help me over the ridge, boys."

When they got to the top of the hill, they looked down the other side. The caravan was waiting at the bottom. Ellie and Becky pointed up. They started running up the hill, smiling.

"Come now, Pappy; we'll carry you down," Josh said.

Pappy sat down on a large rock. "It ain't no use. I ain't got much more road ahead of me." Ellie and Becky were close, almost in hearing distance. "I don't want to die with a bunch of folks cryin' and moanin' 'round me. Let me handle this."

"We heard the avalanche!" Becky said. "Is it blocked?"

"We got it blocked up real good," Pappy said. "They ain't gonna catch us, now."

"You can see the stream Jericho said was the border," Ellie said, pointing north. "You men coming?"

"In a little while," Pappy said. "I'm a bit tired. I think I'll rest awhile. Josh and Caleb will stay with me. We can talk over our next move. Lester, why don't ya go back down with these ladies; and ya and Jericho can start movin' everyone to the stream?"

Lester looked into the eyes of the old man. "Pappy, I . . ."

"It's all right, Lester. Now be a good boy, and do as I says."

Ellie walked over and placed her hand on Pappy's forehead. "Are you all right, Daddy?"

He looked up into her worried face. "Ya know, ya be as pretty as your momma. Now go. I'll be fine."

"You sure?" Becky asked.

He smiled at her. "How's my grandbaby doin'?"

"Just fine, Pappy. I've been feeling the quickening lately real strong, makes me think it's a boy."

"I don't know," Pappy said. "The women in this family are might strong." He reached out and put his hand on her belly. "Thank ya, pumpkin for givin' me such a wonderful gift and for bein' who ya is." He turned to Lester. "We be wastin' too much time on sentimentalities. Lester, get these two down below and get everyone movin' north."

The three started down the hill. When they were out of ear shout, Pappy slumped forward. Josh reached out to hold him up. The old man looked up into the eyes of Josh and Caleb and placed his hand on each of their arms

"Josh, Caleb, ya is as much my sons as if ya come from my own flesh and blood. I want ya both to get this family up north and see that they get settled. Josh, ya be the oldest, so ya will be head of the family. Caleb, help your brother, Josh; and both ya take care of my girls, Ellie and Becky. Promise me that."

Both Josh and Caleb nodded. "We will, Pappy," Josh said.

"I want ya both to bury me here, facin' north so I can watch over ya all."

Pappy looked to the sky. His eyes went wide like he was seeing something not of this world (something wonderful). He let out his last breath, his eyes closed, and his body went limp.

They stood in silence; the only sound, a gentle breeze rustling the tall grass at there feet. Together they lifted him gently. They did as he'd asked (his last command as patriarch of the family and true owner of the Bush Plantation) and...buried him at the highest point, facing north.

# Chapter Twenty-nine

# A Long Way to Go

Josh and Caleb found the two horses the others left for them tied to a bush at the northern base of the hill. They rode full gallop to catch up; both men secretly dreading the moment they would face the others and tell them that Pappy was gone.

They found the others waiting for them along the edge of the stream. Josh dismounted and walked to Ellie. She saw there were only two of them, and was just about to ask where her father was, when the look in her husband's eyes stopped her.

If two people who are very much in love spend years together, they reach a plateau of understanding, often without words. Ellie and Josh had reached that point. She read the sadness in Josh's eyes and knew they contained only the worst of news. She had no idea how, but she knew something had happened to Pappy and that she'd never see him again. Ellie collapsed in Josh's arms.

"Where's Pappy?" Becky asked Caleb.

He didn't answer; the words caught like sand in the back of his throat.

"Caleb, where's Pappy?" Becky insisted.

"He's gone, Becky. The bullet that caused the avalanche was from the Taylor brothers. It got Pappy. He's dead. Josh and I buried him atop of the hill."

"That's not true; we just saw him," Becky moaned.

"He didn't want you to go through watching him die."

"No…!" Becky shouted, pushing him away when he tried to hold her. Once the feelings of anger and betrayal left her, a wave of sadness like she'd never known washed over her and she rushed ahead, sobbing heavily into her husband's arms.

Word spread through the camp. Some fell to their knees; others stared blankly, but most cried.

Josh stood up in one of the wagons. "Everyone, listen. I know how heartbroken you are; but now's not the time to give up. If Pappy were here, he'd tell us to go on; and go on we must. Get ready to forge this stream!"

Josh walked to edge of the stream, followed by Lester, Jericho, and Caleb.

"It ain't wide, but that water's movin' mighty fast. It must have rained recently,"

Lester said. "We'll never get the wagons across."

They stared at the rushing waters, their minds racing for a solution.

Finally, Jericho spoke up. "I'm a strong swimmer; I can swim across."

"What good would that do?" Caleb asked.

"We've still got all that rope," Jericho continued. "Tie a long piece of rope around my waist. If I can't make it, you can pull me in. but if I can make it, I'll pull the chains across with the rope and we can attach folks to the chain and they can work their way across."

"We can use the shackles to make the chains all one length," Caleb announced.

"Sounds like a harebrain plan," Josh said, "but it's all we got. Let's get it done."

They tied the longest rope around Jericho's waist. He took off his shoes and slowly lowered into the stream. Immediately, the force of the rushing water washed him downstream. Five of the strongest men they had held onto the rope. They reeled him in like a fish. Josh bent down, offering his hand to help Jericho out of the water.

Jericho wiped his wet hair back and out of his eyes. "No, Josh, I can do this. It just took me off guard. I know I can do this."

He backed away from the bank and slowly started out, again. He kept his arms high for balance. The water rose to his neck. When he was halfway across, he went down under the water. They were just about to reel him in again when Josh stopped them.

"No, wait, give him a moment."

Jericho's head appeared above the water. He was three quarters of the way across. All eyes fixed on him. Slowly he continued. The water level was again at his neck, then his chest, his waist, his knees. He collapsed on the opposite shore, exhausted.

"Jericho, are you all right?" Josh shouted.

Still trying to catch his breath, Jericho waved that he was fine.

Josh turned to those around him. "Quick, get the shackles and chains and link them up."

When they had formed all the chains and shackles into one long strand, they tied it to the end of the rope. Jericho pulled it across the stream and tied the end of it to the base of a large tree. On the opposite shore, they tied the other end of the chain to another large tree. They took other lengths of rope. Some they cut and made into small hoops that they tied around the chain. They'd use these as guides to keep them attached to the chain, when forging across. They cut larger pieces of rope and tied the children to the backs of all the able bodied men. Everyone got a length of rope that they tied around their waist and tied the other end into the loop of rope on the chain. They forged across in groups of three and four to minimize the strain on the chain. It was a long and slow process; it took nearly an hour; but everyone made it to the other shore safely. They lay on the shoreline, wet and worn out. They were able to carry little food; what each person had on their backs was all they had left in the world. Still, they had made it. They'd passed over the Mason Dixon Line. They'd made it north to Yankee Territory, the Union, to Freedom.

They camped along the water's edge. Everyone sat close to the fires to dry off. What few morsels of food were left, they gave to the children...not enough to fill their bellies, but enough to escape hunger and let them sleep. Everyone fell asleep praying. Being down to nothing, they knew their future was no longer in their hands, as if it ever was.

In the morning, they began marching north. They came to a clearing at the edge of a thick wooded forest. Suddenly, there appeared Confederate soldiers at the edge of the wood, dozens of them. Each of them held either a long knife or an ax.

"We're too far north," Caleb said to Josh. "Why are there so many Confederate soldiers?"

If the soldiers rushed them, they would be defenseless and all would be lost. Then out of the blue, a group of Yankee soldiers on horseback appeared.

"Get back to work. I want five foot of forest cleared away by the end of the day," a Yankee sergeant shouted. The rebel soldiers returned to work, hacking at the bushes and chopping at the trees. The sergeant turned and saw the marching caravan. "Well, what do we have here?'

He rode over; Josh stood in the front. The sergeant looked down on him. "You're in the Union now, boy. Slave tradin' is illegal in these parts."

"We're not slave traders," Josh said.

"Well, we'll just see about that," the sergeant said. He turned to the other mounted Yankee soldiers. "Gather 'em up, and let's bring 'em to the captain."

A group of armed Union soldiers surrounded them and slowly herded them to another clearing where there were army tents and a corral full of horses. They took the horses out and tied them to nearby trees. They placed the caravan in the corral. One at a time, they guided some of the older folks into a large tent. When they returned, they spoke of questions asked by one of the superior Union officers. An hour and a half later, they guided Josh into the tent; a lone Yankee captain sat behind a folding table.

"I presume you're Mr. Nunn, Joshua Nunn?" the man said, standing up and folding his arms.

"Yes, sir, I'm Joshua Nunn."

"I've questioned some of your people, and I'm convinced you are not a slave trader. In fact, I find it a most amazing story."

"Yes, sir, we left our lives in the south to come north."

"I see," the Yankee captain said. "Well, you are free to go."

"Thank you, sir," Josh said. "Before we go, could you find it in your heart to give us some food?"

The captain unfolded his arms, placed his fists down on the table and leaned forward. "Let me make one thing perfectly clear, Mr. Nunn. I'm a Union officer. I'm obliged to follow the laws of the Union, of which I have. I may have to do it, but I don't have to like it. Personally, I find your kind distasteful. The sooner you get your black wife, your half-breed daughter, your bleeding heart white-trash, and those inbreed savages off my compound the better. Do you understand me, sir?"

Anger like no other he'd ever known possible swelled up in him; but for the sake of the others, Josh remained silent.

"Do you understand me, sir?" the captain insisted.

"Yes, I understand."

"Good, now get out of my sight."

Josh left the tent and went back to the corral where Yankee soldiers were releasing everyone. Josh walked to the front and pointed forward. They all began to march north, again. Ellie walked alongside her husband.

"What's the matter, Josh? You look sad. We're free! This is a great day," she said.

"Free?" he questioned. "We've come so far, Ellie; but we still have a long way to go."

## THE END

### Connect with the Author
www.michaeledwinq.com

Michael Edwin Q. is available for book interviews and personal appearances. For more information contact:

Michael Edwin Q.
C/O Advantage Books
P.O. Box 160847
Altamonte Springs, FL 32716
michaeledwinq.com

To purchase additional copies of this book visit our bookstore website at:
www.advbookstore.com

Longwood, Florida, USA
*"we bring dreams to life"*™
www.advbookstore.com